W9-ARA-813

"JUST HOLD ME FOR A MINUTE, BRANDON."

JoBeth rested her cheek on his shoulder. His arms tightened and he began to rock her back and forth. The comforting motion was all she needed. Her fears and hesitation fled. This was where she was meant to be. She raised her eyes. "Thank you, Brandon. Now I think I'd like that kiss."

He chuckled. "Would you now?" He was a little puzzled at the tenderness he felt, the need to make this first kiss something special.

JoBeth's eyes closed; she could feel his mouth lowering toward hers. But when their noses bumped, her eyes flew open. Nose to nose, they began to laugh. It was the catalyst that released their inhibitions, and still laughing, they fell onto the bed, both determined to fulfill their dreams.

FRED'S BOOK EXCHANGE

413 1/2 PEARL ST.
SIOUX CITY, IA 51101
PH. 255-6236

ABOUT THE AUTHOR

Final Payment is the fourth in a series of books by
Evelyn A. Crowe. Readers will be happy to see
that the central characters from *Summer Ballad*,
Charade and *Moment of Madness* gather for a
wonderful reunion scene in this Superromance.
Like the others, it is set in Houston and is
brimming with action and colorful characters—
Evelyn's trademarks.

Books by Evelyn A. Crowe

HARLEQUIN SUPERROMANCE
112–SUMMER BALLAD
160–CHARADE
186–MOMENT OF MADNESS

These books may be available at your local bookseller.

Don't miss any of our special offers. Write to us at the
following address for information on our newest releases.

Harlequin Reader Service
901 Fuhrmann Blvd., P.O. Box 1397, Buffalo, NY 14240
Canadian address: P.O. Box 603,
Fort Erie, Ont. L2A 9Z9

Evelyn A. Crowe

FINAL PAYMENT

Harlequin Books

TORONTO • NEW YORK • LONDON
AMSTERDAM • PARIS • SYDNEY • HAMBURG
STOCKHOLM • ATHENS • TOKYO • MILAN

Published October 1986

First printing August 1986

ISBN 0-373-70233-7

Copyright © 1986 by Evelyn A. Crowe. All rights reserved.
Philippine copyright 1986. Australian copyright 1986.
Except for use in any review, the reproduction or utilization of
this work in whole or in part in any form by any electronic,
mechanical or other means, now known or hereafter invented,
including xerography, photocopying and recording, or in any
information storage or retrieval system, is forbidden without
the permission of the publisher, Harlequin Enterprises Limited,
225 Duncan Mill Road, Don Mills, Ontario, Canada M3B 3K9.

All the characters in this book have no existence outside the
imagination of the author and have no relation whatsoever to
anyone bearing the same name or names. They are not even
distantly inspired by any individual known or unknown to the
author, and all the incidents are pure invention.

The Superromance design trademark consisting of the words
HARLEQUIN SUPERROMANCE and the portrayal of a Harlequin,
and the Superromance trademark consisting of the words
HARLEQUIN SUPERROMANCE are trademarks of Harlequin
Enterprises Limited. The Superromance design trademark
and the portrayal of a Harlequin are registered in the
United States Patent Office.

Printed in Canada

This one's for *me*.

CHAPTER ONE

BRANDON DESALVA DROVE the rented compact onto the shoulder of the four-lane highway and sat staring at the painted sign that proclaimed the entrance to the Santana Dude Ranch. His gaze shifted to the road ahead, and for a second he contemplated the illusion of a great blue ocean created by heat waves rising from the hot asphalt. Only April, yet the relentless sun promised to make the Texas spring a living hell. The advent of summer was too unbearable even to think about now.

How typical of JoBeth, he thought, to be where you least expected. While everyone worried himself sick about her, she was living in the lap of luxury, being waited on hand and foot like a queen. Who would have thought she'd have stayed in this country after everything she'd been through? They'd hunted out every jet-set playground and hot spot in Europe for some trace of her.

Damn irritating woman! The more he thought of what she'd put him through, his relieved expression changed to a fierce scowl. He snarled out loud and jammed the car into gear. For almost a year he'd had a private detective on her trail, but every time they had a lead it turned out to be false. Then, three hours ago, Masters Security had finally located her, and without a thought or plan as to what he would do or say, he'd boarded the company jet and headed for the mountains of West Texas.

"Bitch," he grumbled to himself. One would have thought that by the age of twenty-seven she'd have developed some sense of responsibility. Certainly he, at thirty-three, should have realized JoBeth could never change. She'd been a thorn in his side since she was six and he was twelve. Always tagging after him and his brother, always hanging around him—always seeing through his stories and evasions and lies with those unforgettable smoky-gray eyes. His mouth twisted into a thin smile. Those incredible eyes that seemed to hold some deep secret that haunted him . . .

Brandon forced the memories away, checked the highway behind him in the rearview mirror and waited for the mammoth eighteen-wheeler to roar past, grimacing as the small car rocked in its wake. Before pulling out onto the road, he once again glanced at the folded Houston newspaper beside him. He touched the smudged article, his talisman, and prayed he wouldn't screw up this meeting as he'd managed to do so many others in the past.

"HELLO, BETS!" The husky, masculine voice was like a whisper of cool velvet caressing her sweaty cheek. In the dank, gloomy barn JoBeth shivered with longing. A dream—a wish—she told herself, but how she'd yearned to hear Brandon call her by that absurd nickname. Her shoulders sagged as she realized she'd imagined him there so many times that her mind was beginning to play cruel little tricks. She heaved the pitchfork and angrily stabbed another section of hay away from the bale, tossing the fresh straw into the clean stall.

"Ignoring me won't make me disappear."

There was a remembered hint of laughter in the deep voice that brought her head up with a jerk. She wasn't dreaming this time. Every muscle froze, the paralysis suspending the pitchfork in midair. Then she slowly turned; her pulse raced wildly and her eyes narrowed as she searched every dark corner.

Brandon stepped through the open doorway into a pool of golden light, and her breath caught painfully in her chest. He was here and he was real. God, she'd loved this man for as long as she could remember. Her vision became blurred by tears as she thought how unfair life was, but she quickly blinked them away. He mustn't see her cry at the mere sight of him.

"Don't call me 'Bets.' You know how I hate those ridiculous nicknames of yours." Her voice was so choked and raspy she doubted if he could make out her words.

From her shadowy vantage point she could devour him with hungry eyes without revealing her love for him. And though she'd never forgotten one tiny detail of how he looked, she knew that her memory didn't do him justice. Vibrant, alive, he had a compelling sensuality that left women shocked at their lust for him. Tall, lean, he stood unmoving, and the sunlight gleamed like jet stones in his thick black hair. Sharp sapphire-blue eyes that usually danced with humor and devilment were wary and cautious now. Even though he tried to appear nonchalant to cover his own uneasiness and tension, knowing him as well as she knew herself, she recognized the signs of strain.

As if in defiance of JoBeth's muteness and the feel of her eyes on him, Brandon let the silence stretch as he slowly slipped off his jacket and threw it over his arm. He unbuttoned his vest and tugged at the expensive tie already hanging loose around his open collar. Then he shot her a sharp look from under thick black lashes.

Her heart jumped and pounded. She'd seen him use that glance on his legions of women, but this was the first time she'd been the recipient of that come-hither look.

"It's time to come home."

JoBeth frowned. Just what was he up to?

"Your running days are over, Bets."

Are they? she wondered, as her hopes began to soar. Home! She no longer had a home or anything left of her previous life—except her love for this elegant, wealthy man standing a few feet from her. For the past year she'd thought she had only his pity and disgust. Now, here he was, smiling and seducing her as if the past had never happened. She set the sharp metal points of the pitchfork on the cement floor and crossed her hands over the handle. Resting her chin on her knuckles, she waited and watched as Brandon shaded his eyes against the glare.

"Damn it, JoBeth, come out here where I can see you."

She took a deep breath for courage, then exhaled. With precise movements she leaned the pitchfork against a post, closed the stall gate and took a few shaky steps before she forced herself to a stop. She had to get control or she knew she'd end up in his arms blubbering like a baby.

Brandon's hand came up again to shade his eyes as he watched her moving toward him. Steeling himself not to grab her and shake the devil out of her for the worry she'd caused, he quickly reviewed the sarcastic speech he'd planned. But as she stepped into the light the words stuck in his throat, and he assured himself it was only because she looked so different. He detected a sadness in the depths of her smoky eyes that tore at his heart. She was too thin, too controlled. "What the hell have you done to your hair?" It was the first thing out of his mouth and he could have kicked himself. But his anger helped hide the ache in his chest.

"I'm sorry you don't approve, but Mr. André doesn't make house calls in West Texas," she sniped. "I've had to forgo some luxuries, as you can see." Self-consciously she smoothed back the short cap of light brown hair. She wanted desperately to joke about this being the first time in twelve years she'd seen the natural color, but the gay laugh she'd intended stuck somewhere in her throat. "What are you doing here, Brandon?"

"Well, that's a hell of a welcome. Here I've come all this way—to say nothing of the time spent trying to find you—so I can give you this." He handed her the newspaper he'd manhandled for hours. "You're free, Bets. All your father's debts have been paid." He took a deep breath and went on. "You're a stupid fool. Do you know that? You didn't have to…ah, hell." He watched her read and saw the fat tears welling in her eyes. She glanced up, then away, but not before he saw the pain and hurt and…yes, the shame there. "Oh, Bets." He took a step toward her, reaching out, but when she pulled back he withdrew his hand and ran his fingers through his hair. "Is there somewhere we could talk? Your room?"

JoBeth, lost in thought, nodded and took off down the paved walkway with Brandon alongside. Free! She swallowed. The newspaper article proclaimed her a modern-day heroine. A savior of twenty-five middle-class families that her father, with his wheeling and dealing, had virtually bankrupted. She thought she'd lost everything, but maybe not. Glancing at the man beside her, she stopped, her lips twitching with amusement. They'd come to a fork in the walkway: one path led to the employees' cottages, the other toward the main quarters of the dude ranch. Brandon, his head down, deep in thought, had automatically started up the path to the main house. A laugh of genuine amusement escaped her lips, catching Brandon's attention and halting him in his tracks. She watched confusion flit across his handsome face, and her smile grew. "Wrong way." Her thumb jabbed the air toward the line of small cottages. It tickled her to see that he hadn't yet realized that she worked on the ranch and was not a pampered guest.

"My God!" The truth of her status struck him like a staggering blow in the solar plexus. He trotted back down the path and was forced to break into a run to catch up with her as she unlocked the door to her cottage. "My God!" He stepped into the tiny, grim room, his eyes everywhere, taking in everything from the narrow single bed with its faded and worn corded bedspread to the screen that divided the bathroom from the rest of the room. "My—"

"Don't say it again, for heaven's sake. So it's not the Ritz." The air conditioner rattled a strange series of noises, then suddenly spit a spray of fine mist into the room.

The action so expressed Brandon's feelings that it brought him out of his shock. He lunged for JoBeth and captured her hands, only to groan out loud as he felt the calluses. Without thinking, he pried her fingers open and brought the work-worn hands to his lips.

The warmth and tenderness of Brandon's kiss was her undoing. A deep racking sob fought its way upward, and as she tried to force it back she hiccuped. Bright sapphire-blue eyes twinkling with laughter and memories met hers, and she hiccuped again.

"I remember when you were little and I did something to hurt you, you'd do that very thing. You'd hold back your tears just to prove what a big tough girl you were." She hiccuped once more, losing the battle with her tears. He dropped her hands and gathered her into his arms. Other than dancing together, this was the first time he could ever remember holding her so close. A frown marred his smooth forehead as it occurred to him that though he was a toucher and a hugger, he'd never been so with JoBeth. Why? he wondered. But his thoughts were interrupted as the warm, earthy fragrance of her disappeared when she pulled free of his hold and stepped back.

They stood only inches apart, staring at each other, each lost in the past. Brandon grinned and sniffed. "New perfume, Bets? Can't say much for it."

She returned his smile weakly through tears that she was frantically trying to wipe away with her shirt cuff.

"I didn't realize things were so tough. You should have stayed in Houston instead of running away. Just why the hell did you run?" he growled, his anger mounting with each word. "And why didn't you come to us after your dad shot himself?" He saw a fresh stream of tears on her cheeks, and cursed long and low at his callous stupidity. "Damn, I'm sorry." He stepped backward and slumped down into the only chair in the room.

JoBeth struggled to compose herself. She turned her back on Brandon, wrapping her arms around her chest as a deep shiver shook her body. For as long as she could remember she'd wanted him to hold her, to love her, but she'd never wanted his pity. She'd never asked for anything from him, nor had she ever let him see how much she loved him. Oh, his family knew, but Brandon had always been a blind fool. Closing her eyes, she recalled the one time she might have gone to him for help, but because of her own misguided sense of importance she'd destroyed her chances of ever appealing to any of the DeSalvas for help.

"JoBeth, I'm talking to you."

"Sorry, what?"

"I said, I want to know what happened so that only two days after your father's death you found it necessary to hide out, then skip town. But most of all, I want to know why you didn't come to us for help." He shifted his weight on the worn leather chair to avoid the insistent nudge of a sharp spring.

JoBeth swung around, her arms dropping from their death grip on each other. "You want to know.... You brought the newspaper—you know exactly what happened!"

"That's not the whole story, damn it...."

Suddenly all the fire went out of her and she flopped down on the end of her bed. "Oh, Brandon, it was all so horrible." She clasped her hands together till the knuckles shone white through the tightly drawn skin. "For months before, Dad..." She swallowed, then went on. "For months, Dad was acting funny. He kept telling me he'd had everything transferred to my name, and when I'd demand to know what he was up to, he'd twitch my nose the way he always did when he was trying to be cagey with me. You know how he was when he was in the middle of putting together one of his 'big deals.' This one worried him, I could tell. He wouldn't confide in me. Then . . .'' She shook her head as if to wipe away the horror of finding her father in the library, a bullet through his head, except it was a memory she would never be rid of. ''It happened on the day Lucas and Jennifer's twins were born. You remember how bitterly cold it was? I think the whole state of Texas had come to a standstill, and I was worried about you driving all the way to the ranch. I'd even tried to call you several times to talk you out of going, but I remembered how excited you were about having a niece or nephew.'' She gave a low laugh, her eyes soft with joy for Brandon's brother and his wife. ''They certainly fooled you, didn't they? They gave you one of each. . . .''

Her voice trailed off and Brandon let the quiet calm his frayed nerves. He watched her closely, trying to figure out how one person could have changed so much in barely a year. She seemed to have grown up, and for some reason he bitterly regretted not being there to see it happen. She amazed him. Even in her grief and hurt and pain she was controlled. For a fleeting second he missed the empty-headed butterfly who could chatter on for hours about nothing more important than a new dress or hairstyle.

JoBeth picked up the Houston newspaper she'd thrown on the bed. Solemnly she studied the picture of herself, trying to figure out why and how the reporter had gotten hold of the story. ''I haven't seen a paper since I've been here. Is everything really gone?'' she whispered.

''Everything,'' he confirmed. ''The minute my family found out you were liquidating all your holdings, we assisted your attorney by contacting a few friends we thought might be interested in the properties. The River

Oaks mansion in Houston went first, then the home in Monte Carlo, your winter home in Gstaad, the London and Paris apartments and finally the ranch.'' She hiccuped loudly at the last bit of information and Brandon bit back a grim smile. ''Lucas bought the ranch, honey.'' He nodded when her head jerked up and another hiccup broke from her stiffly held lips. ''It would have been stupid of him not to, since your ranch is only across the highway from ours.''

''Yes,'' she said softly. ''I'm glad he bought it. At least I'll feel as if it's still in the family.'' She threw the newspaper down. ''All gone.'' Her voice cracked and she cleared her throat.

''Come on, Bets, finish telling me what happened.''

Her hands began to rub up and down her thighs nervously, and she glanced up and met his eyes. The genuine concern in them gave her courage. ''I found Daddy, you know? I thought he was still alive and I called for help.'' She rubbed so hard she felt the heat from the friction. ''Then, all I can remember is that people were everywhere—police, doctors, the reporters. The next thing, Hal Goodwin, Dad's attorney...'' She met Brandon's eyes again and quickly looked away, feeling sick at the pain she saw there. She'd forgotten how close he was to her father, how much they'd liked to joke and laugh.

''Hal was there trying to warn me to expect the worst. But I guess I was in shock and couldn't take it all in. It wasn't till the next morning that that awful story broke on television. Daddy had put together one of his 'big deals' again. Something to do with steel and oil. Except this time, instead of using his rich cronies as investors, he'd organized a group of men he knew nothing about. Middle-class men with families and mortgages and children to put through college. They trusted him because of his reputation and invested their life savings and their future. He lost it all—every penny they gave him. He ruined twenty-five honest, hardworking families." She shook her head, the sleek cap of brown hair swinging in mute acknowledgment of her distress.

JoBeth met his gaze once more, and this time she didn't look away. "I know what you're going to say. That they knew the risks when they invested. But that's just it, Brandon. They didn't. They'd been told by some of Daddy's friends—bankers and oil investors—that it was a sound investment. Anyway, the next morning I started getting frantic phone calls from these men, some even threatening. I went to Hal, told him to sell everything—property, jewels, furniture." Her hands were extended palms up in a helpless gesture. "Everything. Even my stocks in U.S.A. Oil."

Brandon sucked a strangled breath through his teeth, making a hissing noise like an angry snake.

"What's the matter?" she asked. But he only stared at her in response, so she went on. "Well, you needn't be concerned. Hal refused to discuss the matter. Besides, I remembered my Uncle Tramble telling me years ago that I couldn't sell those shares to anyone but him. I guess Hal realized that, because he told me I could only sign over the royalties toward repaying those men."

"Smart Hal," Brandon mumbled.

"What?" The tone of his voice alerted her that something had changed.

"Your uncle has lied to you for years, Bets. You can sell your forty-percent share in U.S.A. Oil anytime you want to, to anyone. Hal knew that, but my guess is he was trying to salvage some future for you, not knowing how long it would take to pay back those investors or how long it would be before all your property sold. But Hal told me that no sooner had you disappeared than your uncle was at his office, demanding to know where you were and offering to buy your forty percent of his oil company.''

"But why would he want to buy my shares?" she asked, confused. "I know him well enough to know that he would never have done anything to help me. Besides, he's had a power of attorney authorizing him to vote my shares since Mom died and I inherited them from her.''

Brandon reached out and stopped the movement of her palms on her thighs, holding her hands tightly in his warm grasp. "He was scared to death you'd find out that you could sell them and would act upon it. He knew he hadn't endeared himself to you over the years, and that the hostility he had for your father wouldn't help his cause.''

"What cause?" She tried to pull her hands free, but it only made him tighten his grip. Gazing at him, she realized that the softness in his face had disappeared, leaving an expression she knew only too well. "What do you want, Brandon? Why are you here?''

Now that she'd given him an opening, he felt his throat close and found the words hard to speak. "Part of the reason, Bets... The reason... Damn. Listen, sweetheart, I know this is going to sound callous, but let me explain it all before you say anything." He took a breath and looked her straight in the eye. "I'm here... Part of the reason is I want to buy all your shares in U.S.A. Oil Company.''

"That's why you've been looking for me?"

"Yes, but—"

"You want my shares?" She felt as if there were a viselike grip on her heart, squeezing the life out of her. Why, she silently cried, had she allowed herself to hope that he'd come for her, that he somehow missed her, that there was more hidden under that teasing manner than a shaky on-again, off-again friendship? She hiccuped loudly, twice in a row. Damn him to hell!

CHAPTER TWO

"Now, Bets! Just listen...."

JoBeth surged to her feet, jammed her tightly clenched fists on her hips and glared down at him. "I've heard 'now, Bets' from you for as long as I can remember, and it's always *me* who suffers. 'Now, Bets,'" she mimicked sarcastically, thinking of the thousands of times she'd heard those two dreaded words, then began reminding him of just a few incidents. "'Now, Bets, crawl through the cave *first,* never mind the spiders and bats....' Or '*Now*, Bets, would I lie to you? Just taste the ants. I swear they're good.' And, 'Grab hold of the tire and swing out into the middle of the river. You'll be okay, I'll catch you.' Hah! I almost drowned that day, and would have if it hadn't been for Lucas."

Brandon chuckled and eased back into the depths of the big chair, only to leap suddenly to his feet with a yelp of pain. "That thing bites," he exclaimed, looking at her accusingly. When she tried to push him back down he dodged out of her reach and sat on the side of the bed, patting the space beside him. "Come on, Jo, sit here and let me explain why I've come."

"Don't you dare call me 'Jo,' damn you." She took a swipe at him, but he grinned and ducked. "You only came for my shares."

He thumped the bed again. "Stop being pigheaded. It's a long story and your shares are only part of the reason I'm here." His hand captured hers and tugged her down. "That's better. I've missed you, you know?"

"Don't ruin this so-called happy reunion with more lies."

"And don't you start." He returned her glare, then took a deep breath to avert an all-out argument, yet the thought of one of their brawls strangely excited him. All his carefully laid plans kept slipping slowly away the longer he stayed around her. Why he'd ever thought he could carry on a calm, civil conversation with her was beyond him. In her absence he'd probably deluded himself by giving her a halo. Heaven knows that for every dirty trick he pulled on her, she'd always managed to repay in kind. Like when he was fourteen and she'd caught him and Lorna James naked in the hayloft. Brandon flinched, still smarting at JoBeth's laughter and his father's stinging reprisal. "I've come a long way and spent a lot of my valuable time on this. Please, just hear me out. I promise I'll explain everything as simply as possible so you'll understand."

"Bastard," she grumbled. "Insensitive—"

"Now..." he interrupted, then grinned as she scowled at him. "You know, of course, that after Lucas and Jennifer married, Lucas turned over the running of DeSalvas to me. The worldwide electronics company, the vast oil wells and exploration company, the real estate company were all mine to run. He kept only the ranch, the breeding companies for the cattle and quarter horses, the citrus farms in the Rio Grande Valley and the bank in South Texas. At the time I didn't think anything could make me happier. It took a couple of months before I realized the position offered no challenge. Lucas had hired a select group of men, tops in their fields, to head the various departments. DeSalvas runs like a well-oiled machine without the help of an eager president, even if he's been the corporate attorney for years.''

Brandon gave a disillusioned laugh. ''I had such big ideas. Lucas gave up the company to take up his dream of running the family ranch with his wife and children and handed me my dream in the process. But it was nothing but ashes in my hands. There was nothing for me to contribute. Hell, even the computerized offshore drilling rig is well on its way to being completed and needs only my supervision. You did know that Kane Stone's father, Max, died and left Texas-American Oil to him, and that Kane bought the design of the new drilling rig for the company?''

''No, I'm sorry, I didn't know about Max Stone's death. I haven't read a newspaper in months.'' She didn't want to tell him that any news of home and friends hurt too badly. Reaching out, she patted his thigh, surprised when his hand covered hers and held it there.

''That's where it all started—at Max's funeral. Kane had talked to Lucas, and I guess he learned how dissatisfied I was. Anyway, Kane asked me to help him take over U.S.A. Oil and form a merger with Tex-Am Oil—''

JoBeth's laugh interrupted Brandon, but she sobered when she saw just how serious he was. ''My uncle would never allow that. He's a fanatic about his company. I remember Dad telling of the fight Uncle Tramble and Mother had when she married. He hated Dad, thought he was nothing but a fast-talking, redneck opportunist with his sights aimed directly at U.S.A. Oil. Dad said Uncle Tramble raised so much hell over Mother's stock and the fact that Dad wanted to vote her shares that he finally had to give in and allow Tramble to retain Mom's proxy just to keep some peace. Dad knew Uncle Tramble wasn't going to do anything to jeopardize U.S.A. Oil, and any profit for the company was only money in their pockets. So Dad let the situation stand to save Mother and me the grief of having to deal with Uncle Tramble any more than was necessary. But to think Kane could take U.S.A. Oil away from my uncle is not only laughable, it's insane! Why would Kane Stone want it, anyway? He's the least likely businessman I know, especially with his background. So—"

"Damn it! If you'll let me finish, I'll explain all this." Brandon squeezed her hand to emphasize his exasperation.

Her lips snapped together like a trap and her soft gray eyes sparked with fire. "Well, I'm listening. Go on—tell me."

"So help me, Bets!" The muscle along his jaw began to twitch.

"How are Kane and Shasta, anyway?"

"Fine," he growled.

"Are they still working for the government?"

Brandon tried to cover his surprise at her statement, but with more gruffness than he intended, he answered, "They never worked for the government."

"Yes, they did, and still do as far as I know."

"JoBeth, they don't. They work for themselves."

"Wrong!" she said firmly, and grinned at his narrowing look.

"They did—do not. Damn!" He closed his eyes. It was like old times. "Listen, quit changing the subject. This is all very important."

"Well, go on. But hurry it up, will you? I have to get back to cleaning the stalls." She glanced at her watch. "Then I have a children's riding class to teach."

The muscles in Brandon's jaw jerked spasmodically. Maybe, he mused, appearances were deceiving and JoBeth hadn't changed as much as he'd first thought. "Bets, Kane and I are going into business together. He's giving me forty percent of Tex-Am Oil."

"'Giving'?" she questioned, suspicion raising her eyebrows and widening her eyes.

"Yes, with some stipulations."

"Ah. My shares?"

"Yes," he snapped. "Will you shut up and let me explain this? Kane has already acquired eleven percent of U.S.A. Oil on the open market. He has a pledge of two percent more if he needs it. So, with your forty percent we'll have fifty-one percent of your uncle's stock—controlling interest. We can neatly step in and take U.S.A. Oil away from Tramble." He paused to allow all he'd said to soak in, and tried to gauge her reaction. "Don't frown, Bets. You know very well you can't stand your uncle. And what better way to get back at him for the way he treated your family all those years? Revenge, if handled properly, is sweet. Besides, the money from your shares will make you a wealthy woman again. You can return to Houston with your head high and take up your old life."

JoBeth studied Brandon as he told her of his and Kane's plans, spying a youthful eagerness she hadn't seen in years. It suddenly struck her that this new business venture, the excitement of merging two companies and the fight that would ensue, was just what Brandon needed. He would revel in the challenge. She also realized he wanted this as much as he had once wanted the

DeSalvas corporation. This was a whole new set of dreams for him, and she could tell by his stubborn expression that he was capable of and willing to do anything to make these dreams come true. Anything! The word reverberated inside her head.

She freed her hand from his, climbed quickly to her feet and walked over to the window, raising the shade to let in the bright West Texas sun. "There's more to this than just a hostile stock takeover, isn't there?"

"Yes!"

"Are you going to tell me?"

"No, not yet."

"I see. Not until you have a guarantee that I'll sell you my shares?"

"Yes, but only because it's not my story to tell—it's Kane's. But he told me if you were your usual stubborn self and needed more convincing, I could tell you. I have my reasons, too, Bets. Your uncle has been doing everything he can to stop Tex-Am and DeSalvas from building our computerized offshore drilling rig. His games are getting nastier by the day. And he's also systematically firing a large number of his veteran employees, getting rid of them just before retirement. That, my dear Bets, is only part of the way he's voting *your* forty percent. Cheating hardworking, loyal men out of their pensions because they're eating into U.S.A. Oil profits."

"And nothing can be done?"

"Yes, if you help Kane and me with this takeover."

The air conditioner's sputtering and spitting filled the room as Brandon fell silent and JoBeth continued to gaze out the window. She squinted, staring off toward the Davis Mountains, which erupted from the earth in jagged peaks and rounded boulders. Bigtooth

maples growing in the sheltered canyons splashed their
brilliance on the dark cliffs, and creeks glinted in the
bright sun as they tumbled down the valley. Finally she
shifted her gaze to the ancient, giant, gnarled cotton-
woods that the wild canyon winds had tried to destroy
but had only managed to disfigure. In each tree's
twisted ugliness there was a serene beauty that never
failed to mesmerize her. The cottonwood had withstood what nature and man had wrought and had
proved to be a hardy survivor—like her. She, too, had
learned to bend with the wind.

Brandon's voice snapped her out of her reverie, and
she smiled, trying to control the quaking inside. Her
decision was made. Now all she had to do was find the
courage to go through with it.

"Don't be muleheaded, Bets. This life is not for you.
Take the money and come home."

"How much?" He named an amount and she silently whistled. It was indeed enough to make her a
wealthy woman. But was that all she wanted? She
wasn't noble or self-sacrificing. Looking down at her
callused hands and her short unpainted nails, she grimaced. She hated physical labor and wasn't ashamed to
admit that she was different from these hardworking
people. Oh, she respected and admired their grit, but
she wasn't cut from the same cloth, and managed to
clash with everyone, including the guests. The money
Brandon offered was more than tempting, yet she hesitated. Her old life wasn't appealing, either. Confused,
dissatisfied, she couldn't figure out what was happening to her.

"JoBeth, do you understand everything I've told
you?"

Her tiny smile slipped and her lips slowly turned down at the corners. She knew he held a low opinion of her intelligence. Over the years her defense against his indifference, his teasing barbs, had been a charade of defiance she'd cultivated to a fine art. If only he'd cared enough to look beyond the endless social chatter, he would've realized that it took brains to organize the social events, parties and charitable soirees she'd managed over the years.

She knew the right people to bring together for an evening, and it had never surprised her that friends came to her for help when there was trouble with a business merger. Multimillion-dollar deals were confirmed at some of her well-planned social functions. She had to know about oil companies, political manueverings, stock ventures, international and local politics.

Her world had been full of gossip from men and women: who was whose current lover, who was divorcing whom. That sort of news told its own story of how and where millions or billions of dollars were being moved, traded, or quietly transferred to Swiss accounts. Friends and acquaintances gave her an insight into the world of high finance that could seldom be acquired anywhere else.

JoBeth clenched her teeth. Brandon DeSalva had never taken the time to see her as a real woman. Instead he'd assumed she was a plastic social puppet. Maybe it was time to open his eyes. And maybe it was time he found out that his plans were going to cost him more than money.

Brandon studied JoBeth closely, waiting for her to say something. As she stood at the window with the sunlight silhouetting her, his imagination began to run rampant. The soft sheen of her hair made his hand itch to touch the silky cap; the curve of her cheek invited the brush of his fingertips; the hollow at the base of her neck was kissable and alluring.

Brandon swallowed as his gaze shifted to the thin cotton shirt plastered to her full breasts by the struggling stream of air from the air conditioner. His pulse increased as he noticed her rigid nipples straining against the cloth. His gaze dropped farther, taking in the skintight jeans, narrow hips and endless legs. He squeezed his eyes shut.

Where was his control? Ever since he was a teenager he'd applied mental brakes on his lustful thoughts of JoBeth. After all, she was almost family. And besides, he'd always thought it was Lucas she cared for. Lucas was the one who kissed and patted away the pain of her bruises and scrapes—*he* had put them there. It wasn't until recently that he'd discovered she'd always looked upon Lucas as a big brother. Still, in all those years Brandon had never allowed himself the pleasure of thinking of her as anything other than a friend, one who most of the time was a thorn in his side. Distance was the only way to cope with his feelings for JoBeth and the only way to keep his sanity and his freedom. The last word grabbed his attention, crawling up his backbone like someone's nails scratching a blackboard. Now why would he associate his freedom with JoBeth?

"If there's one thing I've learned this past year, Brandon, it's that I don't want my life the way it was. I want more." She whipped around, her eyes dark with tension and her chin thrust out determinedly. "I'll sell you half of my shares—twenty percent."

Brandon surged to his feet. "Damn it, Bets. Have you listened to anything I've told you? I—" He broke off, noticing the out-thrust chin, the fierce sparkle in her eyes and the stiffly held shoulders. Something about her stance tugged at his heart. There was so much vulnerability hidden behind that proud posture. Then suddenly he remembered. How many times had he been confronted with that look?

The first time was when she was six. Her family had only lived across the road a little while when her mother grew ill and died of cancer. Harold Huntley, distraught and unable to cope with the daily care of a little girl, turned to Catherine DeSalva for help. Brandon's mother had been more than willing to take in a motherless child while Harold tried to work out his business difficulties and his life. One bright morning JoBeth stood stiffly as his mother introduced her to the family. With one hand clutching the woman at her side for dear life and the other holding a grubby stuffed rabbit, JoBeth had turned those gray eyes, drowning in fat tears, on Lucas, and smiled such a sweet smile that he had caught his breath. Then she had turned to Brandon and studied him for a long time with dry eyes, and suddenly for no reason other than he'd crossed his eyes at her, she stuck out her tongue and kicked him hard on the shin. It was the first of many times he'd lost his cool with her, until he'd learned to control his temper. And heaven only knew how much restraint that took....

Brandon sighed heavily, then suddenly had an uncontrollable urge he hadn't had since his childhood. An urge to give her a frog on the arm. How many little boys had given that particular tight-fisted, raised-knuckle jab on the arm to little girls? And how many times had the boys walked off, leaving the recipient with a goose-egg-size knot on the muscle of a scrawny arm? The screams and tears had been a balm to a young boy's ego—they'd proved that girls were unconditionally the weaker of the two. Looking down at the fist he'd made, he grinned sheepishly. What was he thinking of? He shook his head to clear the webs of the past from their clinging hold. "You know twenty percent won't help a tinker's damn."

She could feel the trembling begin in her legs and travel up her body until she was forced to wrap her arms around herself. What she was about to suggest was totally insane and he would only laugh at her. But for once in her life she had to take a chance. "I know twenty percent won't help, but it would if you had my power of attorney to vote the other twenty percent."

Brandon's eyelids drooped a fraction, and his expression of patient disgust changed immediately to one of suspicion. "Yes..." he said thoughtfully, trying to control the growing uneasiness tightening his every muscle. "Why do I have this feeling there's a rope attached to your deal and the noose is secured around my neck?" he joked feebly, then fell silent. It had been a long time since he'd seen that half scared, half brave look on her face. A feeling of doom crept over him. "What's going on in that head of yours, Bets? What scheme are you cooking up now, and what do I have to do for that twenty percent?"

Her resolve was diminishing with each passing second. She rubbed her damp palms on her thighs and opened her mouth to speak, but nothing happened. Swallowing hard, she inhaled deeply, and was more surprised at the sound of her voice than the words that came out. "Marry me!" She couldn't look directly at him, and after a long agonizing moment, the silence punctuated only by the gasping air conditioner—or was it Brandon's breathing—she finally chanced a glance at him. "Marry me and you'll have the forty percent and your dream.'' Figuring she'd gone far enough, JoBeth bit down on her next words: that she'd trade one dream, his, for her own. She waited.

Marriage! It was the one word he'd managed to dance away from all his adult life. He paled, the sarcastic rejoinder dying on the tip of his tongue as their gazes locked and he realized she was serious. If he wanted her shares he'd have to marry her. He paled even more. This was ridiculous. Of course he wasn't going to marry her. He opened his mouth to tell her so but then something strange happened. He felt light-headed, as if his mind and body were no longer in sync with each other. And as if in a dream, he watched his arm slowly ascend, his hand reach for hers, and they shook. Realizing suddenly what he'd agreed to, Brandon yanked his hand from hers as if her fingers were bands of fire. He stumbled backward and sat down heavily in the chair, too numb to feel the sharp bite of the broken spring.

"Bets,'' he mumbled. A wave of giddiness washed over him and he rubbed his face nervously. What had he done? All his life he'd dodged marriage-minded females with an expertise he was profoundly proud of. But now he'd agreed to marry as easily as if it were something he did every day. Baffled, he shook his head. And to JoBeth of all females! Good Lord, she'd been a constant irritant in his life for as long as he could remember.

Brandon quickly glanced up, catching her meek acceptance with a jaundiced eye. He'd been had! He, Brandon DeSalva, with all his experience with women! He'd lost control of the situation and let that empty-headed butterfly trick him. He quickly weighed his chances of backing out and laughing the whole mess off as a joke, yet something stopped him. "I hope you know what you're doing. Hell, Bets. I wouldn't make a very good husband—'' He broke off, refusing to plead for understanding. She'd made her bed; now let her lie in it.... That thought caused a wave of desire to wash over him, and he immediately tried to force it away. But it was still there, like a devil prodding his imagination toward uncharted heights. Was he totally mad? A fierce scowl pleated his forehead into lines of frustration. He *was* mad! He'd just given up his bachelorhood—his life—and it seemed his mind wanted only to run rampant with images of bedding JoBeth. Slowly, carefully, he climbed to his feet. ''Get packed. I'll go up to the ranch house and settle things with your boss, then come back for you.''

He was almost at the door, when she found her voice. ''What are we going to do? Where are we going?''

Brandon stood with his hand on the doorknob for a long moment, his back to her. ''We'll fly to Las Vegas, get married, then go home.'' He stepped outside, shutting the door quietly behind him.

JoBeth was going to get what she'd always wanted, but at what price? The thought that Brandon might end up hating her was too painful even to contemplate. She sighed, relief relaxing her stiff body. What had she done? She gulped, then like a crazy woman, giggled. The most amazing thing was that she was finally going to be Mrs. Brandon DeSalva. But then she realized just how disastrously her scheme could turn out, and her bubble burst. She flopped down on the edge of the bed, doubts assailing her. *I'll make him a good wife if it kills me,* she vowed, *or if he doesn't kill me first.*

JoBeth stared at the chair Brandon had just vacated, her eyes narrowing with suspicion as she wondered why he'd given in to her demands so easily. There had been no outrage, no sarcastic remarks about her unfitness to be his wife and questions as to why she wanted to marry him. Brandon DeSalva was an elegant tomcat used to his freedom. She gnawed at her bottom lip, trying to figure out what he was up to. There was no doubt in her mind that in some strange way she'd fallen into her own trap. But why had Brandon slammed the door shut between them? She didn't trust him one inch. He was definitely up to something. All she had to do was to figure out what, and how it was all going too blow up in her face.

CHAPTER THREE

JOBETH PICKED UP the queen of hearts, laid it over the king and smiled, her thoughts a million miles from her game of solitaire. "Mrs. Brandon DeSalva." Her new name rolled off her tongue in a whisper as sweet as honey. She glanced sideways to see if Brandon had heard. He hadn't. As she turned over another card, the smile grew. Her husband, still buckled into the airplane seat, was sulking.

She shot him another glance, and her eyes collided with blue slits. She swallowed hard. That look meant nothing but trouble. *He's plotting something,* she thought. *Something that I'm not going to like.* Pulling her gaze from his, she turned her attention to the endless expanse of darkening sky.

Their wedding hadn't been what she would have arranged, but beggars couldn't be choosers. Still, he had gone through with it when she'd expected him to renege at any minute. Everything went smoothly, like a well-oiled machine, once he'd made the decision. That's what bothered her most—the ease with which Brandon had accepted his fate. JoBeth remembered other occasions when he'd seemed to accept his due, only to retaliate at his leisure and with devastating results.

She removed the two of clubs from its wrong position and tapped the corner of the card against her teeth. She wanted desperately to ask him what he was up to, but she knew better. Brandon was as quick-witted as a mongoose, and though his manner was usually teasing, he had a stiletto-sharp tongue and sarcastic tone that could cut to the bone. She gave him another sideways glance and relaxed when she saw that his eyes were closed and his head was resting on the back of the chair. Maybe a short nap would ease the anger she'd sensed building in him.

Brandon felt her gaze again, yet this time refused to open his eyes. He just couldn't believe he'd done it—married JoBeth. A curse formed in the back of his throat and he had to struggle to force it down. Damn her to hell! She'd done what numerous other females hadn't. But, then, he rationalized, none of the others had forty percent of U.S.A. Oil.

He rolled his head away from her and opened his eyes a fraction of an inch. Who was he kidding? He'd let the oldest emotion in the world cloud his judgment. A merciless laugh was smothered in his chest. Cloud his judgment! Sex had blinded him completely. He'd heard of men doing anything to get a woman, but he'd always been in control, so he'd never believed the stories. Yet for some reason his libido had gone haywire and he'd had this unmanageable, irrational and absolutely insane need for JoBeth. He tried to tell himself it was just sex, but a little voice mocked him. Still, he shied away from the truth and strengthened his resolve to accept the inevitable.

The Lear jet hit an air pocket and rolled slightly sideways, sending JoBeth out of her seat, grabbing for the sliding cards. *This is a hell of a way to spend my honeymoon,* she thought. The word made her suddenly very nervous. *Honeymoon* meant lovers and making love, and though she'd wanted Brandon for years, this wasn't the way she'd envisioned having him. The plane pitched again and she felt her stomach leap to her throat, but the sickening feeling had nothing to do with the turbulence. Brandon wouldn't want to make love to her tonight, would he? Surely he'd allow them to become more comfortable in their new relationship—after all, they didn't know each other that way. She felt her panic growing. Maybe he wouldn't want her at all. Then what was she to do?

JoBeth moaned out loud, bringing Brandon out of his own thoughts. "Come back to your seat and buckle up, Bets. The pilot just warned me that we're heading toward some thunderstorms." After a few exasperating moments of watching her fumble with the buckle, he brushed her hands away and fastened her tightly into the seat. "You women amaze me. You can unhook a complicated catch on an expensive necklace with a snap of the fingers, but give you something as simple as a seat belt and you're all thumbs." He shook his head, refusing to look up when he heard her chuckle. "Your hands are as cold as ice. Are you going to be sick?"

"Yes...no," she mumbled. His concern and the warmth of his breath on her cheek made her realize just how vulnerable she was. But she couldn't show her feelings, not yet, not until she made him love her in return. Their relationship was going to be shaky enough without him having the added advantage of knowing she loved him. Give Brandon a weapon and he'd use it.

"JoBeth, are you all right? Here." He forced a plastic bag into her hands.

She would treat him like a dear friend, do everything he wanted with a happy smile, not argue with him or cause him to lose his temper. She'd be the best damn wife any man could ask for, and when the dumb ox realized how much he loved her, then and only then would she allow any lovemaking. She would totally control the situation.

With her resolve firmly in place, she grinned secretively. Men were always swayed by their physical urges. She'd have to be the strong one and stand up for what she knew was best if they were going to be able to live together. All she had to do was keep him so happy he'd never want to leave her.

Wasn't it his mother who had told her that Brandon was an elegant tomcat? But all cats thrived on their creature comforts and always returned to the security and tranquillity of their home. Well, by God, she'd make his home a hotbed of contentment.

"Where are you, Bets?" Brandon snapped his fingers before her dazed eyes.

JoBeth shoved the plastic bag aside and scowled. "I'm fine. Here, put this thing away. It's like waving a red flag to my system."

Brandon did as she ordered, chuckling as he remembered her weak stomach and the awful tricks he used to pull when they were kids.

She knew exactly where his memories lay from the devilish twist of his mouth. Her whole body stiffened. "You wouldn't dare." All it took for her to be sick was the gross sound he used to make. It was a wicked thing to have done to her and one that had never failed to get him the severest punishment.

"*Really*, Bets. I outgrew those despicable habits years ago." He pulled a blanket from the facing seat, arranged it around both of them, then leaned back in his own seat. "Tell me something, honey. Why, after your father died, didn't you come to me, Lucas or Dad?"

JoBeth snuggled under the plaid cashmere blanket, her mind working furiously to come up with all sorts of evasions and lies. But if they were to start off their married life right, she was going to have to be honest— or as honest as she thought was good for him. "After all that had happened I didn't know how to ask for help." She sensed his annoyance and stayed his interruption with a quick squeeze of his thigh. "I know what you're going to tell me—that Lucas and Jennifer forgave me for trying to break up their relationship. But damn it, Brandon, I was so ashamed."

"Yes, and we all know that. But remember, we also knew you were tricked by Lucas's so-called best friend into thinking Jennifer was nothing but a gold digger. Jean-Paul Arnaud did a number on all of us and, with the help of Susan McCord, managed to steal more than a million dollars from DeSalvas. Be reasonable, Bets. No one holds Jennifer responsible just because Susan was her stepsister and a thief. Nor does anyone hold any resentment toward you for trying to protect Lucas. Hell, how could they? You didn't accomplish what you set out to do, anyway."

"I know. Still, I was so disgusted with myself and there was such upheaval in my life at the time." She hadn't removed her hand from his thigh, and without thinking, she began to run her fingers slowly up and down the muscles, loving the way they tightened under her touch. Lifting her gaze from the middle of his chest, she suddenly found herself drowning in a sea of sapphire blue. Her breath caught sharply and she had to force herself to continue.

"Lucas had given up heading DeSalvas, Jennifer was expecting the twins, everyone was ecstatic over their arrival and you were totally wrapped up with the presidency of DeSalvas. It just seemed everything was going right for everyone after so many years of unhappiness.'' And there had been too many years of pain with the heartbreaking deaths of Catherine and Elizabeth DeSalva. She'd been close to his mother and sister and suffered with the family every day that passed.

"You had friends, Bets. Why didn't you go to them to hide? Why did you run away?''

"You don't really believe anyone would have stood by me during the scandal of Dad's suicide and the bomb that followed with the disclosure of that horrible business deal, do you? I might have had a lot of casual friends, Brandon, but none were willing to expose themselves to the censure of the press to the extent Daddy received.''

"Maybe," he said, his voice a little rough around the edges as he removed her hand from his thigh and lifted it gently from under the blanket they shared. "But I wish you'd come to me just the same. After all, we were like family, Bets, or almost—'' He broke off. "Well, we are actually family now, I guess. Seems you got what you always wanted, doesn't it, Bets?''

Her heart slammed against her ribs. Surely he didn't know how much she loved him? "What do you mean?''

"Why, you'd always wanted to be a member of the DeSalva family, and now you are.''

"Of all the insulting . . ." She sat up straight. "Listen here, mister, you were the one to come looking for me with your crazy scheme. So don't yell 'foul' if you got caught in your own trap." She inhaled deeply, trying to calm down. She told herself this was not the way to start off their marriage, and recalled her earlier promise that she wouldn't argue with him. But his smug expression was too much!

"Okay, okay." Brandon smiled and held up his hands in mock surrender. "So we both got what we wanted. There's nothing wrong with that. I just hope you know what you're doing."

JoBeth's frown deepened. "That's the second time you've said that to me. Is it a warning of some sort? Or a threat?" She didn't give him time to answer before grumbling, "I hope you know what you're doing, too. After all, *you* agreed to marry *me*. You could have said no. But then you wouldn't have gotten my shares of U.S.A. Oil, would you? And that's all you care about, isn't it?"

"I . . ."

"Well, isn't it?"

"Shut up, Bets, or so help me I'll gag you." He was truly angry now, his eyes shooting blue fire.

She laughed in his face. "You needn't get mad at me for telling the truth." The airplane bucked and rolled and JoBeth grabbed the lapels of Brandon's coat. "Are you sure Lucas isn't flying this?"

Brandon threw back his head and laughed, not only at her ability to change the subject quickly when it no longer pleased her, but at the fact that almost everyone in the family had been prisoner at one time or another in a plane with his brother. "If Lucas were at the controls, we'd more than likely be standing on our heads."

He sighed and gave in to the impulse to take her in his arms. But only, he told himself, because she looked cold and tired. "Put your head down, Bets." He glanced at his watch as he made her comfortable against his chest. "We have about two more hours till we reach Houston, and you might as well get some rest." Brandon smiled into her fragrant light brown hair. He didn't want to reveal the surprise he had in store for her. His smile grew as he remembered that last phone call he'd made before leaving West Texas.

THE RAIN HAD WASHED the streets of Houston clean, and a copper glow was cast over the city as the red ball of the sun began to set through the dusky clouds. Jo-Beth glanced around hungrily, her gray eyes dark with the emotion of coming home.

Brandon expertly wove in and out of the traffic, the wide tires of his Corvette hugging the slick road. Even the congested freeway was a welcome sight, and she sighed deeply. No more wide-open spaces or majestic mountains to gaze at in loneliness. Here was her town, her home. Concrete and steel, densely wooded parks, stores unequaled by any in all the places she'd traveled. The restaurants, the polo field where she'd spent hours sipping champagne and watching Brandon play.

She turned her head, her eyes taking in the skyline of downtown, then with a quick flick she was staring at the approaching Galleria. The DeSalvas Building wasn't far; she could just make out the penthouse floor that would be her home. She shivered, wanting to hug herself with the sheer joy of being married to Brandon. Yet she was nervous, uneasy with her happiness.

She shot a quick look at her husband. Brandon had been entirely too quiet. He hadn't even commented on her limited amount of luggage as he stowed it away in the trunk. Instead he'd only laughed when she explained that designer jeans weren't constructed for horseback riding, nor was silk made to withstand sun, sweat and hard labor. The only item of her old wardrobe she'd taken to West Texas and managed to salvage was the turquoise-silk Valentino dress she had on now—her wedding dress. With infinite care she smoothed the light, luxurious material over her knees. "Brandon?"

"Hmm?" he absently answered, and when no question was forthcoming, glanced at JoBeth. "What?"

"Just what exactly was Dad's deal that bankrupted so many investors? The lawyer said something about oil wells and steel, but at the time I was too upset to pay attention to specifics."

Brandon was quiet for a long moment, wondering how much of her father's dealings she was cognizant of, or if she was capable of understanding all the intricate details. "In some ways your dad was a lot like Kane, Bets. They both figured that the oil-gas-consuming public were getting a raw deal from the big petroleum corporations. Harold Huntley was a visionary, I believe, because years ago—about the time of the gas crisis—he told me we were heading for big trouble. We depended on the Middle East oil suppliers too much. That's about the time he began to dream of setting up his new company—G & S Corporation—Gas and Steel, a company working with a three-part plan. The first part involved drilling new wells. Your dad was the best damn wildcatter in Texas, but he ran into a streak of bad luck when he sank thirteen dry holes. Then he leased old salt caverns in Louisiana for oil storage, but they began to leak. Finally he invested in a couple of steel mills up East, but they closed."

"Why steel mills for heaven's sake?"

"That was the beauty of his dream, Bets. With the oil crisis of a few years ago, it didn't take long for American oil companies to realize that even if they wanted to drill for more oil, they couldn't because all their rigs were in the Middle East. We had no surplus of rigs, nor the steel to build them. Of course, that's the very position the Saudis wanted us in—dependent and willing to pay through the nose. They raised the price of oil per barrel, the oil companies raised the price of gas and the consumers paid the outlandish prices.''

''Yes, but that was years ago. Things have changed.''

''Have they? The price of gas at the pumps is still high, higher than it should be. We're supposed to have a glut of oil in reserve, yet there are fewer rigs pumping oil than ever. The big oil companies are raking in the money, diversifying into other companies and shuffling their money around. Your dad predicted another crisis and wanted to try to forestall it. Kane sees the same crisis coming, but because of the extensive traveling he's done he has a broader view of the situation. He says if just one major oil company can drill, produce, supply and pass on at a cheaper rate, it will force the fat-cat oil barons to come down off their thrones and explain to their consumers what's happening.'' Brandon's expression was filled with knowledge and the hunger of challenge.

''That's why you and Kane want to take over U.S.A. Oil and merge with Tex-Am Oil?'' She shook her head. It sounded all well and good, but a little too noble for her taste. ''What about profits? Are you telling me the two of you and the stockholders are willing to give up lining their pockets?'' A deep frown etched her forehead. ''I'm part stockholder, and I'll tell you right now I'm not a charitable organization.''

''No, no. Listen, Bets, it's all very complicated, and I don't have time to explain fully.'' He pulled the car into the outdoor parking lot of DeSalvas and slowed before heading down the ramp and into the private underground parking.

"You don't think I will understand, is that it? You think I'm a dummy?"

"Hell, no. Listen..."

She turned her head away so he wouldn't see the hurt in her eyes. Nothing had changed, and she wondered disgustedly why she'd thought marriage would instantly make him see her in a different light. Her tear-filled gaze traveled up the twelve stories of the bronze-and-glass building that was DeSalvas, until it finally came to rest on the penthouse floor. Home didn't look so bright all of a sudden.

"Bets."

"I understand perfectly, Brandon. You never thought I had any brains. Why should things change now?"

"That's not true. I just never looked past your pretty face." He tried to joke away the insult.

"Thanks a lot." The car came to a stop and she picked up her purse, ready to jump out, but Brandon's hand clamped down on her arm.

"There's something I want to settle between us, JoBeth." He shifted in the leather seat, uneasy with her glaring at him. "I don't want anyone to know *why* we married."

JoBeth's eyes opened wide and stared innocently at him. "Oh, do you mean you don't want anyone to know you married me for my shares of U.S.A. Oil? Or is it that you don't want anyone to know that an empty-headed social butterfly netted the infamous bachelor and trapped him into marriage? Or—"

"Shut up, Bets." Angrily Brandon shoved open the car door and unfolded his tall body from the bucket seat. "Damn smart-mouthed woman," he mumbled as he swung her large suitcase out. He took her arm with a little more force than he normally would have and led her into the elevator. "Don't pout, Bets. It doesn't become you."

"I never pout."

Brandon laughed, dropped JoBeth's suitcase, grabbed her shoulders and spun her around to face him. "There's one other thing."

The steel doors closed and the elevator crawled swiftly, silently upward. "Damn it, Brandon! More rules?" Shrugging out of his hands, she moved away till the cold wall touched her back and stopped her retreat.

They glared at each other, ignoring the fact that they had reached the penthouse floor and that the elevator doors were bouncing open and closed, accompanied by the loud blare of the warning bell.

"This is important, JoBeth." Brandon's hand shot out, his fist slamming against the button to stop the ear-splitting racket. He shook his finger angrily, then dropped his hand when her lips tightened and her expression shifted into a look he knew of old. She was about to become as unreasonable as any other female being ordered to do something by a man. Brandon sighed and softened his tone, making sure to add a note of pleading to his voice.

"Bets, honey...." Her lips pulled tighter, and against his will his eyes began to sparkle with mischief. How many times, he wondered, had he seen that very look? And how long had it taken him to learn not to laugh, or he'd be talking to a stone wall? He wiped the mischief from his eyes and forged on. "Under no circumstances are you to let on to your uncle what's going on. I'd really prefer you didn't talk to him at all. By now he's only aware of some activity in U.S.A. Oil's stock. He's not to know until we're ready who's behind the acquisition of the shares. This is a dangerous game we're playing, and Kane has gone to a lot of trouble setting it up. Don't blow it, Bets. And please don't give me that stubborn look. This is vital to everyone's future and health.''

JoBeth shot him her dirtiest glance, then strode through the doors and headed down the long peach-carpeted hall past Lucas's old suite to Brandon's door.

"I want your solemn promise."

She hesitated, her tapping foot making a muffled thudding on the thick carpet. "I know Uncle Tramble has some unsavory habits, but really, Brandon, from your ominous tone you make him sound like a murderer."

"That's just what he is!"

JoBeth gasped, but before she had time to completely absorb his statement or demand an explanation, the suite door swung open and she found herself smothered in the arms of Matthew DeSalva. A loud hiccup sent everyone laughing.

Brandon's father tightened his hold, and she lifted tear-drenched eyes to look at Lucas, Jennifer and Shasta Stone as they stood in the entry hall, their faces alight with laughter. Another hiccup forced its way from her throat. She tried to smile, but her lips quivered and she bit down hard, grinning crookedly.

Matthew tenderly brushed away a lone, fat tear from her cheek with a roughened fingertip. "No more waterworks, baby. This is a happy occasion." He smoothed back a thick strand of hair from her forehead. "You don't know how glad I am that you're truly my daughter now. Catherine and I always loved you, you know?" He chuckled softly. "She predicted this, God bless her."

JoBeth bit harder on her lip to keep from making a fool of herself, and blinked rapidly. "I love you, too," she said, and turned with Matthew to see Brandon being congratulated by his brother and sister-in-law.

Matthew retrieved his cane from the crook of his arm and with slow stiff steps led JoBeth into the living room. He slipped his arm free of hers and left her to face Shasta, then made his way to the long gray leather couch to watch the show that was sure to come.

Shasta Masterson Stone quickly stood on tiptoes and kissed JoBeth's cheek. "Congratulations," she said, but there was a lack of joy in her greeting, almost a note of defiance.

JoBeth's smile froze and the thank-you never formed as she stared at Kane Stone's diminutive wife and her best friend. There was a glittering hardness in Shasta's velvet brown eyes that she'd never seen before. "What's the matter, Shasta?" Her eyes searched the room hurriedly before returning to the small, stylishly dressed woman before her. "Where's that gorgeous husband of yours?"

Shasta brushed the question aside with a sweep of her hand. "I guess by this marriage, Brandon now has your U.S.A. Oil shares?" She inhaled deeply. "Why couldn't you have stayed lost just for a few more months?"

Shasta's quick, waspish tongue cut JoBeth to the quick, taking her breath away. Totally at a loss as to why she was Shasta's target, she looked around frantically for Brandon or Kane to come to her rescue. "I don't . . ." she tried, then demanded, "Where's Kane? He can explain."

"My husband—" Shasta spit her spouse's title as if it were an obscenity "—is at Tex-Am's offices downtown. The man now has oil in his veins instead of blood."

Then the expressive pixie face was suddenly wiped clean of all emotion, leaving a pale mask so completely out of character that JoBeth knew something was seriously wrong and that this was not just a display of Shasta's famous temper.

"Shasta?" But she didn't get any further as Jennifer interrupted them and Shasta walked away. JoBeth's frowning gaze followed her friend as she moved toward Brandon.

"Don't worry about Shasta. She and Kane are going through a few rough spots, but they'll work everything out." Jennifer smiled hugely, her violet eyes sparkling. "Can you imagine Kane giving her up?"

"No," JoBeth murmured. It was common knowledge that the decadent and jaded Kane worshiped his sharp-tongued wife. If there was trouble it wouldn't last long. Kane would see to that. He had a way of clamping down on Shasta's overactive imagination that always amused his friends.

"JoBeth, are you all right?"

Jennifer's question jarred her out of her thoughts. She turned, gazed blankly at her new sister-in-law, and a stillness settled between them.

The awkwardness was broken by Jennifer's hand lightly touching her arm. Then she suddenly smiled, grabbed JoBeth's hands and kissed her cheek. "Welcome to the family. Though you've always been a part of the DeSalvas, now it's official. Lucas and Matthew have been absolutely beside themselves ever since Brandon called earlier. We wanted to meet you in Las Vegas, but Brandon vetoed that idea. Instead he suggested we be here when the two of you arrived."

"Listen, Jennifer..." JoBeth interrupted, her voice urgent with distress.

"Don't say it—you don't have to." Jennifer squeezed the cold hands in hers. "What's past is best forgotten. Besides, I know what you did was only to protect Lucas." She tried to look stern, but her eyes glowed with joy and confidence. "After all, you loved Lucas first...like a brother, of course."

JoBeth's happy grin grew into a genuine smile of pleasure. "Of course." Then suddenly he was there, his strong arms surrounding her with the same strength he'd given so freely all her life. She was in Lucas's arms, her head pressed to his shoulder, tears dampening his coat. "I always seem to be blubbering all over you," she mumbled.

"That's what brothers are for." He tugged on a strand of hair until she was forced to look up. "I don't know how you did it," he whispered, "but I'm proud of you. Now wipe that frown off your face and don't worry. Brandon is an intelligent man. He'll soon come around and realize what everyone has known for years."

"I've gambled my life and happiness on your convictions. I pray to heaven you and Matthew are right." She smiled shakily. "I don't think I could stand it if you turned out to be wrong and he truly didn't love me."

"I'm never wrong where my brother is concerned. Now cheer up—here's Jenny with a glass of champagne. Drink it, honey, you've got a good life and wonderful future to toast."

CHAPTER FOUR

THERE WERE ONLY SIX PEOPLE, including her, in Brandon's living room, yet with the laughter and everyone talking at once it seemed as if fifty voices filled the air. Empty champagne bottles sat on tabletops, sharing space with a few small plates, barren of the hors d'oeuvres Jennifer had thoughtfully sent out for.

JoBeth, lost in thought, was brought back to reality by Brandon's laughter. Lucas was describing the twins' latest antics. Little Matthew and Elizabeth were at an inquisitive age and stirring up enough mischief to drive the whole household crazy. She smiled, her eyes on Brandon as he chuckled at the details his father interjected every so often. She loved to watch Brandon, his gestures, smiles, the way one eyebrow climbed higher than the other, the way his eyes sparkled, the way he moved. There was nothing phony about him. He was always relaxed and at ease, taking people as they came, no matter the situation. Maybe, she mused, that was why women fell all over him. He took them at face value, yet was gifted with a special knowledge of their needs and desires. A small crease settled between her eyes as she realized for the first time just how calculating and manipulative he must be to be so wise in the ways of women.

JoBeth brought the fluted baccarat champagne glass to her lips and shifted her gaze to the pale foam, watching as it quickly receded to a clear honey liquid. Suddenly the room tilted a little to the left and she squeezed her eyes shut until the light-headedness passed. Her stomach rumbled inelegantly, a reminder that she hadn't eaten anything but a couple of hors d'oeuvres since breakfast. Sunrise seemed a decade ago and a million miles away from where she was now.

As unobtrusively as possible, she slid from the curved-back black leather chair and stood. Relieved that no one had noticed her movements, she gave her friends one more brief glance before turning toward the kitchen. But before she took a step, her attention was captured by the room's decor. She winced. Italian art deco. Linear, heavy furniture in glass and chrome was combined with glove-soft leathers in black, gray and white and accented with bold splashes of tomato red and electric blue—all the very latest designs. It was awful, she thought, and her stomach twisted painfully as if in agreement. As she slipped unnoticed through the kitchen's swinging doors, she promised herself that the very first thing she was going to do was to get rid of everything. She didn't care how loudly or vehemently Brandon protested, she couldn't live in someone else's nightmare.

JoBeth shrugged the distasteful task away. Her mind focused only on one thought: food. She yanked open the refrigerator and eyed the typical bachelor fare disgustedly. Two bottles of very expensive champagne, a half-empty bottle of vodka and some soft drinks. She grabbed a can of Coke, popped the tab and took a sip, her gaze still searching the sparse shelves.

Her nose wrinkled as she spied the open packages of lunch meat behind the bottles, coated with a green mold that would have done a medical laboratory proud. She

closed the fridge and was about to test the freshness of
a loaf of rye bread that was sitting on the counter, when
movement caught her eye and she glanced up to see
Jennifer squeezing through the swinging doors.

Jennifer was smiling, but her hands were over her
eyes, shielding them. She sighed, dropped her arms and
gazed around as if absorbing the soothing cream-and-
peach decor. "Oh, my, that room . . . It's so, so . . ."

"Busy. Loud." JoBeth grinned.

"Yes, and more. How is it possible for Brandon to be
so conservative in some ways . . . ?" She trailed off,
glancing over her shoulder toward the living room. "It's
so out of character."

Shaking her head, JoBeth wondered the same thing.
Brandon had obviously made the change since she'd
been gone.

"Shelly Ann Summers," Shasta offered helpfully as
she came through the doors, her big brown eyes dancing with mischief. "Summers Interiors Limited," she
added, noticing the puzzled expressions turned toward
her. "I'd say he dated her about two weeks too long!"

They all laughed, and it was Shasta who finally broke
the mood. "JoBeth, please say you forgive me for what
I said to you earlier and for being such a bitch. I took
my personal problems out on you. Please . . . I'm sorry,
and to prove it I'll even go shopping with you, any day,
anytime."

Shasta's pleas shocked both JoBeth and Jennifer—
they knew how much their friend loathed shopping of
any kind. JoBeth nodded, a smile playing at the corners of her mouth. "I'll hold you to your promise."
Shasta's slim shoulders slumped dramatically and they
all laughed. "Now help me find something to eat and
tell me why Kane's not here."

Once again the brown eyes that seemed to speak before any words were formed went suddenly blank, "There was an emergency problem at the Tex-Am downtown offices." She shrugged as if the matter were of little importance. "He said he'd try to make it over, but I wouldn't look for him anytime soon." JoBeth studied Shasta's stylish black-and-green silk suit and neat appearance skeptically. And as if Shasta could read her mind, she glared furiously and retorted, "Okay, so he laid my clothes out before he left." Looking down at herself, she wiggled a loden-green leather pump.

About to make a caustic comment, JoBeth paused as both she and Shasta caught Jennifer's furtive movements. "What's that?" JoBeth pointed to a shopping bag that Jennifer's foot seemed intent on pushing through the doorway leading to the dining room. "Jennifer DeSalva, what are you doing?"

"Me? Nothing, nothing." She gave the bag one more shove, but when it caught on the edge of the Persian rug at the entrance to the dining room she yanked it up and crushed it to her chest. "No, JoBeth!" she warned as both women converged on her. "Shasta, stop her. JoBeth, you don't want to see." But all three were laughing and the bag was wrestled from Jennifer's embrace. "It's just a few things Brandon asked me to remove."

Silence filled the kitchen as JoBeth pulled out a diaphanous silk and lace nightgown. Shasta whistled appreciatively and held up a black lace teddy, cut low in the bodice and high in the legs.

Jennifer and Shasta prepared themselves for JoBeth's reaction, but she only laughed and said, "Well, at least he was considerate enough to ask you to remove these." She dropped the nightgown back in the bag of lingerie. "I'm not crazy enough to think he lived a life of celibacy before our marriage." Her words and the picture they brought to mind of Brandon denying himself the pleasures of the female body were so ludicrous that all three began to giggle.

"Hush." Shasta threw a quick look toward the living room and began to stuff the teddy back into the bag. "They'll hear us and be in here in a flash."

True to her predictions, Lucas, Brandon and Matthew were soon walking into the kitchen, demanding to be enlightened as to the cause of their amusement. JoBeth munched rye bread and finished her Coke while everyone stood chatting for a few minutes. Then Jennifer's suggestion that they all leave hit her with the force of a blow. She was about to spend her first night alone with Brandon—her wedding night. She followed everyone to the door, absently thanking them and kissing them goodbye.

Granted, she reassured herself, she was his bride, but not his wife—that would come much later. Still deep in thought, she picked up her suitcase, which Brandon had dropped earlier, gave one last wave to Lucas and left the two brothers talking. She only made it to the length of the hall where it divided—one way leading to the guest bedroom, the other to the master bedroom—and had just started toward the guest room when Brandon's hand stayed her.

"Wrong way, Bets."

"What?" She jerked around, gazing down at his pointing finger. "But..." Dear heaven, surely not? Maybe he'd misunderstood. "But, but..."

"But what, Bets? You didn't have some crazy idea we were going to conduct a platonic relationship in this marriage, did you?"

The blood rushed to her head, staining her cheeks bright red. Brandon's eyes sparkled and hers widened, then she swallowed—hard. That was exactly what she'd thought. What in heaven's name had happened to all her plans? This was all wrong and she had to stop it before it went too far. "But, but..."

"So articulate this evening. Come along." He removed her suitcase from her hand, struggling a little to loosen the fingers gripping the handle. "And no more buts, Bets," he teased, leading her toward the master bedroom. Yet, for all the humor he gained from Jo-Beth's shock, there was a banked fire in the depths of his sapphire-blue eyes, a low flame waiting to be ignited. "Nothing more to say?"

She didn't like his smug smile, nor his tone, and was about to retaliate, when Brandon pushed open the door and the cavernous room yawned before her. The bed, big and wide, seemed threatening, and she balked, digging her heels in the thick carpet. But Brandon wouldn't let her escape, and like a mechanical doll she was pushed and prodded toward the adjoining bathroom. Once inside, she spun around to face him, but Brandon stepped back, smiled, then shut the door in her face.

"I'll shower in the guest bathroom," he said. There was a long pause, then he called out with laughter lacing every word. "Don't be too long... dear."

"BETS, HAVE YOU TAKEN ROOT and sprouted in there?"

She frowned at the closed bathroom door, adjusted the large towel wrapped around her and took a deep breath. Her fingers touched the brass knob and then she pulled back, suddenly afraid of what was about to happen. For years she'd dreamed of this moment. Why was she so scared now? Because, she told herself, the rest of her life teetered on the next few hours. She mustered up her courage, clasped the knob and yanked the door open.

"I was beginning to think I was going to have to call in the emergency squad to pry you out of there." His eyes gleamed as he took in her bare flesh, fresh-scrubbed face and the damp ends of her hair. It had been years since he'd seen JoBeth without all the trappings of a sophisticated woman. Standing there, she reminded him of the little girl with mousy-brown hair and flying pigtails who was always tagging along behind him. And for some unexplainable reason, though he knew it was silly, she reminded him of a virgin. Brandon shook his head. God, that was a laugh. JoBeth had had men trailing after her all her life, and the affairs must have mounted over the years. Yet there was an uncertainty in her eyes that gave him pause. He reached out and gently clasped her shoulders, restraining the urge to yank her roughly to him. Her skin felt warm, and as soft as silk. "Do you realize that we've never kissed?" he asked, his voice surprisingly husky.

Why, she wondered, had she never noticed that Brandon had predatory eyes: hot and hungry? She wanted to say something funny, anything to break that unnerving, hypnotic gaze. Her knees were shaking and she felt weak and warm all over. She cleared her throat. "Actually, we have kissed before."

His thumbs had been moving lightly back and forth over her collarbone, circling lower and lower with each stroke, but at her words they stopped. He smiled and let the tips of his fingers trail across the tops of her breasts.

"When I was ten and you were sixteen—at Christmas." At Brandon's caress the last word caught in the back of her throat and her towel loosened and slipped a fraction. "I caught you under the mistletoe and everyone teased you so you had to kiss me." There was too much male skin exposed, even though a towel was wrapped around his waist. He was too close and the heat from his body did strange things to her senses. "You wiped the kiss away with the back of your hand afterward."

"Let's try it again, shall we? This time I promise I won't wipe it away."

JoBeth studied his face, seeing something she'd never seen there before—desire. At least, she'd never seen it directed at her. He was devastatingly handsome. Now she knew why women said he had only to look at them and they'd follow him anywhere. She took a step, bringing herself into his embrace. "Just hold me for a minute, Brandon."

She rested her cheek against his shoulder, inhaling the clean male scent of him, and closed her eyes. His arms tightened and he began to rock her back and forth. The comforting motion and his nearness were all she needed. Her fears and hesitation fled and she snuggled closer, loving the feel of being in his arms. This was where she was meant to be. She raised her eyes. "Thank you, Brandon. Now I think I'd like that kiss."

He chuckled. "Would you now?" He was a little puzzled at the tenderness he felt, the need to make this first kiss something special. But the restraint he was having to exert over his desire was even more puzzling.

JoBeth's eyes closed. She could feel his nearness, his mouth lowering toward hers as she eagerly moved to meet him. But when their noses bumped, her eyes flew open. The movement was so awkward and unexpected that, nose to nose, they began to laugh. It was the catalyst that released their inhibitions, and still laughing, they fell backward onto the bed, seeking the feel of flesh against flesh. Her towel bunched around her and she murmured a protest. Then suddenly they were both naked and she couldn't seem to get close enough. She wiggled in his embrace. The move brought a groan from Brandon and she smiled to herself. Yes, he wanted her. The evidence of his desire nudged against her with a velvet firmness that was unmistakable.

"How lovely you are," he whispered in her ear, his eyes touching her everywhere.

She was thinking the same thing about him. With his tall body, the whipcord leanness and the pattern of veins that played over the muscles, he was sexier than any man she'd known.

"Where are you, JoBeth?" He rolled her onto her back, covering her with his warmth.

"I was thinking about the past," she lied. "About the time—"

"Well, stop it, Bets. If you think too deeply about the past we're liable to start arguing, and this is definitely not the time for that." His head dipped and his mouth covered a pert nipple, savoring the taste of her skin.

JoBeth's mind lost all hold on the past, the present and the future as Brandon assaulted her senses with his expertise. She murmured his name, alternately cursing and pleading with him to stop playing with her. He seemed to want to test his power over her, and she realized he had total control of the situation. He was all male, tender, rough—sweet and demanding. And she reciprocated with her own brand of torture and reward, making him call her name in the darkness and loving the husky plea for release in his voice.

Moments later, spent and exhausted, Brandon shifted JoBeth's limp body closer to his and asked, "What are you thinking, Bets?"

She sighed as one of his hands cupped her breast with a possessiveness that thrilled her. Closing her eyes, she could still feel the cloudlike drifting of her mind and body.

"Don't go to sleep, Bets. I want to talk."

She chuckled at the notion. "I wouldn't have taken you for a talker."

"Most times I'm not, but this is different. You're my wife and I want to know what you're thinking."

"I was thinking about the time I caught you peeking through the bathroom window while I was taking a bath."

"I never!" he returned indignantly, then laughed. "You little devil, you knew I was there and you stripped for me." He still remembered what the sight of her, even her budding thirteen-year-old body, had done to him. As punishment, his hand slipped between her legs and when she laughingly tried to wiggle away he held her firmly, growling in her ear as he heard her breathing catch. "You didn't have too much to offer a nineteen-year-old. I had more mature girls on my mind then."

"Oh, yeah? Then why...?" She trailed off with gasp. "Stop it, Brandon!"

"Why? Don't you want to make love again?"

"Yes, but, but..."

"You're just full of buts tonight, Bets. It's not like you to be at a loss for words. What's the matter?" he taunted, then shifted his body over hers and slid into the warmth she offered. "I want you again."

JoBeth watched the play of shadows as the clouds moved across the moon's surface. She'd never realized how open the penthouse suite was with its two walls of windows extending from floor to ceiling, making her feel as though a huge hand cradled them in its palm and was stretched toward the stars. She sighed softly and eased the covers up over their naked bodies. If the world stopped tomorrow she wouldn't cry at its loss; she'd been loved by Brandon. And if anyone were to call it "just sex," she would argue that there had been too much feeling and passion between them to consider their experience merely sex. Maybe Lucas was correct and Brandon did love her; he just hadn't realized it yet. Suddenly, like a snapshot, an image flashed in her mind. A picture of herself at nineteen. She'd been in Switzerland at finishing school when she'd received one of her father's infrequent letters. Her world had fallen apart as she'd read that Brandon had become engaged. Two hours later she found herself suffering from too much to drink and in a young Swiss's bed. She'd lost more than her virginity that night: she'd lost all hope. The next morning while she sat in the head mistress's office, awaiting a call from her father to tell him she'd been expelled and to come and get her, she faced up to what she had done. She'd saved herself for the man she'd loved and he'd thrown her aside. No matter that Brandon didn't know she existed or that she was no more than a nuisance. She made up her mind then and there that he would never make her cry again, nor would she ruin her life over him. A week later, when her father was able to leave his Middle East negotiations, she learned that Brandon's engagement had only lasted three days. She wanted to kill him. How could he have done that to her? JoBeth grinned at the memory of the irrational and illogical thoughts of a teenager and wondered how she'd managed to survive those long, agonizing years.

"Want to tell me what's so funny?"

"Oh! Just a memory."

"I hope not of another man?"

She turned over and tried to make out his expression in the moonlit room. "I have to tell you something." She wanted to change the subject as quickly as possible, knowing Brandon's ability to extract information. She refused to let him know that she'd been daydreaming about the past. "Brandon, satin sheets are really tacky."

The bed began to jiggle, and she reached out and touched his shaking shoulders as he buried his head in the pillow. After a few seconds of muffled laughter, Brandon lifted his head, his eyes gleaming brightly in the shadows. "I know, and they're damn hard to sleep on, too. The last time I dived into bed, I landed on the floor on the opposite side. Maybe you'll buy something decent tomorrow?"

"I take it when you had the place redecorated the bedroom was not neglected."

There was a long silence as Brandon realized the significance of her question. "Right," he answered curtly. When he could feel the next question coming, he forestalled it. "I don't ask about your past, so don't delve too deeply into mine. We'll manage better that way."

Now she really wanted to change the subject. "Brandon, you intimated earlier that my uncle was some sort of criminal. Would you tell me what you meant? Also, you were going to tell me why Kane is so eager to oust Uncle Tram. I think I'd like to know that, too."

"Now? My God, Bets, it's four o'clock in the morning. I'm sleepy and worn out." He wrapped his arms around her, tightened his hold and tried to roll her over him to the other side. But JoBeth suddenly became uncooperative, all legs and arms, refusing to be removed from her spot. Momentarily giving up the battle, he said, "Come on, Bets, crawl over so I can go to sleep."

"I don't like that side of the bed, Brandon."

"Listen," he growled softly, "I don't sleep with my back to the door. Now move your butt."

JoBeth giggled as a picture flashed into her head. "Does the big gunslinger wear his .45s to bed?" A pillow was stuffed in her face and she only had time to yank it down and murmur, " 'Back to the door.' Really Brandon, you'd think at any minute you expect a burglar to come in here." She finished the sentence on a squeal as she was bodily lifted and dropped on the opposite side of the bed. "I'll never close my eyes sleeping on this side," she lamented loudly.

"Try."

THE SOUND OF THE SHOWER woke her the next morning. With heavy eyelids she crawled out of bed and stumbled disorientedly to stand in the open bathroom doorway. Her confusion disappeared as Brandon began to sing in perfect tone. A sleepy smile played around the corners of her lips as she remembered the previous night, and the smile grew when the importance of what had happened in the past twenty-four hours struck her. She was Mrs. Brandon DeSalva. She tiptoed across the warm tile floor, yanked open the shower door and slipped in before Brandon could catch his breath to protest. Wrapping her arms around his soap-slick flesh, she rubbed against him, loving the immediate response from his body. She lifted her head and kissed him while her hands ran up and down his wet back, then came to rest on the hard muscled mounds. "You've got nice buns."

"What?" He nearly choked on a mouthful of hot water.

"Buns. You know—your behind. I've always admired it." She rubbed her palms across the tight flesh, then patted him a couple of times.

"Not in the shower, Bets. I'll kill myself."

"Oh, I don't know, I think there's more to you than you let on. Come on, sweet cheeks."

Brandon was racked with a coughing fit. " 'Sweet cheeks'?" he whispered. "You sexist— What a thing to call your husband, especially at eight o'clock in the morning." But any further comments died on his lips as he gave in to the fact that JoBeth's nakedness was driving him crazy. His mouth captured hers and he crushed her swollen breasts to his chest. Then suddenly they were both screaming and jumping apart as the water switched from hot to ice-cold, immediately extinguishing their desire and turning their warm flesh to cold goose bumps.

He hopped from the shower and pulled JoBeth with him, laughing as he wrapped a towel around her and used another to dry her hair. A few minutes later she emerged from the fluffy folds, and he grinned. "The way you look now reminds me of the time you *slipped* and fell into the manure pile...."

"I was pushed," she retorted.

Brandon shrugged, his lips twitching at her fierce scowl. "All right, pushed. Anyway, you have that same surprised look as you did then, after I pulled you out of the river."

"Lucas rescued me. *You* threw me in." She struggled with the towel that was wrapped loosely around her body, trying to hold it up with one hand while the other was busy fighting the poorly secured towel on her head. One side kept slipping over her eye, and she finally gave up and pulled it off with a snap. "Where are my clothes?"

Brandon fought to keep his expression straight and pointed toward the closet, not trusting his voice to remain steady. "I'll go and make some coffee."

JoBeth smiled sweetly. "Oh, do you mean to tell me you actually have something in this place other than the trappings for seduction?"

Brandon stopped in midstride and turned around. "Don't push it, Bets."

JoBeth stared at his retreating back. Well, everything wasn't as bright in paradise as she'd thought.

Finally dressed in what she had termed lately her security blanket—worn jeans and white Western shirt—she entered the kitchen ready to do battle for some answers. But her words were cut off as the aroma of freshly brewed coffee assaulted her empty stomach. "Is there anything to eat around this place?"

"Caviar, crackers—rather stale, I'm afraid—three kinds of pâté."

"Ugh." She made a horrible face at him.

He handed her an oversize mug of hot coffee and waved at her to sit down across the table from him. "I guess you'll have to go to the grocery store today."

"Me! Where is your housekeeper and the cook you had?" Silence filled the kitchen as she watched him struggle for an explanation he thought fit for his wife. No matter that before he wouldn't have hesitated to tell her that because of all his affairs he needed more privacy. She was just thrilled that he wanted to protect her from his past. Her heart beat faster at the thought, then slowed to a more normal rate at his next words.

"I've been busy setting up the computerized drilling rig and was never home, so I let them go. I guess if we eat it's up to you. You can cook, can't you?"

JoBeth looked him straight in the eye and lied. "Of course. Your mother taught me." She continued her bluff. "Don't you remember?"

Brandon shook his head, then took a sip of coffee, eyeing her over the rim. "All I recall is being forced to eat burned chocolate-chip cookies and brownies that were like bricks."

JoBeth raised the mug to her lips and murmured, "Oh, how soon we forget." She thought it prudent to change the line of conversation and asked, "You don't truly expect me to clean and scrub, do you, because if you do you're in for a big shock."

Brandon chuckled. "No, do whatever you like. Hire someone. I'll have my secretary send you over some money and I'll make sure she contacts all the stores so you can charge. I'm sure you want to buy some new clothes."

She looked down at the well-worn jeans and shirt, realizing she would miss their comfort. Maybe she wasn't ready to part with them. "I think I'll wait till you give me the money for my stocks before going on a buying spree."

"Like hell." Brandon's mug hit the glass table with a sound that made JoBeth flinch. "You're my wife. You'll spend my money. I mean it, JoBeth. The money from your shares is to be invested. No clothes, jewelry, furs or cars are to be bought with that money. Do I make myself clear?"

"Yes, but—"

"No buts, Bets." Then he laughed, surprising her with the bright sparkle in his eyes. "There are entirely too many 'buts' from you lately." He looked down at his watch and started to rise.

For the first time JoBeth noticed that he was dressed in a three-piece suit. "Where are you going?" she asked, frowning.

"Work." He reached across the table and laid his finger on her lips. "Please don't say 'but.'"

JoBeth knocked his hand away, hurt beyond belief that he was going to leave her on their honeymoon. Then she had to remind herself that she'd forced him into this sudden marriage and that he didn't consider this day any more special than any other. She bit down on her lip to keep it from trembling. "Well, what am I supposed to do with myself?" she demanded.

"Now how the hell would I know? Do what you always used to do." Slowly he climbed to his feet, reluctant to leave her when he'd hurt her feelings. "Listen, Bets. I have to go. There are people waiting on me."

She followed him to the door with dragging steps, and when he turned around she refused to look at him. Instead her gaze took in the living room, and she winced. If she was going to live here the whole place would have to be changed.

"Bets, are you listening to me?"

"No."

"Then please do. This is important. You are not to talk to your uncle."

He opened the door and walked down the corridor, JoBeth at his side. "And what am I supposed to do if he calls me? You don't think our marriage is going to remain a secret long, do you?"

"No, actually the announcement is in this morning's paper, thanks to Lucas!" He slipped the keys from his pocket and opened the door leading to the roof, holding it wide for her.

JoBeth realized where they were and stopped Brandon from continuing up the stone steps by blocking his way. "Where are you going?"

"I told you, Bets, to work." Exasperated with the delay, he grasped her shoulders to move her aside, but instead suddenly found her in his arms, her mouth against his. For a fraction of a second he thought of resisting, but the taste of her lips was too intoxicating. "This is not fair play, Bets," he whispered against her eager mouth. "I have to go. The helicopter is here to take me to the offshore oil rig."

JoBeth eyed his suit, shook her head and laughed. The lawyer in him refused to change, and his conservative attire suddenly irritated her enough to let him go. She stepped back and followed him to the roof, where the company helicopter waited. "When will you be home?"

Brandon frowned, unused to answering to anyone for his actions. He was about to tell her it was none of her business then stopped when he realized that it was not just JoBeth demanding to know, but his wife. He wasn't sure if he liked having to account for his time and actions to anyone else. He glared at the ground and spun around without answering. Once at the helicopter, though, he glanced over his shoulder, hating himself for the lost look he saw, even though she tried to disguise her hurt by shielding her eyes from the morning sun. He felt like a heel as he strapped himself in and signaled to the pilot that he was secure, yet he refused to give in and wave. After all, she'd forced him into marriage, hadn't she? She'd just have to accept what he offered.

JoBeth watched her husband lift off, and stayed on the roof as the aircraft circled the Galleria and headed south toward the Gulf of Mexico. Damn his arrogance! She'd show him.

But once in the suite the quiet drummed heavily in her ears and she knew she couldn't stay there. She was just about to call Jennifer to see if they were still in Lucas's old suite, when the phone rang. Her hand hovered over the instrument, itching to pick it up, but Brandon's warning came back to her and she only glared at it. Then angrily she yanked it up, swearing to herself that Brandon DeSalva was not going to make a slave of her and tell her who she could speak to or what she could or could not do. "Hello!" The static was terrible and she yelled, "Who is it?"

"If you need something to do today," Brandon hollered over the helicopter's phone, "why don't you have something done about your hair. You don't have the temperament for mousy brown. Besides, I prefer you as a blonde."

The static and Brandon's voice were suddenly replaced with a soft dial tone, and JoBeth slammed down the receiver. She was going to get even with him. Looking around at the atrocity he called home, she rubbed her hands together. When he walked through that door this evening he wasn't going to recognize the place.

She was on her way to the bedroom to collect her purse, when she realized he'd gotten away without answering her questions about her uncle. He hadn't told her what had happened to make him think Uncle

Tramble was some kind of criminal. That was just another little item on a long list that Brandon DeSalva was going to have to explain to her, and soon.

CHAPTER FIVE

JoBeth heard the sound of a key in the door and frantically glanced around the bare living room, its Italian art deco furniture replaced with cedar wardrobe cases. She set down her glass of wine and slowly stood, being careful not to catch her white silk Charmeuse jump suit on the rough wood of the case she'd been sitting on.

"Bets, what the hell is going on?" Brandon dodged a tall wardrobe box, came to the entrance of the living room and stopped. He stood speechless for a long minute, taking in the stripped room, then turned his unbelieving gaze on his wife. "What is all this?"

"Some clothes I had in storage."

"And this?" He waved his hand, indicating the bare room.

"I didn't like the decor."

"So I see." His expression altered and suddenly he sprinted toward the master bedroom, JoBeth on his heels. Once there he sighed with relief. Though the room had been redecorated, there was still a bed. The wild gray-and-red bedspread had been replaced with a muted floral cover, and where there had been uncomfortable chairs there were now lovely wing chairs in a pastel mint green. "Bets, where is the living room furniture? And is this the only room you've seen fit to redecorate?"

She gave him a Scotch on the rocks and led him back to the living room. "Actually, after I had a good look at the dining room, I decided I like the black lacquer chairs and table."

"Thank you. I picked them out." He took a hefty slug of his drink. "Now would you mind telling me what happened to the other furniture and when this room will be in order?"

JoBeth lifted the wineglass to her lips, then lowered it without taking a sip. She might as well tell him now. "I miscalculated a little, Brandon. I thought Hastings Interiors could have the items I picked out delivered today." She laughed a little despairingly. "I guess I don't have as much influence as I used to. There was a time—"

"When?"

"About a week." She turned her back on him, leaned down to pick up the bottle of wine from the floor and murmured, "Or two."

"I heard that, Bets!" Brandon stopped, ran his hand through his hair and sighed heavily. A year's absence hadn't changed her any. She was still as scatterbrained as ever. "What was all this business about disrupting the whole building this afternoon?"

JoBeth studied her freshly manicured nails, then smoothed the waist of her jump suit. "I want you to know I don't like that new secretary you hired. She's a tattletale. Where's Cleo?"

"Never mind Cleo. And Sue Parkinson is a top-rate legal secretary. Now what happened?"

"Do you know you went off without giving me any keys to the private elevator? If Lucas and Jennifer hadn't still been here to rescue me I'd have been locked up in this suite all day."

"JoBeth!"

She gulped some of her wine, hoping for a little more courage. "Well, Brandon, the penthouse elevator is *so* small. I called security and we commandeered the public elevators for a short while." She took a breath and went on before he could interrupt. "Do you have any idea how heavy all that Italian junk was? The movers could only get one or two of those monstrosities in the elevator at a time and every minute was costing you a fortune. So they made short trips, filling the penthouse elevator, unloading it on the twelfth floor, then transferring full loads to the two main elevators."

"So you tied up every elevator in the building for three hours? People had to use the stairs if they wanted to get from floor to floor?"

She stared at him, her gray eyes wide with an innocence they both knew was false. "I didn't think it was three hours, sweet cheeks. Your secretary exaggerated a tiny bit."

Brandon couldn't help himself; he began to laugh at the nickname. "If you ever slip up and call me that in public...so help me." But he didn't finish as he grabbed her and pulled her into his arms. "You'll never change, will you, Bets?" His lips captured hers before she could answer.

When Brandon finally raised his head, he smiled and stroked the bright blond hair. "Thank heavens you went to the beauty shop. I was beginning to despair of ever seeing the old you again. What else did you do today, or should I ask? And I'm starving. Are we eating here or do we have to go out?"

With his hand in hers she led him to the dining room and watched with excitement as he took in the beautifully laid table. She'd managed to get, among other things, her mother's fine china and crystal out of storage. "Have a seat and I'll bring the salad."

He was half seated, then suddenly jerked upright. "Can I help?"

"No!" She'd almost yelled, and had to calm herself to answer again. "No, no. I have everything under control." Hurrying through the wide swinging doors, she waited until they stilled and then let her breath out.

She would have to be very careful until she could hire a cook. Still, it would be better not to let him find out she was as incompetent as he accused her of being. JoBeth thanked her lucky stars for the microwave, frozen entrées, vegetables and desserts. She'd planned the next few days' meals with the precision of a military maneuver.

As she quickly punched holes in the thick plastic package and shoved the shrimp with lobster sauce into the oven, she had to fight back a giggle. The maintenance man had looked so confused when she'd lamely told him the loud bell on the microwave made her nervous.

Now all she had to do was time the food by her watch and she'd be able to serve Brandon good hot meals without his being any the wiser. Of course, she reminded herself, she'd have to keep him away from the stuffed freezer, too.

With two green salads in hand she backed through the swinging doors and sat down. "The white wine is behind you in the cooler." With a satisfied snap of her napkin and a quick peek at her watch, she smiled across the table.

He'd seen that look before and was instantly suspicious. "You wouldn't try to poison your new husband, would you, Bets?"

"Of course not." She picked up her fork and began to eat. "By the way, I gave the furniture to the Salvation Army." Looking up from her plate, her eyes sparkled and her lips refused to be still. "Though I had to talk them into carting the stuff away. Really, Brandon! How could you have let any woman talk you into buying that junk?"

"You're treading on thin ice, Bets. Let's just drop it, shall we?" He was eager to change the subject and wondered what husbands and wives talked about at the dinner table. Then he almost laughed aloud. He'd never had any difficulty with dinner conversation before. Why was he struggling now? "How was your day? What did you do besides redecorate and go to the beauty shop? Did you call any of your old friends?"

JoBeth grinned as she realized what he was doing. She picked up her Waterford wineglass and gazed at the pale liquid. "I called my attorney and instructed him to rescind the power of attorney Tramble has over my stock. He sent the papers late this afternoon for my signature and said he'd have them delivered to Uncle Tram by courier first thing tomorrow morning." She chuckled as she remembered her attorney's enthusiasm to rid himself of any further dealings with Tramble Carter Baldwin. But her amusement faded when she caught Brandon's scowl.

"I wish you hadn't done that yet."

"Why? For heaven's sake, Brandon, you were the one who told me that Uncle Tram was using my shares for his own gain. I would have thought firing men who had been loyal for years just because they were approaching retirement would be reason enough to stop him *now*.... Oh, I see." She glanced at her watch, jumped up and grabbed their salad plates. "You don't want to rock the boat till you and Kane are ready. Excuse me."

Once in the kitchen she slammed down the plates, grabbed the scissors and went to work on the plastic pouches. Once their dinner plates were heaped with rice and shrimp with lobster sauce, she backed through the door again. "Just a minute." In and out once more, she returned with a silver basket lined with linen and lace and heaping with hot French bread. "Where was I?"

"It's okay, Bets. I wasn't thinking about Kane or our deal, but that you and I have to get our business straight before we take on anyone else." He took a bite of the shrimp. "This is good." He took another bite and amended his words. "I take that back. This is great. Where in the world did you learn to cook like a Cordon Bleu chef? I know Mother never taught you anything this complicated. You were too young."

JoBeth ducked her head, staring at her plate with eyes that sparkled entirely too much. "Finishing school. I learned to cook in Switzerland. But your mother taught me the basics." It was true. Catherine DeSalva had agonized over the fact that JoBeth could never keep her attention off Brandon long enough to learn the art of cooking.

She fought to retain control of her expression and finally was able to look up. "May I have some more wine?" He was gazing at her strangely and she could only hope her frozen smile didn't give anything away.

With all his compliments over the dinner, she felt like a heel and the meal seemed to drag on forever. This was definitely not going as planned. It was with relief that she stacked the dishes in the sink and joined Brandon on a crate in the living room.

"Would you like me to show you how to load the dishwasher?"

"No. I hired a maid today. She'll be here in the morning and can clean up the kitchen then."

He poured her a Drambuie and a cup of coffee and came back to sit beside her on the crate. "I've brought some papers that need your signature, Bets." Picking up his briefcase, he placed it across his knees and snapped open the locks.

For some reason the sound made her heart plummet. She'd allowed herself to live in a fantasy world for the past two days. Now reality was about to intrude and the real reason for this marriage would be staring at her in black and white. She quickly lifted the snifter to her lips and took a hefty sip of liqueur to wash away the sorrow that was beginning to choke her.

The fiery liquid eased the ache in her throat, but did nothing for the ache in her heart. She accepted the piece of paper he handed her, jumped to her feet and walked to the high wall of windows. Houston's skyline was before her as the long day slipped away under the setting sun's red glow.

She looked down at the check in her hand. After all was said and done, after all the laughter and what she'd mistakenly thought was the beginning of love, it all came down to an impressive series of zeros on a check.

"You need to sign this, Bets. No, read it first, though it's just a simple sale transaction of your twenty percent share of stock." He watched her as she quickly walked back to him, read the document and scrawled her signature with a flourish. He sensed something was deeply wrong, yet was at a total loss as to what or why. Then he silently berated himself. When had he ever understood JoBeth? This was what she wanted, the way she wanted it. Damn it! Then why did he have this feeling of loss?

Brandon handed her another sheet of paper, his voice now gruff as he explained, "This is a statement granting me your power of attorney on the remaining twenty percent. It gives me full voting rights over those shares, but I won't receive any monetary gain from royalties."

After she had signed and handed the papers back, Brandon poured them both a generous amount of liqueur. He hesitated a second, shrugged, then pulled more papers from his briefcase. "These are our wills. I had my secretary draw them up for us today. They're really quite simple. If I die, everything, excluding my interest and holdings in DeSalvas, is bequeathed to you. Your will is virtually the same, making me your beneficiary to everything except your shares in U.S.A. Oil and any other investments and stock you acquired before our marriage."

"Covering all your bases, Brandon?"

"Goddamn it, Bets, that's not fair."

It wasn't and she wanted to take back the words the minute they had left her mouth. This was the lawyer in Brandon—she'd seen it a million times over the years—and like all lawyers, he liked loose ends neatly tied into an acceptable package. "Sorry." But she couldn't muster up a smile. "Where do I sign?" Making a grab for the papers, she found she was playing a game of tug-of-war with him.

"You're not to sign this until tomorrow in front of witnesses. Your lawyer should go over it with you first, check everything out, make any changes you want."

"Fine. Let go!"

"No, not until you understand." She released her hold on the documents and he sat down carefully, avoiding the protruding nail on the corner of the crate. "Stop scowling, Bets. I'm not going to murder you in your bed."

"Not even for the other twenty percent?" Her mouth twisted in a parody of a smile.

It was Brandon's turn to frown. "JoBeth, did you *ever* read your grandfather's will?"

She shook her head, sat down on the thick carpet and reached for the liqueur bottle. For the first time in her life she wanted to get blessedly carefree and forget what she'd done.

"Did your dad's attorney ever read it to you?"

"No." She gazed at him, her eyes blank.

There was a long thoughtful pause as Brandon studied the far wall, working out the reasons behind his fellow attorney's somewhat unethical silence. "Then you really never knew you could sell your shares in U.S.A. Oil anytime or to anyone till I told you?" She nodded and he went on. "I suppose your lawyer, realizing your state of mind after your dad's suicide and the scandal, thought it best not to go into too much detail. But, Bets, if you were to die tomorrow, next week, or thirty years from now, your shares would automatically go to your legitimate heirs, your children. And if you have no heir, as stipulated in the original will, your stock reverts back to your family—Tramble. That's why I've tried to impress upon you to be very careful where he's concerned."

"That's about the third or fourth time you've either hinted at or accused Uncle Tram of being some kind of monster. Come on, Brandon, he's an old man, for God's sake."

"But not so old that he couldn't hire someone to kill you. He's done it before. The fact that you're his niece and blood kin wouldn't bother him in the least. If you stood in Tramble's way, he'd simply have you removed.''

She couldn't believe her ears. Her uncle was no saint, but then what multibillionaire who'd managed to hold on to an empire was? "Enough! I want to know what you have on him that makes you hate him so."

Brandon slid off the wooden crate and settled on the carpet across from JoBeth. "Oh, I don't hate him. I'm just a realist who knows that when you corner a rat, no matter how small or how big his opponent, the rat will turn and try to devour his enemy. Your uncle is no different." Without a word he removed the crystal liqueur glass from her hand and gave her a cup of coffee. "Do you remember about two years ago when Kane came back to the States and began dating Shasta?" He waited for her nod before going on, making sure he had her undivided attention. "Well, Kane didn't come back just because he had a yearning for America. He returned to find a murderer—or as he says, 'the power behind a murder.' It seems he'd become friends with a former employee of U.S.A. Oil, a scientist who had discovered a synthetic fuel formula. Kane was very close to the old man, and when he was run down in some back street in France, Kane found a lead and followed it, straight to U.S.A. Oil and your uncle. I know it's hard to believe, but, Bets, you have to understand how financially disastrous the discovery of a successful synethetic fuel formula would be on the oil industry and U.S.A. Oil. Kane doesn't know how Tramble found out what was going on, but he says he ordered his men to retrieve the formula at any cost and eliminate the scientist. Now Kane and I want to develop and distribute that fuel.''

JoBeth rubbed her hand across her forehead, suddenly angry with herself for drinking too much. What Brandon was telling her was important. She knew he wasn't making it up, but still, she couldn't believe her uncle was a cold-blooded killer. Her skeptical expression warned Brandon that she doubted him.

"Damn it, JoBeth! This is no fairy tale. I wouldn't make up a story like this just to get voting control of your stock. Ask Kane—or better still, ask Shasta. Your uncle tried to kill her, too."

"What?"

"He tried to have her run down. It seems Tramble has a penchant for hit-and-run accidents."

Horrified, she studied him. She was torn: she knew he was telling the truth, yet she just didn't want to believe it. "If what you say is true, then why hasn't he been arrested?"

"No proof. Not the kind that would hold up in court, anyway, but he's guilty, Bets."

She leaned forward, rested her elbows on her folded legs and covered her face with her hands. "I don't know. I just don't know. This is all so crazy." Weary and a little tipsy, she dropped her hands and stared at Brandon. There was more to her exhaustion and worry than what he'd told her about her uncle. She realized that something had changed between her and Brandon tonight, and it wasn't for the better. Climbing slowly and a little shakily to her feet, she mumbled, "I'm going to bed. Maybe there I can think this all out." When he started to get up, too, she said, "Good night, Brandon," hoping to discourage him from following her.

She needed to be alone for a while to try to come to grips with the news that her only living relative was responsible for the murder of one man and had threatened the life of one of her close friends. Most of all, she needed the time alone to figure out how she was going to alleviate the coolness that seemed to have entered into her relationship with Brandon.

Those damn shares and the agreement—all her fault, of course. Until tonight he'd seemed to have forgotten the way she'd forced him into marriage. But now, with everything signed, sealed and delivered, there was no need to kid themselves that their marriage was anything more than a business agreement. She stripped off her clothes and crawled into bed, ignoring the fact that she was on his side. Then she closed her eyes, letting her mind drift with the effects of alcohol, until she finally fell asleep.

A SUNNY, CHEERFUL DAY and an empty bed greeted her the next morning. Her eyes felt gritty, as though they were filled with sand, her head pounded relentlessly, and the inside of her mouth... That was beyond description. But two hours later and with great difficulty, she managed to pull herself together enough to dress, then to eat some toast. Glumly she gazed rather glassy eyed at the clear blue sky, wondering what she was going to do with herself. Not only today, but every day from now on.

She needed to get out of this place and have a few laughs. The first person who sprang to mind was Shasta, and JoBeth was just reaching for the phone when it rang. Snatching up the receiver, she answered, "Penthouse."

"Mrs. DeSalva, there's a Mr. Baldwin in the lobby, wanting to see you. May I send him up?"

Her heart rocketed to her throat. Uncle Tramble! Panicking, she glanced around as if help were hiding in a dark corner or lurking beyond a wardrobe packing crate.

"Mrs. DeSalva, are you there?"

Between her reluctance to see her uncle and hearing herself called Mrs. DeSalva for the first time, she forgot Brandon's warning and threw caution to the wind. "Yes, send him on up."

The few minutes she stood at the penthouse's open door seemed like an hour. A light began to blink, announcing the arrival of the elevator. She held her breath.

All her life she'd let this man intimidate her. Though his advice was always good, his arrogance in dispensing it galled her. She knew he'd always despised her father, calling him a roughneck wildcatter and an opportunist. There had been fights behind closed doors that she had never learned the outcome of, but they'd always left her good-hearted father depressed and angry.

"Married life must agree with you, honey. Your mind is a million miles away."

"Hello, Uncle Tramble." JoBeth fixed a smile on her face and stepped back, allowing him to enter. She'd used those few seconds to study him. Tramble Baldwin hadn't changed in the least since as far back as she could remember. His portly body always moved with deceptive swiftness; his whiskey-and-tobacco voice could hold so much contempt that it could freeze his victim. But it was the honeyed endearments in the gravelly tone that always made her uneasy.

She followed him and watched as he surveyed the stripped living room. "We're redecorating."

Tramble took off his Stetson and ran a hand spotted and veined with age through his thinning gray hair. "I'll have to give it to you, honey. You fall in a pile of manure and come up smelling like a rose. Yes, sir. Brandon DeSalva is quite a catch." He smiled, showing a mouthful of even white teeth. "'Course, with his reputation with the women, I wouldn't get too attached. However, these days married couples go their separate ways, don't they?"

"No." She was immediately defensive. "Did you come up here to make slurs on our marriage or to wish me well?"

His dark eyes narrowed, the creped lids making him look suddenly sinister. "Neither. Is there somewhere in this damnable place where an old man can sit down?" He followed her into the dining room and pulled out a chair, lowering his overweight body slowly onto the cushion. With a sigh, he fumbled in his breast pocket and extracted a thick cigar. Recalling years of smelling the obnoxious smoke, she pushed him an ashtray and waited. But Tramble didn't seem disposed to hurry, and the delay gave her time to compose herself. He was just an old man, she reminded herself, and her uncle at that.

Tramble chewed the cigar from one side of his mouth to the other until he found a comfortable position for it. "Sweetheart, you're not naive enough to believe a man with Brandon's appetites will be content with one woman, are you?"

She tried to interrupt, but he continued talking, his loud voice drowning out her objections.

"It was all very noble of you, girlie, to almost bankrupt yourself by paying off Harold's bad dealings, but I hope you'll be smart enough now to get some of that DeSalva money in your back pocket before Brandon goes on to greener pastures in his pursuits."

"Uncle Tramble! Brandon and I love each other."

"Sure, and a dog doesn't have fleas." He laughed, a raucous sound of disbelief and amusement. His rotund girth shook and his pale face flushed. Then suddenly his skin turned a pasty white.

"Uncle Tram, what's the matter? What's wrong?" She leaped to her feet and hurried around the table to him.

Tramble waved her away and in a choked voice asked, "Some water." When JoBeth returned from the kitchen he popped the top off a bottle he was gripping tightly and shook out two white pills. After the water washed them down he sighed. Then, from a small gold box, he carefully extracted a tiny pill and placed it under his tongue as he'd done with another one when she was out of the room. He closed his eyes.

"Uncle Tram?"

"I'm all right—just nerves—give me a minute."

JoBeth waited and watched anxiously. When his eyelids finally lifted, she found herself gazing into gray eyes just like hers. But his were glaring, filled with a cunning hate. She blinked, surprised by the depths of emotion radiating from him.

"I'd like you to explain this, girl." He yanked a single sheet of paper from his coat pocket and slammed it down on the table between them. His hand balled into a tight fist beside the document and his big diamond ring flashed and winked.

She knew what the paper was without looking. Swallowing her apprehension and remembering Brandon's warning, she straightened her shoulders, refusing to show him that she was quaking inside. "I thought it was time I took control of my life."

"That's all fine and good." He sucked angrily on his cigar a moment. "I've been running U.S.A. Oil for forty-five years. I don't need some female sticking her fingers in my business. Now you just ring up that fancy lawyer of yours and rescind this." He shoved the paper at her, scowling fiercely.

"I can't do that." Brandon had put her in an awkward and dangerous position. She couldn't back down now and do what her uncle wanted because she'd already given control to Brandon. She couldn't tell her uncle she'd sold half of her holdings, either. All she could do was try to bluff her way through this meeting the best way she knew how.

"'Can't'! The word is not in my vocabulary. Of course you can. Just call and have the changes made— *now*."

She had to get him out of the suite. "Uncle Tram, I have an appointment. I just can't think about this now." A little empty-headedness wouldn't hurt. She rose and he followed her to the door. Then suddenly she was ashamed of herself for being such a coward. "A year away has taught me a great deal." She reached the door and opened it. "I've heard some upsetting things about loyal men at U.S.A. being fired before their retirement came up. That's despicable! And as owner of forty percent," she lied, "I want it stopped."

He shoved his face close to hers, the malice thick in the air around them. "I don't know what you're playing at, girlie, but if I were you I'd back off. Nobody— I mean nobody—runs *my* company but *me*." He smiled, a chilling stretching of lips over white teeth. He clamped down on the cigar, and his smile broadened as he saw her shudder. "You play with fire, you're liable to get badly burned—and that doesn't exclude Brandon. Think about that while you call your lawyer."

JoBeth closed the door after him and leaned back against it. Her breath came hard and fast, her knees trembled and her mouth was as dry as cotton wool.

Fear had entered her life: fear for herself and for the man she loved.

CHAPTER SIX

THE DARKNESS PRESSED DOWN on her like a smothering hand, and sleep evaded her efforts again. Frustrated, exhausted, JoBeth eased out of bed, careful not to waken Brandon. She slipped on her red silk robe, gave the slumbering man another longing look, then padded quietly out of the room. The panoramic view offered by the expanse of windows in the living room once more beckoned her with a promise of peace. How many times in the past two weeks had she found herself here in the early hours of the morning? Too many.

She reached the wall, pressed the hidden button and watched as the curtains slipped open with the rustling sound of silk taffeta. A thick blackness still embraced the city, and the few lights below made her think of the DeSalvas Building as a giant candle atop a birthday cake, except the flame had been extinguished.

JoBeth tore her gaze from the night beyond and turned around. She'd worked hard on redecorating the suite. Now it resembled a home, warm and welcoming. Except her husband was never home long enough to appreciate it, nor her. Her shoulders slumped as she thought of the past two weeks.

Granted, Brandon had warned her that he was going to be busy with the computerized offshore drilling rig, but lately, some of the problems with it seemed insurmountable. A series of accidents, lost material and general screwups had cost Brandon and Kane a lot of time and money. Something was fishy, and they intended to find out just what it was.

She understood his concern for his business problems, but what she couldn't comprehend was his attitude toward her. She simply didn't seem to matter. But, then, what did she expect? She'd planned to have the time to make him see that he did love her, but time together was being denied her. She pulled a comfortable armchair close to the window and sat down. "The best laid plans of mice and men..." she reminded herself disgustedly, a fitting maxim, since her plans had certainly gone astray. She curled her cold feet under her and propped her chin on her hand.

Damn it, she hadn't even been able to tell him of her uncle's visit. But, then, she hadn't really wanted to tell him about it, knowing that if she did she'd have to repeat the conversation word for word, and then he'd know of her uncle's threats and her silly fears. She frowned. She'd also neglected to tell him that a few days after Tramble's visit a Mercedes with dark windows had run a red light and nearly hit her. The sound of screeching brakes and blaring horns and the memory of that relentless oncoming car were still fresh in her mind. Nothing unusual had happened since then, so she'd told herself it was simply an accident, a coincidence after Brandon's warning. Brandon, Kane and Shasta had simply misjudged her uncle.

She closed her eyes, trying desperately to convince herself of that. Yet something nagged at the back of her mind.... All at once it came to her: the look in her uncle's eyes, the cunning hatred aimed at her. A hard shiver crawled over her skin, and she tried to shake off her fear.

Stop it! She opened her eyes and stared out the window blindly. When was her mind going to stop going around and around in circles and give her some peace? She'd tried everything—lunches with old friends, shopping; she'd even started charity work again, attended a couple of parties alone because Brandon couldn't make them—but nothing helped. She was more lonely here than when she'd been isolated from everything and everyone in West Texas.

A fat tear splashed on her hand and she angrily wiped at her wet cheeks. Damn it, now she was crying like a baby. The old JoBeth had never cried, had never been lonely or at a loss for ways to fill her time. Marriage, she thought sadly, had done her more harm than good.

"Bets, what are you doing sitting in here in the dark at this hour, crying? Here—" he hunkered down beside her chair and handed her the end of the belt to his robe "—wipe your eyes and tell me what's wrong. Is it because I didn't go to the Hills' party with you yesterday?"

She sniffed, hating herself for her weakness. "Partly... No, not really."

"Then what?"

"I don't know what to do with myself," she wailed. "I never had to worry about my time before. There were always things to do, places to go, people to wile away the hours with. But now... I don't know what's happening to me." She scrubbed her damp eyes with th silk tassels at the end of the belt. "Do you know that lunch the other day with four of my old friends I w actually bored out of my mind! All they could t about was who was having affairs with whom, wh husband had a new mistress, or how much money own husbands spent on some piece of jewelry."

She looked at him with gray eyes filled once more with tears, making them luminous, and as bright as diamonds. "They're boring, Brandon. Silly, petty, vain women with nothing better to do than backbite their friends. Oh, I'm not saying all my friends are like that. Gail Higgins and Mary Jean Clark aren't."

The smile that Brandon had been holding in check blossomed all over his handsome face. "Didn't Gail and Mary Jean work before they married into money?" JoBeth gazed at him in confusion, so he explained. "Gail was a model, wasn't she? And Mary Jean was a school teacher? Though neither of them work full-time anymore, I believe Gail still models for charity events and other occasions, and Mary Jean does volunteer work for the school board."

"So," she said belligerently, "what does that have to do with me?" Sighing dejectedly, she slouched farther in the chair. "I just don't know what's wrong. Maybe I've changed."

"Ah. Now there is the crux of the problem, Bets. ʼʼu've changed. Your year away taught you some- ʼg—a sense of responsibility and worth. You're bet- ʼan most of your fair-weather friends. You have a ʼind. You just need to use it more often." He ʼa flying fist. "Go find a job."

ʼWork?" She was horrified at the thought. ʼ be mad!"

ʼ? I do, and so did you for the past year." ʼe always worked, and West Texas was ʼopped, lost in thought for a second. ʼlo, for heaven's sake? I'm not trained ʼ important than giving parties and ʼharities. There's no market for a ʼiver." Something clicked in her head, a memory of her conversation with Gail and Mary Jane. "You know... No, no, it's outrageous."

"What?" He stood, captured her hands in his and pulled her up to stand beside him.

"It would never work," she mumbled.

Brandon slung his arm around her shoulders and led her back to the bedroom. Once in bed, warm and comfortable with her in his arms, be began to place light kisses along her jaw.

"It might work!" She pushed up on one elbow and looked down at him, her eyes gleaming in the moonlit room. "Mary Jane, Gail and I were having lunch at Tony's the other day, and for some reason we started watching some of the new crowd there—young executive types."

"Oh!" Brandon froze; his wandering hand stilled on her thigh. "Eyeballing the younger men, were you?" It was meant as a joke, but the question came out accusingly. He still hadn't asked her why he'd come home one evening and found the place stinking of cigar smoke, and she'd said nothing about having a visitor.

JoBeth absently brushed his hand off her leg. "I wasn't man watching, if that's what you're implying. But you know the type of executive I'm talking about, young urban professionals? What do they call them...yuppies? Lots of new money and not sure what to do with it but make more. Anyway..." She moved away from lips that nibbled a path down her arm to the sensitive bend of her elbow. "Quit it, Brandon."

He gave up and flopped back with a mournful sigh. "It's your fault, waking me up at this hour. You know how horny I get in the morning, and yet you cruelly push me away." Sighing loudly, he watched her from the corner of his eye, hoping she'd have pity on him.

JoBeth flopped back angrily. "Well, damn! If you don't want to hear what I'm going to do... Men!" She snorted with disgust. "All you think about is sex. My life is teetering on the brink of destruction—"

"Bets—"

"And you want me to soothe your libido. You come creeping home every day sometime before dawn, crawl in bed and wake me up from a sound sleep with your wandering hands and sweet words."

"I never creep," he told her, chuckling into the warm curve of her neck. "Sneak, maybe."

She shrugged his insistent lips away reluctantly. "I never get to talk to you. The only time we get to have a conversation is after we make love, and you know I can't think that early. And that's another thing—" He cut off her protest with his mouth. Lost in the kiss, she wrapped her arms around his neck. If passion was all she was going to get from him, then so be it.

For two weeks it had been this way. Each day problems and circumstances seemed to team together to keep them apart, but at night they would reach for each other. Subconsciously, they sought the closeness, the affection they couldn't share during the day.

BRANDON FELT like a heel. Worse, he was guilt ridden over his treatment of JoBeth. It had been nearly a week since he'd found her crying, and because of the numerous responsibilities heaped on him lately he hadn't made an effort to have a long talk with her. But what nagged at him more than his own negligence was her attitude. She didn't seem to care as she once had. He still left home every morning before she awoke and returned long after she'd gone to bed. Yet before, they'd managed to make a little time for conversation—no matter that it was after they'd made love and the words were incoherent sometimes. She had always been a willing listener. Now she simply rolled over and went back to sleep.

Brandon pulled into the underground parking lot and jumped out of the car carrying two shopping bags. He smiled when he thought of the reception he'd receive, and sprinted for the elevator. It was only three o'clock and they had the rest of the afternoon and into the night to make up for lost time.

AT TEN MINUTES AFTER TWELVE Brandon looked at his watch for the thousandth time that evening. The candles on the table had burned down to small flickering flames. The bottle of champagne that was supposed to have been for a celebration sat half empty and sadly flat. Where the hell was she? There had been no notes by the telephone telling him of an engagement she had, no messages, nothing but a missing wife and the lurking, growing suspicion that she might be with another man. After all, JoBeth liked parties, always had. She wasn't the type of woman who enjoyed being alone.

As the time passed, Brandon's imagination played havoc with his memory. He thought of all the men he'd seen her with in the past. He took a quick sip of the flat champagne and grimaced; the bad taste reminded him of what had happened when he'd dropped by the River Oaks Country Club on his way home that afternoon. Could JoBeth have already heard? Gossip traveled fast in his set. He conceded what he'd done was wrong, but hell, just because he was married, he didn't have to cut himself off from his old haunts and friends.

"Fool," he grumbled out loud. "You know very well why you went to the club for a drink. You felt married!

For some foolish reason that particular institution seemed tantamount to prison this afternoon. At least, that's what you used to think.'' Brandon felt a complete fool, sitting alone, talking to himself. He clamped his lips together.

What was even worse about going to the club alone was knowing that his friends and acquaintances there were aware of his recent marriage. But it was Carmen Walters, an old rival and viper-tongued enemy of JoBeth's, who brought his mistake home to him. The first words out of her bright red mouth made him see that he had done JoBeth an injustice by going there by himself so soon after their wedding. Carmen had intimated loudly enough for several people to hear that he was already tired of his new wife and on the prowl. Of course, it was absurd. He hadn't even thought of another woman since he'd married JoBeth, and truth be told, that bothered him more than anything.

He glanced at the silver-wrapped present he'd bought to soothe both her anger and his guilt once he told her what had happened. But how could he be forgiven if she didn't come home, and soon? The sound of a key in the door made him sit up straighter.

Whistling, JoBeth shut the front door and glided down the hall. Her evening had been rewarding, and more productive than she'd ever thought. Pulling off the sequined jacket, she slipped out of her shoes and kicked them out of her way. She stopped just long enough to work the difficult zipper down her dress—when she froze.

"Just where the hell have you been till one o'clock in the morning?"

"Hi, Brandon." She peered in the direction of his voice, trying to pierce the darkness "What are you doing sitting with the lights off?'' She took a few steps and flicked on a lamp, the glare momentarily hurting her eyes.

"Answer my question!"

She stiffened. No one talked to her in that tone of voice. "What do you care?"

"Don't start with me, Bets. Where the hell were you?" He saw her glance at the brightly wrapped package and the bottle of champagne and wished he'd thought to remove the evidence of his guilty conscience.

Oblivious to the storm brewing, JoBeth grinned. "Is that for me?" Before he could deny it, she pounced, tearing away the paper and ribbon. He couldn't help himself and began to smile at her childlike enjoyment and excitement.

It was the first present Brandon had ever given her, discounting the garter snake when she was ten, and she couldn't control the wild beating of her heart. The peach box with its raised monogram was from an exclusive and outrageously expensive lingerie shop. With oohs and aahs, she pulled the handmade nightgown of the palest of pale, shimmering green, delicate Charmeuse satin from the box. But it was the appliquéd tulip in buttercup yellow and mint green that widened her eyes. The flower covered one breast, its long stem winding around the side to end in beautifully shaped leaves. She knew those leaves were placed so they would fall on one cheek of her buttocks. It was an exquisite, one-of-a-kind gown, and she clutched it to her breast, then leaped onto his lap. "Oh, Brandon, what a wonderful gift." She kissed him long and hard, feeling the tension drain from his stiffly held shoulders.

"Where were you, Bets?" he murmured against her lips, wanting to sound stern but failing as her warm body pressed against his. "I was worried."

"I told you two days ago I was going to a meeting." She slid off his lap, avoiding his hands by hopping out of reach. "You don't listen, sweet cheeks." Shaking the sexy nightgown before him as a matador would with a cape, she backed away. "I'm going to take a shower. Want to join me?" With that, she spun around and sprinted out of the room.

Brandon didn't waste any time lunging after her. He told himself he'd get the answers to his questions one way or another.

FOR SOME REASON he never got around to asking those questions. Leaning close to the mirror, studying what he could see of his face behind the mask of thick white cream, he wondered why he'd given in so easily. His reflection told him nothing, so he rocked backward to finish shaving. As he did, the array of brushes, bottles, tubes, pencils and other strange containers and instruments caught his eye. *His* space had been invaded and her paraphernalia multiplied daily. Brandon's lips tightened as he spotted the mangled tube of toothpaste. How many times would he have to ask her not to squeeze it in the middle? Did his brother have to put up with these problems? Did all married men?

Brandon picked up his brush, saw the long blond hairs in it and stomped from the bathroom with the offensive object held out between his forefinger and thumb like a distasteful piece of trash. When he reached the side of the bed he paused, ignored the innocent face of his wife in deep slumber and dropped the brush on her stomach.

"Wha—what?" JoBeth jerked awake and groggily took in the angry face above hers. She looked down at the brush lying beside her and then back at Brandon. "If you're trying to be funny you failed miserably."

"It wasn't meant to be a joke. Your things—" He broke off as the telephone began to ring, snatched it up while he continued to glare at her. "Hello!" he bellowed.

JoBeth glared back. "What's the matter with you this morning?"

He waved her to silence with a sharp movement of his hand as he strained to hear the low, husky voice on the other end. Whether male or female, he couldn't tell. But as the person repeated the message an angry flush tipped Brandon's ears a fiery red. "Who the hell is this?"

"It doesn't matter," the hushed voice murmured smoothly. "Why don't you ask your wife where she was early last evening and whose bed she graced? You didn't think marriage would change anything, did you?"

Brandon slammed down the receiver so hard the clock and his watch on the bedside table almost bounced off. His sapphire-blue eyes darkened as he stared at JoBeth, trying to tell himself the caller was just some crank. But little things from the past that had begun eating at him lately came to mind once again.

"Brandon?"

"Wrong number," he snapped. Giving her one more look that defied comment, he spun around and walked away, shutting the bedroom door softly behind him.

Fifteen minutes later, muffled, rich male laughter sent JoBeth scrambling from the bed. She snatched up the new nightgown from the floor and slipped it over her head, struggling to pull it down as she rushed to the door and dashed out. Still half-asleep, she halted to get her bearings, cocking her head to one side as she heard Brandon laugh again. A few hurried steps brought her to a stop once more, but this time every muscle in her body stiffened.

Brandon, perched on the kitchen countertop, a coffee cup in one hand and surrounded by packages of frozen dinners, was laughing his head off. "Shrimp with lobster sauce—delicious. Beef burgundy and rice—super meal. But you outdid yourself with the stuffed flounder." He kissed his fingertips, savagely enjoying her bright red cheeks. "And the chicken Kiev. Oh, life is never dull with you around."

JoBeth glowered at him, at a total loss for words. She grabbed the package from his hand. "I never got around to the chicken Kiev. *You* are never here for dinner anymore." She gathered up the frozen dinners, carried them to the freezer and placed each in carefully, taking her time as she frantically searched for an excuse. Brandon hated liars, and she'd started off her marriage with a whopper.

Embarrassed, humiliated and caught in one of her own traps, JoBeth said the first thing that popped into her head to throw him off the track until she could come up with a good reason for her lie. "Is there supposed to be fidelity in this marriage?"

Brandon's smile quickly faded and the color drained from his face. "Yes."

"On both sides?"

"I would hope so, yes. Are you thinking of taking a lover this soon, Bets?"

She shut the freezer door and turned around. "Will you draw up the papers or whatever it takes to start a company in Texas? You know, name, owners, etc."

"Bets, you can't just jump from infidelity to corporate papers!"

"Why not?"

"Because I haven't had my second cup of coffee yet." He smiled. She grinned. Then they both began to laugh. And though she had sidestepped his question about a lover, he just added it to a growing list of others he wanted to ask her. "Are you going to tell me more about this company or are you going to leave me wondering what you're up to?"

JoBeth retrieved a cup from a cabinet and filled it with coffee. "Are you sure you have time to listen?" she asked a little sarcastically.

"I'll make time."

She smiled over the rim of her cup and murmured, "That will be a new experience."

"Don't start, Bets. Just tell me your news."

Her eyelids closed to slits and her mouth tightened. "Okay. Do you remember me telling you about having lunch at Tony's with Gail and Mary Jean?" He nodded. "Well, we were watching some young men eating, and Brandon, their table manners were atrocious. I'm sure these were wealthy young men with positions of power, or they hoped to be, but they either ate like pigs or couldn't figure out which silver to use." She was frowning and chuckling at the same time. "One man ate his fresh oysters on the half shell with his salad fork, his salad with his dinner fork, and when the finger bowl was filled he totally ignored it. We could tell he had absolutely no idea what it was for. I couldn't believe it. Here were men hoping to further their careers and they didn't know how to eat at a table set properly for lunch. Can you imagine what they would do at a formal dinner?"

"Outrageous," Brandon teased, but when he saw how serious she was he immediately sobered.

"Are you going to make fun or listen?"

"Sorry." He bit the inside of his lip. "Go on."

"Well, during lunch we discussed how today's children are no longer taught correct manners or etiquette. One thing led to another, and we decided to start a business to right this wrong. Gail, Mary Jean and I are now partners in Etiquette, Inc." She grinned, pleased with Brandon's stunned expression. "We were going to call it DeSalva, Higgins and Clark, but decided that sounded egotistical. What do you think?"

Brandon snapped his fingers. "Just like that, you three are starting a business?"

"Right." Her brow was beginning to furrow at his tone. "What's wrong with that?"

"What about office space? Advertising? Material? Employees? I take it you will employ others to help out?"

"Yes . . . of course."

"And where will you get your customers?"

"We've already enrolled twenty children from the ages of six to thirteen." She was glaring now, angry with herself for feeling so hurt at his lack of confidence in her. "Last night we decided—"

"That's where you were? At a meeting to get this company started?"

"Damn it, Brandon, don't you ever listen to me? I told you about it days ago. We met last night after Gail's cocktail party for the new heart specialist at the Medical Center. Mary Jean's husband owns those two partially empty buildings near the Galleria and Saks Center. We, actually Mary Jean, talked him into giving us free office space for one year, plus one large room to make into a mock restaurant. He's also allowing us to use his three restaurants to give the students on-site training when they're ready. She turned away, pulled up a chair and sat down in front of him, her smile spreading with each inch his mouth dropped open.

"We're all going to chip in our extra china, crystal, silver and linens. So, you see, everything is taken care of except filing the necessary papers and opening a corporate bank account, which we want you to handle. You will, won't you? You're the only husband of the three that's a lawyer, and Gail's and Mary Jean's husbands have both contributed."

Brandon shook his head, a little numbed by the speed at which these three women seemed to work. It was a little frightening, too. He always took his time to think through any problems that might arise, but JoBeth and her friends seemed ready to just jump in without a second thought. "And what has Gail's husband contributed?" He had asked lightheartedly, but when she began to tell him he nearly choked on a swallow of cold coffee.

"Oh, Douglas? Well, we were all going to chip in an equal amount of money to start the company, but after he heard what we were up to he advised us to borrow the money rather than use our own. Something about write-off taxes and things. Anyway, his bank is willing to lend us what we need." She named a figure.

" 'Write-off taxes and things'?" He couldn't believe his ears. In a matter of days they had space, supplies, a loan that made his ears ring and customers.

"Oh, there's more."

"More?" he asked faintly.

"Last night Jean decided that it was time we expanded." JoBeth's eyes were glinting in the morning sunlight that poured in from the kitchen window. She wanted to dance with happiness. For the first time in her life she had totally dumbfounded, confused and impressed Brandon. "Since it was those yuppies in the restaurant that gave us the idea in the first place, Jean thought we should branch out to include them in our venture. Executive Etiquette, Inc. We'll teach them etiquette, table manners, how to climb the social ladder with all the social graces. What do you think?"

He was quiet for a long time, then he smiled. "I think if Douglas is willing to give you a loan and Jim is willing to let you have office space and the use of his restaurants to experiment in, then the least I can do is act as your company lawyer." He pulled her from her chair and wrapped his arms around her warm body. "You never cease to amaze me, Bets," he murmured in her ear as his hands began to wander down over the silky gown and the firm mounds of her behind. He squeezed, bringing her between his legs, and his mouth swooped down on hers.

JoBeth pulled away, breathless and laughing. "God, the morning really does wild things to you, doesn't it?" She glanced at the clock on the wall and moaned, "I can't, Brandon." Pulling away, she turned and began walking out of the kitchen.

"Why not?" He trailed after her, his eyes bright with desire.

"I promised Jennifer I'd meet her at Tiffany's to pick up the guests' presents for the DeSalva Charity Auction and Ball!" She eased the gown up over her head, dodging Brandon's hands, and ran into the shower.

He followed her to the bathroom and stopped only to consider whether he wanted to take a shower with or without his clothes. His decision made, he unbuttoned his shirt and was hopping around on one foot struggling with a stubborn shoe, when she stepped out—naked, wet and immensely sexy. He felt his desire grow, but she eluded his grasp once again. "Stand still, damn it."

JoBeth laughed as she wrapped a towel around herself. "I've got to meet Jennifer, and I don't want to be late."

Brandon stopped, then gave up and flopped back on the bed to watch her dress, letting the fire in his loins cool. "You're not upset that Jennifer is hosting the party, are you?"

JoBeth paused in the act of fastening her bra and thought. The DeSalva ball, held every two years, was an international social event. The proceeds from the black-tie, five-hundred-dollar-a-plate dinner were donated to the Children's Hospital. There was also an auction of prize horses, cattle and Western art. The exclusive gathering was for two hundred of the wealthiest elite—politicians, movie stars, European aristocrats, friends and businessmen—and was an event that she had always hostessed after Catherine DeSalva's death. "I won't lie and tell you it doesn't matter, because it does. I'm a little jealous, but I think Jennifer will do a fine job, and I'll help all I can."

Brandon jumped off the bed and slowly came toward her. She backed away. "Now, sweet cheeks, I told you I'm in a hurry." She struggled to get her panty hose up as he continued to advance.

But instead of gathering her in his arms, he reached out a long finger, hooked it under her chin and brought her face to his so he could kiss her tenderly on the lips. "I'm crazy about you, Bets."

It was the closest thing to a declaration of love that she could hope to get, and she could only smile stupidly and stand there while he picked up his jacket and vest and left the suite. Maybe, she thought hopefully, one had to be a little crazy to fall in love.

Finally coming to her senses, she shook her head and finished dressing. She picked up her purse and was ready to follow Brandon out of the suite, when the telephone rang. She hesitated at the door, telling herself she was going to be late if she answered it. But she had never been able to ignore a ringing phone. She sprinted back to the living room. "Hello."

"I still haven't received the letter reinstating me with your power of attorney. JoBeth, I'm usually a patient man, but my patience is running short today. There's a board meeting soon and I want your shares to vote with mine."

"No." Her grip on the telephone tightened with each passing second of silence.

"I don't believe I heard correctly, sweetheart."

The raspy voice, devoid of any emotion, sent a chill up her backbone, but she wasn't about to let her uncle bully her. "There's nothing wrong with your hearing, Uncle Tramble. You'll have to vote without my stock from now on."

"I understand you feel the need to do something useful and noble after the fiasco your father caused, but this board meeting is not a testing ground. Those shares are not something you can teethe your newfound power on. Go shopping, JoBeth," he said with disgust overflowing his sarcasm. "Buy yourself a diamond necklace or a new fur coat if you must have something to do. Just stay out of my way." He waited a long moment for a reply, but when he heard only her soft breathing he continued, "My assistant and his secretary are on their way over with a letter of reinstatement for you to sign. Do it, JoBeth. Don't make me get ugly."

"I'm afraid that wouldn't do any good. I don't have the power to turn over any shares to you." She could have kicked herself, and bit hard on her lip to keep from groaning out loud.

"Explain yourself, girl!"

"Brandon will be voting for me from now on. He's an unbiased third party and will be fair." A deep shudder ran through her body, and she knew she should have kept her mouth shut. But at least she hadn't told him about the sale of her shares or the impending takeover.

"You best be joking, JoBeth," he growled, ominously emphasizing each word.

Her throat tightened, her lips moved, but nothing came out, and all she could do was shake her head in answer.

As if Tramble could see her, he went on. "You're just like your daddy—stupid. You'll regret this, girl. Mark my words. You'll rue this day."

She flinched when he slammed the phone in her ear, then she held out the receiver and stared at it as if she expected it to bite her. The suite suddenly seemed filled with menacing shadows, and she rushed out, shutting off her uneasiness with the closing of the door. Tramble would get over it, she tried to convince herself. She'd tell Brandon what she'd done and let him worry about it. After all, this was all his fault, anyway. Let him straighten it out.

With her problems resolved to her satisfaction, she headed for the elevator and her meeting with her sister-in-law. As she punched the button and the doors slid smoothly closed, she realized she liked the word—sister-in-law. Her family had always been the DeSalvas, and when Catherine and Elizabeth died in a car crash, something very special had been taken from her. Now, by Lucas's marriage, she once more had a sister, and she knew it was time to show her appreciation for Jennifer's forgiveness and warmth. In more ways than one her returning to Houston was a beginning for all—even for her.

CHAPTER SEVEN

SEATED IN KANE STONE'S OFFICE high above Houston's skyline, Brandon held a nine-carat emerald ring up to the overhead lights. He rotated the ring, and his breath caught at the green fire that flashed from the facets. No wonder history was filled with stories of men killing and women selling their bodies for the magnificent stones. He slipped the ring on his little finger, stretched out his hand and admired it at arm's length, wondering if JoBeth would like it.

In truth, she wasn't much of a jewelry wearer, even in the past, when she'd had tons of it. But they hadn't had time to buy her an engagement ring, and as he was walking past the tiny, exclusive jewelry store on the first floor of the Tex-Am Oil Building, the ring had caught his eye. He had stood there, entranced with the color that sparked to life as the stone turned on its display. He told himself he was only fascinated by its beauty, but the longer he looked at the ring the more his thoughts turned to the past.

He remembered teasing JoBeth years ago, telling her that her eyes reminded him of jewels—diamonds, hard and cold. He hadn't gotten the usual rise out of her. Instead she'd only smiled, her smoky-gray eyes so like sharp, colorless stones that it had been difficult for him to breathe then, too. It was her beauty that had always intrigued him, but it was her eyes that had held him en-

thralled with their ever-changing depths. She'd laughingly told him she'd always secretly yearned for green
eyes, cat eyes, as deep, dark and mysterious as emeralds. So now here he was, having just bought his wife
the mysterious stone on a whim. He shook his head at
his fanciful behavior, and a frown began to pleat his
forehead as he tried to figure out the reason for this new
tenderness for JoBeth. Heaven only knew she'd been a
problem to him all his life, and now look what a mess
she'd gotten them into. Marriage! A low masculine
whistle of admiration jarred him out of his confusion
and he fought to gather his thoughts.

"That is some ring." Kane closed the office door and
walked over to stand beside Brandon. "May I?" As
Brandon had, he held it up to the light. "For Jo-
Beth?"

"Of course." Brandon accepted the ring back, carefully placed it in the box, then slid the box into his inside jacket pocket. He was about to dive into a lengthy,
useless explanation, when they were interrupted and all
thoughts of JoBeth's gift fled as he took in Kane's new
secretary. She was tall, slender, with miles of blond hair
and a face that immediately brought to mind Alice in
Wonderland, but her voluptuous body ruined the image. As Kane introduced them, Brandon could only
stare, speechless, at the contradiction of sensuality and
innocence.

"Brandon, this is Alice."

Stunned, Brandon just nodded as *Alice* handed Kane
some papers and left the office.

"Shame on you, Brandon. Your tongue is practically hanging out, and you've only been married a few
weeks."

He ignored the jab. "You must be out of your mind! Has Shasta seen her yet?" Brandon saw a flicker of uncertainty cross his friend's handsome face before it was quickly masked.

"My wife does not tell me who I may or may not hire."

"Oh, those are brave words, indeed, Kane, but you forget that I've seen Shasta in action." Brandon watched as Kane's silver eyes narrowed and his decadent face went blank. He wondered if he'd said something totally out of line. "Is anything wrong?"

Kane laughed, waved away his concern and sat down behind the desk. "No, but thanks. Shasta's just having a little trouble becoming accustomed to staying in one place longer than a few months. She'll come around." He leaned back, propped his feet on the desk top and grinned. "How are things with you and JoBeth?"

The change of subject was not to Brandon's liking, and Kane knew it. It was almost impossible to gain information from Kane Stone if he didn't seem disposed to giving it, yet Kane had a way of extracting what he wanted to know with a frightening ease. Partners they might be, but they were still feeling each other out and testing the other's strength. Brandon only hoped he didn't come off lacking in any quarter. He never wanted to be on the wrong side of Kane.

The man was as mysterious as his past. Though everyone knew he had been wealthy before his inheritance of Tex-Am Oil, no one knew where that wealth came from. There was talk that when it suited him, and from time to time, Kane did special jobs for some secret branch of the government. After he married Shasta and she gave up her lucrative position as private detective in her family business, Masters Security, she joined him in his dangerous work abroad. The couple had roamed the continents until recently, when Kane's father had died and left him the family company. No one had thought the world wanderers would decide to go into business, or that the ins and outs of the cutthroat oil industry would be right up Kane's alley. But Brandon could tell Kane truly enjoyed the daily challenge of pitting himself against those who stood in the way of his goals.

He thought of how Kane had set the older, conservative members of the oil community on their ears. Kane's fashionable Italian and French clothes and the casual, almost careless way he wore them raised many an eyebrow at the prestigious but stately Petroleum Club. A few members had been brazen enough to suggest that he dress more like his peers out of respect for the older and wiser generations, and also because he had an image to uphold before the public. Brandon had watched those pompous, arrogant do-gooders meet Kane's piercing silver eyes, then, unable to sustain the contempt or laughter there, their gazes dropped and an uneasy silence followed until someone coughed or asked a question.

Kane Stone was about to rattle the cages of the old lions and make them yield to a far more intelligent, fast moving and modern man: a Renaissance man. He was about to break the shackles of mediocrity within the oil industry. Brandon grinned. He planned to share in the shake-up and enjoy the fruits of running alongside a winner. Kane might be an enigma with an aura of excitement about him, yet it was also his magnetism that pulled people to him, people of worth and foresight willing to follow his lead. Brandon knew *he* could never be a follower, but he would be an equal partner.

"If you're through sizing me up, Brandon, let's talk about the computerized drilling rig. Are you still having problems?"

"About as many as you." He wasn't going to let Kane get away with anything if he could help it. "I heard you were out at the refinery half the night, checking the security. What happened?"

"Damned if I know. The new system went haywire for no apparent reason. Masters has checked it over thoroughly a couple of times." Kane shrugged, then rotated his head from side to side to relieve the tension. "They can't find anything wrong, either."

"Do you think someone's tripping it deliberately?"

"That's what it looks like. But why? This is the second time the refinery has been broken into, but they haven't tried to sabotage it or steal anything." He closed his eyes and leaned his head back on the leather chair. "Man, I'm beat." Sighing his defeat, he asked again, "Any more problems concerning the rig?"

"Hell, I couldn't begin to put my finger on everything that's been going wrong. Pieces of equipment disappear, then some turn up later. Tools break for no reason. Men have accidents that don't make sense. The drinking water on the rig gets tainted. The freezer shuts down and the food spoils. Nothing major, just dozens of little things that are driving us crazy and slowing down production. Has Masters Security come up with anything for me?"

"No." Kane picked up a sheet of paper and handed it to Brandon. "You're going to be as thrilled about this as I am. It seems that the ship loaded with the specially treated steel housing for the offshore computers is being held in the channel. The port authorities won't grant permission for it to dock until the complaint is checked out. Can you believe smallpox was reported to be aboard?''

Brandon cursed long and loud, then jumped up and began to pace the thick carpet. "We have to have the housing unit before the computers can go in, Kane."

"I know that. But until the board of health checks the complaint the ship will stay just where it is."

"How long are we looking at?" Brandon asked.

Kane shrugged. "I'll tell you something, though. I see Tramble Baldwin's hand in all our problems."

Brandon stopped his pacing and faced Kane. "As far as the trouble with the rig, yes. But thank God nothing of the takeover has leaked. The only thing Tramble knows is that JoBeth has seen fit to withdraw her power of attorney so he can't vote her shares any longer. He's been remarkably closemouthed about it."

Kane rubbed his face tiredly. "He hasn't contacted her again? He's just taken what she's done without a fuss or a fight? It smells fishy, Brandon."

"He's an old man with a bad heart, and the fight has left him. I don't see him causing any trouble whatsoever."

Kane stared at him, his eyes glinting with suppressed anger as he reviewed the past and what that "old man" had gotten away with. "Nevertheless, we'll keep everything close to our chests till I say we go."

Brandon nodded. "That's fine with me." He picked up his briefcase and was preparing to leave, when Kane's next question brought his head up with a snap.

"Brandon, you didn't marry JoBeth just to get her shares, did you?" He held out his hand to stop the heated answer. "I know you wanted in on this deal and the partnership, but if you did anything you'll regret later I wish you'd tell me. The possibility has been eating a hole in my gut for weeks—to say nothing of Shasta's pestering the life out of me.''

Brandon paused then looked Kane in the eye. "You can tell Shasta I married JoBeth because I wanted to. I've always wanted her. It just took me some time to realize it. End of discussion?''

Kane smiled, a smile that could melt the hardest of female hearts, and was not lost on the men, either. He stuck out his hand. "End of discussion, and congratulations, I hope the two of you are as happy as Shasta and I. Now where are you off to? I need to be able to contact you if some decision is reached about the ship.''

Brandon gripped the hand of his partner firmly and returned the shake, their eyes level, their thoughts as one as they realized they were going to work well together. Male intuition, Brandon thought. "I'll be out in the Gulf on the rig. Use the shortwave to reach me.'' He looked at his watch and frowned. "I have to run. My pilot is waiting on top of DeSalvas and it will take me thirty minutes just to get out of downtown this time of day.''

Kane walked him to the door. "I know being downtown is a pain in the ass, but this is where the action is, so learn to live with it. Have Alice give your pilot a call and tell him you're on your way. Have a good flight, and be careful.''

BRANDON LOOKED DOWN at the lazy swells of the Gulf of Mexico and tried to relax his ramrod stiff body. The wind pulled at his hair and whipped against his face. The tangy scent of the sea almost choked him and his fear was so tangible he could taste it.

"Mr. DeSalva!'' the pilot yelled as the cockpit began to fill with the sharp smell of smoking electrical wiring. "We're going to have to ditch this baby. I'll try to put her down as softly as I can while you sing out a couple of loud and clear Maydays." He shouted their coordinates several times as he struggled with the listing helicopter.

Brandon did as he was told, then instead of watching the water rush closer, he tested the pilot's straps on his life jacket, making sure they were securely fastened before he checked his own. *JoBeth will never let me forget this.* He almost laughed out loud, but caught himself, realizing the man next to him would think him hysterical. She'd dig out every detail, every emotion, and harp and tease him for years to come—if he lived.

"The wind is picking up, Mr. DeSalva. Hold on. We're going to hit hard."

Brandon could just make out the whitecaps as the helicopter turned around crazily like a drunken, circling bird before it struck the surface with a sound like a giant's hand slapping the water. An instant of hissing steam boiled around them, then the warm sluggish waters of the Gulf sucked the aircraft down into darkness.

THE WHITE-HOT SUN BURNED every drop of moisture from the usually humid atmosphere, sending people scurrying for air-conditioned shelters. The Galleria, with its restaurants, ice-skating rink, theaters, hotels and specialty shops, seemed to swell with the crowds. Restaurants prospered as the lines formed out the doors and halfway down the corridors. The small restaurant in Neiman-Marcus was just as crowded, with a long line extending far into the main aisles of the store itself. But the customers already seated were enjoying the coolness of the hand-painted delft tiled walls, the crisp white table linen accented with electric-blue napkins, shining silver and sparkling crystal. Voices were held at a respectful, dignified murmur. JoBeth eased her feet from her shoes and pressed hot, aching toes to the cool floor. "God, my feet are killing me."

A soft moan came from behind a menu in sympathetic agreement. "Are you sure you can talk Brandon into wearing all those clothes you bought him?" the voice asked. Then the menu lowered and Jennifer DeSalva's violet eyes began to sparkle with amusement. "They're not exactly his style, you know."

JoBeth waved a hand. "He needs an image boost." Brandon's three-piece suits and his dogged determination to resist any change had always driven her crazy. But now she saw a chance to remedy the problem and wasn't about to pass it up. Mentally she shrugged. Never mind that Brandon was going to blow a fuse when he discovered her plan. She frowned as her sister-in-law shook her head. "Now what's the matter?"

"I'm just amazed at your audacity sometimes."

"Oh, pooh! Brandon will bitch and gripe for a while, but he'll come around." She picked up the menu with a groan as her stomach made its empty state loudly known. "I'm starving, and there's no telling how long Shasta's going to be. Are you sure she said she'd meet us? You know her aversion to stores."

Jennifer grinned, picked up her glass of ice water and took a large unladylike gulp, almost choking as she tried to warn JoBeth of the old lady bearing down on them. "JoBeth, here comes Abigail Wentworth."

The elegant lady, with her old-world air, her Adolfo suit and her ever-present string of pearls, glided to a stop. Her entourage came to a halt a respectful two steps behind her. "My dear JoBeth, I can't tell you how proud I am of you. To take it upon yourself to repay those poor unfortunates is most commendable.''

JoBeth opened her mouth, but was immediately hushed by a regal wave of a bejeweled hand. Out of the corner of her eye she caught Abigail's cronies nodding with her every word, and she bit down hard on her lip to keep from grinning.

"Contrary to what everyone believes and says, I liked your father. Though he was totally wrong for your mother. She should have married..." JoBeth's facial muscles tightened, and the old lady sighed deeply. "Well, never mind that now. It's neither here nor there. Nonetheless, you are a brave young lady to do what you did and uphold the family honor.''

Embarrassed, JoBeth tried once more to break in, but Abigail thumped her cane on the floor with a couple of dull thuds to show her annoyance.

"You are a true heroine of our times. I would like you to come by for a visit soon, my dear. And if there is ever anything I can personally do for you, please don't hesitate to call.'' Houston's reigning monarch sailed out, the lead ship with her tugboats chugging loyally behind her. In her wake she left numerous women at the surrounding tables gaping after her.

Touched, JoBeth ducked her head and began to dig around in her purse. "Don't say anything, please Jennifer, or I'll start to cry. Irritating old witch. Never paid the slightest bit of attention to me before,'' she grumbled. "Always ignored my parties.'' Then, with pen and paper in hand, she began to write a list for Jennifer, but her thoughts were still on the old lady's words. "'Family honor,' indeed. 'Heroine'! She's my great-aunt, you know.''

She lowered her head again, blinking rapidly as she tried to finish what she was writing. "Here's the list of caterers I used for the ball and auction." Her words were coming fast and clipped as she struggled to gain control over her emotions. "Your idea to have Tiffany's make up gold butterflies as gifts was a brainstorm. Clever lady to connect the name of the ranch and the gifts. Mariposa and gold butterflies...."

She shook her head, but it wasn't at Jennifer's talent. Tears had gathered in her eyes, and she couldn't cry here with all these people still watching. Her lip suffered another hard bite and she flinched.

"JoBeth," Jennifer said softly, and gently patted her hand. She grinned when the hand under hers was snatched away.

"Sorry, I know you mean well, but I can't take sympathy lately. I tear up like a two-year-old. Damn! I never used to cry like this."

"It's all right. You've had a hard year."

JoBeth's head jerked up and she laughed with genuine humor. "You can say that again. Would you believe I shoveled manure and—" But she broke off as she spotted Shasta entering the restaurant. "I don't believe it. Will you just look at her."

Jennifer turned in her chair and sat up straight, craning to watch their friend make her way toward them. She quickly turned puzzled eyes to JoBeth, then back to Shasta, before she caught on to what JoBeth meant.

JoBeth looked down and grimaced. Shasta was wearing the very same Valentino linen dress in white, while hers was red. Her eyes narrowed to slits as Shasta pulled out a chair and sat down.

"Sorry I'm late, but I had things to take care of." She gave her vague explanation in a deliberately mysterious tone, then scowled when JoBeth and Jennifer didn't jump at her hint. Looking from one to the other, she asked, "Okay, what have I done now?" Silence met her inquiry and she caught Jennifer's gaze shifting from her dress to JoBeth's. Her mouth dropped open, and her large brown eyes widened. Then she began to laugh. "I'll have to tell Kane to watch where he buys my clothes from now on." She giggled, a delightful sound that brought smiles to her companions' faces.

At JoBeth's insistence, they ordered lunch, and dug in the second the food arrived. There had always been a conspiracy between JoBeth and Jennifer to withhold their questions to all the hints Shasta threw at them. So they ignored her mysterious tone, making Shasta's eyebrows twist in frustration.

Barely able to suppress a smirk, JoBeth asked, "Has anyone talked to Samantha lately?"

Jennifer, immediately picking up on the game, followed her lead. "She called a couple of days ago, and I must tell you, JoBeth, you are so far down on her black list I doubt you'll ever be able to get off."

JoBeth flinched. Samantha Grey was one of her closest friends, and she knew there were going to be hurt feelings to smooth over after her year of deliberate silence. "How's Boston? And are they still living at the ranch?"

Shasta coughed loudly, but was ignored.

"Boston's fine, and yes, they're all still living in Santa Fe," Jennifer said, forgetting their game as she went on to explain. "He's been out in Los Angeles, shooting some music videos. And before you ask, the answer is no, Samantha was not the producer." Her frown deepened.

"She didn't produce them because Boston didn't ask her to," Shasta butted in, glaring stonily at each woman. "He figured that even with all her help she needed to be with the children. Now listen, you'll never guess what's happened."

Jennifer's eyes met JoBeth's and silently they decided the game wasn't over yet. "Something must be wrong, though. You should see one of the paintings Samantha sent to be auctioned off." She whistled softly, letting the suspense lengthen, until both women leaned forward in anticipation. Samantha was now a world-renowned American Western artist. What she put on canvas usually sold for outrageous prices. "Both of you are aware that Boston is half Indian, aren't you?" They nodded. "Well, the painting is sort of a portrait of him, except she's painted him near naked in breechcloth, holding a spear and with his hair long and braided with feathers. I sat and drooled over it for hours until Lucas threatened to burn it. God, it's the most magnificent painting I've ever seen, but I have this strange feeling that Boston hasn't seen it yet, and I doubt he'll approve."

JoBeth smiled. Samantha and Boston Grey were as confusing a combination as Shasta and Kane. Boston, with his beautiful voice that had enthralled millions for years, had retired from the pressures of the music business and married Samantha, tall and leggy, with masses of freckles and an abundance of shocking poppy-red hair. They loved each other beyond belief, and when their firstborn arrived Boston couldn't have been happier. But two years later, at the time of Shasta and Kane's courtship—if that's what it could be called—

Samantha gave birth to quadruplets: four boys. Both parents were stunned, but elated. Now, to hear that Boston was returning to the music world, a world he'd sworn never to enter again, and the stranger news that Samantha was not by his side, was distressing. "Are they coming to the DeSalva ball?"

Shasta thumped her elbows on the table and cradled her chin in her hands. "She said she wouldn't miss it for the world. Now can I tell you what's happened.?"

JoBeth grinned, realizing they'd managed to hold Shasta off until they were halfway through the delicious cheesecake. "I guess you'd better," she said, laughing, "'cause it's going to drive you crazy if you don't." At Shasta's scowl she asked, "Do you know you've put sugar in your coffee? You drink it black. You ate the turkey and broccoli Mornay, and you hate broccoli. Now you've eaten all the fresh strawberries on your cheesecake. Shasta! You know they make you break out in hives."

"Well, why the hell didn't you stop me?" Brown eyes usually filled with mischief and laughter darkened with anger. She threw a quick glance around the restaurant and lowered her voice. "Are you two going to listen to me now, or do you have more trivial news to catch up on? I tell you I've done something— Never mind. You're not going to believe this, though. Do you know what my husband had the nerve to ask me to do the other day? Do you?"

JoBeth and Jennifer shook their heads and smiled. Both knew from past experiences to let Shasta's temper run its course before they tried to get any straight answers from her.

"Well, let me tell you. He wanted me to get rid of my Porsche. *My Porsche*, mind you." She thumped her fist in the region of her heart as if the mere thought were a mortal wound. "'Sell it,' he said, 'and get a station wagon'! I'll grant you he said a Mercedes wagon, but my God, can you see me driving around in a station wagon?" She shuddered, and a crafty smile turned up the corner of her lips, making her look more like a devilish little elf with every passing second.

JoBeth refused to look at Jennifer, knowing if they did they would both be lost in laughter. "What have you done, Shasta?"

"Me?" She opened her brown eyes wider than ever. "Why, I did exactly what the man asked me to do... with one *tiny* change. I went out and bought me the fastest, snazziest, fire-engine-red Lamborghini you've ever seen!" Shasta crossed her arms over her breasts and defied either woman to remind her that Kane had absolutely forbidden her a Lamborghini. It was the only thing he'd ever denied her and she knew it was only because he knew how she drove and was afraid she'd kill herself. Well, she'd shown him.

"Good for you," JoBeth egged her on. "Don't let any man tell you what to do."

"JoBeth," Jennifer warned, "she's going to be in real trouble over this. I know Kane."

"I'm glad someone does," Shasta retorted. "I haven't seen him lately. He's always at that damn oil company." Her smile died and she eyed her friends glumly. "If you only knew what else I've done..."

But their attention was averted from Shasta when JoBeth looked beyond her friend's shoulder and swore, "Oh, hell! There's Carmen Walters." She swore again, bringing smiles from her friends. "She's seen us and is making right for our table."

The brunet seemed to fit her name. Dark and fiery with coal-black eyes that flashed sultry looks and drew men like bees to honey. JoBeth had always disliked her, and when, about two years ago, Brandon had begun noticing her, she developed an instant aversion to the woman. Twice divorced and known as a man-eater, Carmen had seemed to direct her come-hither gaze at Brandon in the hopes of making him husband number three.

"JoBeth, how good to see you. It's been what...a year?"

The sincere tone was belied by the venomous hatred glimmering in her eyes. JoBeth braced herself for what she knew would eventually come. Carmen was out for blood, and JoBeth wondered suddenly if the woman had truly loved Brandon. "Carmen," she said, nodding, striving to sound casual but distantly friendly.

"Why just look at you two—the Bobbsey Twins." Her malicious gaze flickered between JoBeth's dress and Shasta's.

Shasta mumbled something under her breath and JoBeth grinned. Carmen had made more than a few passes at Kane. She glanced quickly at Jennifer and suddenly envied her and Lucas's rather isolated life at the Mariposa.

There was a long silence as the women eyed one another, then finally Carmen said, "I must say, JoBeth, I was rather surprised to see Brandon back at his old haunt yesterday." Her statement met with blank stares and she explained. "You know, the country club. I guess married life hasn't changed him as much as one might have hoped."

JoBeth could feel the hairs standing up on the back of her neck and wondered frantically what Brandon had done. "What are you talking about, Carmen? Ouch!" she yelped as Shasta kicked her shin under the table. The pain deepened as she realized she'd fallen right into Carmen's trap by asking that question.

"Didn't he tell you where he'd been all afternoon?" she asked sweetly, her red, sensuous lips curved like the Cheshire cat's. "Shame on him. He came by the club for a couple of drinks and some company. Dear me, JoBeth. Life must have been hellish for you this past year, having to actually work for a roof over your head—and on a dude ranch of all things." She shuddered delicately. "Brandon and I had a good laugh over the thought of *you* waiting on a guest or mucking out a barn." She lowered her voice and whispered, "I must tell you, I was surprised to see him at the club. But you know how Brandon is. Always on the prowl for someone new and interesting." She pouted prettily, then flashed a pearly smile. "I *was* shocked, though. So soon after your marriage, too, JoBeth. I could never put up with his old ways, but, then, you've known Brandon far longer than I and must be resigned to his little quirks and peccadilloes."

She was going to claw Carmen Walters's eyes out right here and now. Her body felt like a coiled spring ready to snap. She'd just begun to stand, when she was abruptly jerked down by Jennifer and Shasta.

Carmen sensed her immediate demise and her smile slipped as she stepped back from JoBeth's intense, murderous stare. "Well," she hedged nervously for a second, then began moving away. "I best be off."

"How could he! I'll kill Brandon DeSalva." JoBeth looked from Shasta's sympathetic gaze to Jennifer's.

"She could be lying about yesterday," Shasta offered helpfully.

"No. Carmen was entirely too sure of herself. I could just strangle him for doing this," she whispered fiercely, then suddenly gasped as a bone-numbing chill racked her body.

"JoBeth!"

"What's wrong?"

She shook her head as if in a daze, wondering what was happening. She couldn't remember feeling so strange...except once. But that was years ago. Closing her eyes, she tried to capture the elusive memory. She envisioned herself standing before the dark, yawning hole of a cave entrance. She was chewing on the end of one pigtail, crying, calling Brandon's name, only stopping her sobbing long enough to listen for his answer.

She'd eventually given up her vigil, run for her horse and ridden as though the devil were on her tail. Hours later, with Matthew, Lucas and some ranch hands, they'd pulled a scratched and wildly cursing Brandon from the collapsed limestone cave. Of course, his bruised ego had made him turn on her, stoutly denying he needed anyone's help.

Now she experienced that bone-numbing chill. But unlike the past, and because of her hurt and anger, she brushed the feeling away as nonsense.

"JoBeth?"

Shasta touched her arm and she jumped. "I'm all right—just mad as hell." She picked up her purse and yanked out a ten-dollar bill to cover her lunch. "Listen, I'm not going to be very good company. You two go on without me. I'm going to pick up the dress I bought for the ball and then go home." She stood, threw down her napkin and scowled. "Shasta, you don't know where Brandon is, do you?"

Delicate brown curls bobbed a negative answer, and JoBeth spun around and marched out. Why? Why had he needed to go looking for another woman? Dreams, she realized, had a way of turning into bitter reality.

CHAPTER EIGHT

WITHOUT KNOWING HOW SHE GOT THERE, JoBeth found herself driving down Post Oak Boulevard, headed for the Saks Center and the exclusive boutique. Heatwaves radiated off metal, glass and concrete, making every object take on a slightly blurred appearance. She blinked as an intense flash of sunlight struck her eyes like a shard of glass. Tears formed beneath her lids and she swore under her breath, telling herself over and over that Brandon couldn't be bored with her so soon. A horn blared harshly, and she realized she had sat through two green lights. Stomping on the gas pedal, she quickly turned the DeSalvas company car, a yellow Mercedes sedan, into the packed parking lot of Saks Fifth Avenue.

Maybe her marriage wasn't what it should be, or even what she wanted, but she and Brandon made love almost every night. And that didn't lead her to believe he would have the energy or the inclination to take on another lover. For the first time it hit her just what a hell she'd made for herself. She loved him to distraction, and the thought that he might not, or never would, was unbearable. She could never live with herself or him if she believed that was true. She frantically tried to convince herself that time was all they needed to become like normal married couples.

As she circled the parking lot, working farther and farther from the entrance, she laughed hysterically. Neither she nor Brandon was "normal people," and they certainly hadn't started their marriage the way most couples did. Damn it! Everything was her fault. If she just hadn't pushed Brandon. She spied an empty space and swung the car into the slot.

The heat hit her like a slap in the face as she climbed out. She winced, holding the linen dress away from her body and fanning it for some relief. Now all she had to do was pick up her gown, get home, kick off her shoes and wallow in a cold bath and a little self-pity.

Expediency wasn't one of her better traits: an hour later she stepped out into the glaring sun once more. The heat seemed worse after the coolness of the shop. Perspiration popped out on her forehead and the back of her dress was quickly soaked. But even the thought of the car's air conditioner didn't make her foolish enough to run. Sunstroke was not in her plans for the day.

The back of her yellow car sandwiched between two black ones stuck out like a sore thumb. She was almost there and was digging around in her purse for the keys, juggling the long, heavy garment bag, when the shoulder strap of her purse was yanked sharply down her arm. Puzzled, stunned and inattentive to her surroundings, JoBeth jerked back in shock and watched the severed leather strap slither to the ground.

She spun around, the garment bag sliding from her arm. Her heart beat like a sledgehammer as she confronted the young man holding her purse in one hand and a wicked long-bladed knife in the other. She took a step back. "Take it." Wanting desperately to look around or yell, she knew instinctively it would be the

wrong thing to do—she mustn't and couldn't take her
eyes off the shining blade. "Please...go."

The man took a quick step toward her and she tried
to back up once more, but her path was blocked by the
side of her car. Something was terribly wrong. Her assailant should have been far away while she was still too
shocked to scream. But he wasn't. Another step and the
silvery steel made a blurred pass at her midsection.

JoBeth sucked in her stomach automatically, pressing herself flat against the searing metal of the car.
When she realized her attacker wasn't leaving without
some of her blood on his knife, she decided to take her
chances. She opened her mouth and screamed at the top
of her lungs.

In slow motion she watched him come at her again,
and waited this time, wanting only to squeeze her eyes
tightly shut, but the lids seemed frozen wide open. In
horrified fascination she watched, knowing she was
forcing herself to witness her own death.

Sunlight caught the steel and flashed a glint of white
light across her face, making her flinch. Then, suddenly, another hand, large and deeply tanned, was
clamped on her assailant. JoBeth shifted her gaze from
the knife to the two struggling men. Relieved, breathless and scared, she couldn't watch anymore, no matter the outcome. She slid to her knees on the scorching
concrete of the parking lot and closed her eyes. Hanging her head, her stomach knotting in fear, she listened
to the men's heavy breathing and grunts. Then there was
a strange quiet, the only sound one of retreating footsteps.

"Lady, lady?" a deep rumbling voice inquired softly.
"Come on, honey, he's gone. Ran off like a scared

rabbit, and I hope with a broken wrist. Here, let me help you up. You'll hurt yourself down there."

She was lifted by strong hands, turned around and pressed against a well-muscled body.

"Are you okay? He didn't cut you anywhere, did he?"

"No." Her voice came high and squeaky, but instead of trying again, she burrowed her face into the clean smelling white knit shirt. After a long moment she opened her eyes and looked up tentatively, an uncertain smile quivering on her lips. "I thought he was just after my purse...but he came at me with that awful knife. He was going to kill me!"

"Nonsense. You just scared the hell out of him and the vindictive little bastard thought he'd pay you back."

Black eyes as dark as coal gazed down at her. She stared into the strong, rugged face, then realized that she was pressed intimately to his body and his arms were still holding her snugly.

As if he knew what she was thinking, he slowly, reluctantly let her go, but his smile offered more if she was willing. "I think you could use a long cold drink and a place to sit down before you collapse."

"Oh, no...I—"

"Don't say you're all right. You can barely stand, your knees are shaking so badly. I must admit mine aren't in much better shape."

They both looked past his crisp white shorts at tanned, long, well-shaped legs. JoBeth chuckled weakly at the absurdity of those strong knees shaking with fear.

"There, that's better. There's a sidewalk café over there. It's crowded, but I'll see to it that we get a table, and one with a big umbrella."

He'll do it, too, she thought, and allowed herself to be led away.

The cold lemonade tasted like heaven and the wet napkin he'd filled with ice and placed against her forehead and then her neck made her sigh. "Do you think we should call the police?" She opened her eyes and was once again struck by his gentleness; it seemed so at odds with his rugged appearance. She slapped her hand over her mouth. "My God, you saved my life, bought me a drink, and I don't even know your name." He laughed, a mellow, appealing sound that immediately made her rack her brain for unattached friends she could fix him up with.

"Rod Sharp at your service, madam." He bowed his head, his black eyes dancing with laughter as he reached out and clasped her hand. "I didn't save your life, you know. He wasn't going to knife you. And as for the police . . . what would they do? Take your story and a description. Did you get a good look at him? I was a little busy, and he escaped before I had time to take his measure."

JoBeth frowned and thought. "You know, I couldn't tell them much, either. I was more concerned with that knife he kept flashing at me."

"Don't worry about it." He patted her shoulder. "Look." He held up the mangled white leather purse with its severed strap for her inspection. "I did manage to save this."

"I'd forgotten all about my purse! Thank you again, though words are a sorry repayment. I'm convinced that by running that nasty man off before I had a heart attack, you saved my life." Her cheeks glowed and her smile was tender.

Rod picked up her hand and lightly kissed it. "It was my pleasure. Now I must ask you something very serious. Stop smiling. Are you married?" He glanced down at the hand absent of any ring and smiled winningly.

"My ring!" Horrified, JoBeth's gaze froze on her bare hand. "I had it on. I know I did." She glanced up, met the disappointment in his eyes and pulled her fingers from his. "I . . . I guess I've lost it. But, yes, I'm married, and I love my husband very much." She saw the sadness on his face and became even more determined to find someone for this wonderful man. What a catch for some lucky woman.

Rod walked her back to her car and waited until she had opened the door and tossed in her purse and dress before he clasped her shoulders and turned her around. "May I have just one small, insignificant reward?"

She pulled back a little, but he refused to let her go. "I don't think that would be proper, do you?"

He sighed, then smiled. "No, you're right." Then before she could stop him he pulled her into his arms and his lips captured hers in a determined kiss. After a few breathless seconds he released her. "I'm sorry. I see now that you truly are a happily married lady."

JoBeth glared at him, then smiled. She couldn't be mad at a man for trying. Besides, he had saved her life, no matter what he said to the contrary. "If I were to invite you to a dinner party I'm going to give, would you come?" He grinned, but his dark eyes were serious and a little hard, like polished jet.

"Of course." He accepted the pad and pen she handed him and quickly scrawled his telephone number. Then he shut her door, motioned for her to lock up, waved and walked away.

Instead of returning to the safe haven of home, JoBeth pulled into the bumper-to-bumper traffic on Westheimer. Her hands were still shaking and her foot trembled so on the gas pedal that she felt the car should be jumping in tandem with her nerves. She couldn't believe what had happened to her. The horror of seeing the flashing knife sent a cold chill down her spine despite the suffocating heat that had built up in the car.

JoBeth adjusted the vents to blow cool air on her damp face as she wove between cars. When she finally reached the exit to River Oaks Boulevard she sighed with relief. An immediate feeling of peace washed over her as she passed the palatial homes. Trees older than the opulent residences dotted the manicured lawns of the street that led to the River Oaks Country Club.

But JoBeth paid little attention to the familiar scenery. Her gaze was riveted to the sand-colored brick house that rose majestically among verdant trees, flowers of a multitude of colors and shrubs so lushly thick and tall that they camouflaged the tall brick fence. Even the twin turrets with their stained-glass windows did not miss her inspection. As she pulled up in front, a sharp knot constricted her chest and she swallowed to ease the pain in her throat.

The sight of her home brought back an avalanche of memories. Some good, some bad, but all were as much a part of her life as the baccarat crystal chandeliers, white-and-gold Italian marble floors, the curved stairway, Persian rugs and priceless antiques too numerous to remember. She leaned back on the leather headrest and closed her eyes. When she wasn't at some finishing school or traveling all over the world, and was old enough not to have to live with the DeSalvas, this had been her home. A place where she'd thrown parties and entertained everyone from businessmen to European royalty. All for her father and his business interests. This was also, she thought sadly, the place where her father had shot himself because he was unable to face the shambles he'd made of his life.

Yet despite his anguish, his suicide, he'd tried to leave her her world, but she couldn't accept the gift and had sold everything. She opened her eyes and stared at the Huntley estate, realizing for the first time that even though she was extremely wealthy again, she would never try to buy any part of her old life back. She'd changed from a frivolous, useless woman who fluttered through life to a woman with a husband she loved dearly and a life she would give up only to death.

As her thoughts slipped back to the present she began to shake again. Not because of the experience with the purse snatcher, but because of the memory of Carmen's smug face as she left the restaurant. JoBeth's hands gripped the steering wheel until the skin stretched white and thin over her knuckles. How could Brandon have dated that bitch? She forced her fingers from the wheel one by one and flexed them, trying to restore circulation. With the renewed life came pain, and she welcomed it. It gave her something to focus her anger on, instead of planning ways to make Brandon pay for falling into his old routine. Damn him! Would he never realize that he loved her? *Could* he love her as everyone seemed to believe?

JoBeth put the car in gear, gave one last look at what had been her home and drove away. Life went on, she realized, no matter the circumstances. The past was best forgotten. Maybe she'd made a mistake forcing Brandon to marry her, or maybe she had been so wrapped up in her own desires she'd neglected to think clearly. But during her year alone on the dude ranch, she'd learned more about herself than she'd thought possible. Yet one thing had never changed: her love for one pigheaded man. Her absence from him had only made that love stronger. So maybe, she rationalized, just maybe she'd done the right thing. Then again . . . JoBeth shook her head sharply. Her thoughts were like a rat in a maze, going around and around as she tried to convince herself she'd done the right thing.

The tall DeSalvas Building loomed ahead and her drifting attention snapped back. She jerked the steering wheel and squealed into the lot, heading for the underground parking. The events of the day flashed back at her and she stepped on the brakes. She stopped and stared at the yawning dark entrance with a foreboding she'd never experienced before. With a quick spin of the wheel she parked the car in an empty slot near the entrance and jumped out. Just this once she'd give in to her instincts and enter the building through the lobby.

A harassed security guard glanced up from his bank of monitors. "Afternoon, Mrs. DeSalva."

She smiled, nodded and would have passed him by as she headed for the private elevator that went directly to the penthouse suite, but the guard's next words stopped her dead in her tracks.

"The courier from Neiman-Marcus delivered the clothes for Mr. Brandon." He fiddled with a couple more knobs, then looked up, his lined forehead a mass of worry.

Amid all the ruckus she'd forgotten the clothes she'd bought. She also thought of what she'd done earlier and what Brandon's reaction was going to be. "Thanks, Frank," she said absently, and turned to go, but once more his words stopped her.

"And the florist delivered your order." He looked up from the adjustments he was making, smiled at the rows of television monitors as if satisfied, then turned his full attention on JoBeth. "I couldn't take the men up myself. These damn . . . excuse me . . . these blasted screens were on the blink." He scratched his head a moment and continued. "They went as dark as night for about an hour." He saw her frown and quickly went on to ease his conscience about what he'd done. "Your maid was still there, so she let them in. I called up later and everything was okay."

No one was to enter the penthouse floor from the lobby without a security guard to accompany him, or unless he'd been authorized by one of the DeSalvas.

"What florist, Frank? I didn't order any flowers."

"Weren't no flowers, ma'am." Frank's uneasiness increased. He yanked up his sign-in board and all but shoved it under her nose. "Wallman's Florist delivered plants—a mess of them. Took four of their men a couple of trips to carry everything up. I figured with all the remodeling you was doing . . ." He trailed off.

"It's all right, Frank." She could tell from the old man's rapid speech and his fidgeting hands that he was extremely agitated, and she didn't want to disturb him more. "I didn't order them, but maybe Mr. DeSalva did. Anyway, I'll find out. If there's been an error we'll take care of it." She backed away from his troubled expression. "Don't worry, please, Frank."

In a matter of minutes she was standing in the center of her living room, witnessing the truth of Frank's words. But it should have taken twice as many men to juggle these monsters in the elevator and down the hall to their suite. Huge copper pots sprouted small trees thick with glossy green foliage. Terra-cotta urns nestled in beautiful standing planters were graced with lacy ferns. Someone had turned her home into a jungle. Granted, an elegant, artfully arranged jungle, but a jungle nonetheless.

She spent half an hour on the phone before she accepted that her attempts to get an explanation were futile. She wasn't going to get any satisfaction from Wallman's Florist. Yes, they had filled the order and delivered it, but they were not at liberty to disclose the sender as the party preferred to remain anonymous. She slammed down the phone, racking her brain, trying to think who would send her and Brandon such a gift. The problem was, there were dozens of people who wouldn't hesitate to make such an extravagant gesture, but *they* certainly wouldn't have withheld their identity. She glanced at the plants and grimaced. Why did not knowing the sender take all the joy out of the gift? Anonymity suddenly seemed to take on some ulterior motive. She was being silly, of course, but still...

JoBeth surged to her feet, kicked off her shoes and marched into the kitchen. Another display of green fern in a white wicker stand caught her eye, and as she studied it it left an unexplainable bitterness in her mouth. Why did "funeral" pop into her mind? God, she was worse than silly; she was becoming downright morbid. She quickly fixed herself a Coke over crushed ice, and with the cool drink in hand she headed for the bedroom. At the open doorway she stopped and with a caution she couldn't explain, she peeked in, then sighed. There were no offending plants here. But there was something else... a feeling of intrusion.

JoBeth sat down heavily on the end of the king-size bed, brought the sweating glass to her forehead and closed her eyes. She had never been fanciful, though she'd always instinctively known when things weren't right. And now her senses were screaming at her that someone other than her, Brandon and the maid had been in this room. She set the glass on the carpet, walked over to the big double dresser and pulled open one of her drawers. Beautifully arranged lingerie, neatly folded, met her sharp inspection. She laid her hand on a silk gown and frowned. It wasn't exactly as she'd placed it, but was separated from the other gowns a little. She'd always been persnickety about her lingerie, not wanting anyone else to handle it or put it away. Her strict orders to the new maid had yet to be broken.

JoBeth straightened the gown, then smiled. A second later the smile turned into a laugh, and she stepped back and flopped onto the bed. She wasn't going nuts, after all! Of course the room felt as if a stranger had been there. One of the men from the florist's had probably thought he could stash one of the trees in the bedroom, then must have decided there wasn't enough room. As for her lingerie . . . she'd more than likely displaced it this morning while she yanked drawers open looking for her elusive white slip. Still, where was the satin nightgown Brandon had given her? She'd just remembered it wasn't in the drawer where it should be. Well, the maid had more than likely sent it to the cleaners.

With a gusty sigh of relief that she'd worked out part of that problem, JoBeth picked up her Coke, scooted across the bed and stretched out to ponder another: Brandon and his little tête-à-tête with Carmen Walters. The mere thought of that woman getting her hooks into Brandon made JoBeth glare at the ceiling. *Over my dead body,* she vowed.

She was carefully planning and chuckling over ways to rid Houston of that two-legged vermin, when the bedside phone rang. She reached out, then paused, her hand suspended over the receiver as that old troubled feeling returned. Whoever it was on the other end boded ill for her, she was sure. Maybe she ought to ignore it, she thought, but only for a moment. "Hello," she said tentatively.

"I won't play your game much longer, JoBeth. If you've really given Brandon your voting rights over your stock, I'd advise you to rescind your good-natured gesture. You know, sweetheart, your generosity won't keep Brandon from other women's beds. Hell! I'd be willing to bet his eye is already starting to wander. And if my memory serves me correctly, not too long ago he had a hot and heavy relationship with Carmen Walters."

"Hello to you, too, Uncle Tramble."

"Cut the crap, niece. I'm not in the mood." There was a long pause, and as she listened to the raspy, heavy breathing she wondered if her uncle was ill.

"I can't and won't take back my voting rights. Damn it, Uncle Tram, this would never have happened," she lied, "if you hadn't been so gutty and started firing those men right before their retirement."

"Shut your Goddamn mouth, JoBeth. You know nothing of what you're saying. Besides, you never know who might be listening in."

JoBeth smiled hugely. For the first time that she could remember she'd managed to shake her uncle's composure, and she wasn't about to pass up the chance to twist the knife a little deeper. "But it's true, Uncle, dear. You fired several executives in the past two years.

Loyal men who've been with you for as long as you've been in control of U.S.A. Oil."

"Shut up woman," he growled.

She was carried away with her own sense of power. "Brandon is going to make sure you never have that opportunity again. He's promised me he'll ask the board of directors to reinstate those men you fired. He can do it, too, with my voting shares. I'll bet he can even ask for your..." She trailed off, staring at the receiver as the dial tone screamed at her. "Well, of all the nerve. The old goat actually hung up on me."

Then she gasped, realizing what she'd told him. Brandon had warned her repeatedly of the danger of any contact with her uncle. It looked as though he knew her better than she knew herself; he was fully aware that she could never keep her mouth shut. Damn, damn. She'd done it again, but at least she wouldn't have to lie her way out of this one. She hadn't told Brandon about the previous talks with her uncle, and she simply wouldn't tell him about this one, either. How, she wondered, did she get herself into these things without even trying? The crux of her problem was that her troubles never came when she expected them. Each was like a delayed bomb: the fuse was lighted, then unexpectedly it would go out, but the danger was still there, waiting for any small breeze to rekindle the flame of destruction. Had she learned nothing in her year away?

Disgusted with herself and her actions, she jumped off the bed and headed for the kitchen. She had almost reached the doorway, when the doorbell rang and she veered sharply in the opposite direction. Without a thought to safety or security, she swung the door wide. "Kane!" Standing beside him was Shasta, and she grinned at the two, joyously welcoming them. Here were the very people to take her mind off the mess she was in and give her some needed laughs. "Come in, come in." She stepped back and waved them by. "Would you like something to drink?"

"JoBeth," Kane started, then stopped, cleared his throat and gazed pleadingly at his wife. "I can't do it." He marched past them to the living room.

"What's the matter?"

"Come here, JoBeth." Shasta grasped JoBeth's arm and guided her to where Kane stood at the windows.

JoBeth suddenly felt hot, then cold. She yanked her arm from Shasta's grip and began to chatter nervously. "What do you two want to drink? Kane, Scotch, isn't it, or has Shasta got you drinking wine?" She took a quick shallow breath and started again, but the words died on her lips as she saw the look of concern and pity that passed between husband and wife. All at once her knees gave way and she grabbed for a chair. "What's happened?"

Shasta glared at her husband and gave him a tiny shake of her head as if to say she wasn't going to be the one to break the news.

"Please, tell me. Damn it, one of you say something."

Kane began, his voice husky with emotion. "Brandon's helicopter is down." He leaped across the space between them and grabbed JoBeth as she slumped in her chair.

But she batted his helping hand away as the impact of his words hit her. "Where?"

He squatted in front of her, taking her cold hands in his, and started to tell her all he knew. "Somewhere in the Gulf, between shore and the oil rig. The aircraft obviously developed trouble and they had to ditch it, but, JoBeth, they managed to get out a Mayday and their coordinates. The Coast Guard is searching the area now." Shasta came to sit beside him on the floor, and he let go of one of JoBeth's hands and encircled his wife's trembling shoulders.

"I see," JoBeth said calmly, refusing to take her gaze from their clasped hands. "Then there's hope that he's still alive?"

"God, yes. Don't you ever give up on Brandon DeSalva!"

She laughed then, a shaky sound that pierced the hearts of her friends. "I've known Brandon longer than either of you. He'll be all right. Believe me, I'd know if something had happened to him." She looked up and stared Kane straight in the eye. "I *would* know. What do we do now?"

"Wait and pray and hope."

"Yes." She settled back in her chair. "What about Jennifer and Lucas? She flew in this morning and Lucas wasn't going to leave the ranch to pick her up until tomorrow."

Kane slowly stood, feeling as though he were a hundred years old. If something happened to Brandon and he could trace the accident to Tramble Baldwin's door, he would see to it that the old man suffered before he died. But his questions would have to go unanswered for now. This was not the time to badger JoBeth with his suspicions. "I'll go get Jennifer and put in a call to the DeSalva ranch. But Brandon will be all right—you'll see."

She nodded and closed her eyes. "He'll come back. He has to." Damn it, he still hadn't told her he loved her, and there was no way in hell she was going to let him die without knowing the truth. She bit her lip hard to keep from crying. Waiting would be the easiest part; it was the thought of losing Brandon that was unbearable.

CHAPTER NINE

"WHAT TIME IS IT?" JoBeth knew she'd asked the same question at least a thousand times, but she had to know.

"Five-forty-three," Shasta said as she paced the room. Jennifer DeSalva sat beside Matthew, holding on to his frail, blue-veined hand with a tenderness that brought a lump to her throat. How much more suffering could the proud old man take? First, the death of his wife and daughter, and now possibly his youngest son. Lucas stood sentinel at the tall expanse of windows even though the heavy curtains were closed to shut out the sun's blinding glare. Shasta's gaze shifted to her husband, who was speaking softly into the telephone. Everyone waited, each anticipating the end of the conversation with both eagerness and dread. Something should have happened by now.

JoBeth rubbed her hands together as if to ward off a deep chill. She felt naked without her wedding ring. A frown rippled her brow and she immediately ducked her head to keep the others from seeing it; any change would only bring their concern and endless questions. Brandon would be furious with her for being so absentminded and neglectful about something as important as her wedding ring. She could hear him now. *Oh, Bets,* he'd say on a sigh of resignation and laughter. *Think back to where you remember seeing it last.* Those very words had been used on too many occasions over the years.

Those words... Her first memory of them was when she'd lost her little pillow. Brandon had searched for hours, with her trailing behind, fat tears filling her eyes until he found her beloved "lillow" wedged between her headboard and the mattress. There'd been lost dolls, puppies, shoes, books, and her favorite red party dress, which he'd despised. To this day she believed he'd hid it, only to have to find it when she threw a crying fit and his wise mother made him return it. Oh, there'd been a million other little things—even the disappearance of a couple of eager young suitors that she suspected he ran off.

As she sat there lost in thought, she smiled. Brandon had always griped and bitched at how much trouble she was, but thinking back, she realized he'd never failed to find her lost items. Now she'd lost the most precious thing she owned: a simple wide band of gold. *Think back to where you remember seeing it last, Bets.* But she couldn't remember!

"JoBeth." Kane hung up the phone and faced his friends. "The Coast Guard has spotted some wreckage where they think the helicopter went down." Before they could ask, he answered. "No, they haven't spotted anyone yet. But remember, Brandon wouldn't necessarily be with the wreckage. Both he and the pilot will have on life jackets and more than likely be riding the currents. It's just a matter of time now—a little longer wait, that's all."

No one spoke, each too afraid to voice his fears. Anything could happen to a man floating the Gulf waters. JoBeth clasped her fingers together until they hurt. Her chest ached from holding back the tears and anguish she was feeling. If something didn't happen soon she felt she would shatter into a thousand pieces. The phone rang again, and everyone froze, the tension a palpable thing in their midst. She squeezed her eyes tightly shut, knowing this was the final word. One way or the other, their waiting was over. The drone of Kane's voice grated on her nerves and she fought to control her trembling limbs. Then, suddenly, her heart skipped a beat and she relaxed as Kane threw back his head and laughed loudly and joyously.

"Brandon's alive! As a matter of fact that was him, and all he said was he was *damn* cold." Kane chuckled. Brandon hadn't exactly used that word, but he thought he'd better clean up the man's expletives a bit for old man DeSalva and the ladies.

JoBeth jumped to her feet, meeting Kane's shining silver eyes with a fierceness that caused him to sober immediately. "Why did you hang up? You didn't let me talk to him. How do I know you're telling the truth?"

"JoBeth." Lucas spoke softly and waved Kane away.

She was in Lucas's arms, tears of relief streaming down her cheeks. "I'm sorry," she sobbed into his shirt as she struggled to regain control of her emotions.

"Go on and let it all out, honey. You know how Brandon hates to see you cry." Pressing JoBeth's head to his chest, he smiled tenderly at Jennifer. His wife was soaking his father's shirtfront with equal zeal. Even Matthew's eyes were damp. He asked the one question everyone had forgotten to ask. "Where is he, Kane, and how do we go about getting him home?"

Kane, not untouched by the scene before him, slung his arm around his wife's shoulders. "The Coast Guard is going to fly him here." He pulled Shasta closer so he could get a better look at his watch. "They should be landing on the roof helipad in about twenty to thirty minutes.''

THE MERCILESS SUN BEAT DOWN on JoBeth's head until she thought she'd faint. The glare stung her eyes and made them water, and sweat slithered down her sides, soaking the waistband of her wrinkled linen dress.

''JoBeth, come over here in the shelter,'' Lucas said, so exasperated with her stubbornness that the words came out harsh and demanding.

But she ignored him and shook her head, never taking her eyes off the southeast horizon.

''JoBeth!'' This time Shasta tried, and was abruptly waved to silence.

''Quiet,'' she snapped. ''Look!'' JoBeth pointed at the tiny white speck that was making its way toward them. Then, suddenly, the wind from the big Coast Guard helicopter picked up her skirt and whipped her hair against her eyes with a stinging series of slaps. She fought neither, but took a few steps forward and stopped, then quickly brushed the strands of hair from her eyes so as not to obscure her first sight of Brandon.

He stepped down from the helicopter and turned his back on his waiting family as he briefly shook hands with the pilot, then moved back for the door to slide shut. As the aircraft lifted off, Brandon spun around, a smile spreading over his face like sunlight breaking through a storm.

JoBeth covered her mouth with her hand, and through a blur of tears she giggled. He was still in his three-piece suit, though it looked shriveled and shrunk. There was a green blanket wrapped around his shoulders and he was barefoot. The sight of his feet protruding from the shortened pant legs sent her flying into his waiting arms.

"Now, Bets, don't cry." He hugged her to him fiercely and scolded her at the same time. "Come on, Bets, you know I don't like this." She hiccuped loudly and he laughed, and that brought on a new torrent of tears and sobs. "Bets, Bets." He patted her on the back a couple of times, looking helplessly at the people beyond her shoulder.

Brandon managed to shake hands with his father and brother and Kane, and even gave a quick kiss on the cheek to Jennifer and Shasta, all without letting go of JoBeth. Another loud hiccup, muffled by his damp suit jacket, brought a chuckle from everyone. "Enough, Bets. You'll have me as wet as when they pulled me out of the ocean."

"Sorry." She hiccuped, then wailed, "Oh, Brandon! You went out to the oil rig in a suit?" When he gave her an injured look she couldn't help but return it with a weak laugh.

"The fish appreciated it, though, Bets." He yanked up a corner of the jacket and showed her a few holes. "See."

JoBeth's knees gave way as scenes from *Jaws* flashed through her mind.

"No, no. Come on, Bets. Don't you dare pass out on me. Lucas," he pleaded with his grinning brother, "help!"

"Not on your life. Sometimes, brother, you carry things a bit too far."

Brandon supported JoBeth with one arm and patted her cheek none too gently with his free hand as he half dragged her to the rooftop door. "The sun's getting to her. She couldn't have missed me this much."

"How dare you suggest such a thing!" JoBeth jerked upright. "I was half out of my mind. You are..." She trailed off, looked up into his sapphire-blue eyes dancing with mischief and smiled. Obviously his near-fatal experience hadn't done any real damage; he was his old teasing, infuriating self. She gave him one passionate hug, then led the way down the stairs and into the cool penthouse suite.

THEY WAITED in the living room for Brandon to shower and get into dry clothes. JoBeth wanted to accompany him into the bathroom, but decided that she wouldn't embarrass Matthew with her impatience. There was no doubt whatsoever that if she got him alone they'd end up in bed, no matter who waited to hear his tale.

Dressed comfortably in faded jeans, T-shirt and worn tennis shoes, Brandon joined everyone, deliberately drawing out the suspense by quietly gazing around the room before he sat down. He put his arm around JoBeth's shoulders and pulled her close to his side, smiling.

"That's enough son," Matthew ordered. "We're all on the edge of our seats waiting to hear what happened. Besides you've put us through enough this day without making us endure your strange sense of humor."

Brandon's blue eyes sparkled as he took in the faces of his family and friends. He inhaled a short breath and opened his mouth, about to let loose with his jokes, but what came out surprised even him. "I'll tell you this! I was as scared as hell. I may never swim in the ocean again." Fear, he thought, was a difficult thing for a man to admit to, but he'd really been afraid in that endless expanse of murky water. "The pilot, Bob James, is a first-class man. He handled the situation with a calm strength right from the beginning."

"What happened, Brandon? Why did he have to ditch the craft?" Kane leaned forward, his silver eyes fixed on Brandon's, his attention riveted on each word his partner spoke.

"We may never know," he hedged, "but Bob swears he checked out the helicopter before we went up. He told me from the way the craft acted it must have been a valve malfunction," he lied. "There was a popping sound, then the helicopter was spewing fuel and oil everywhere. It's a miracle we didn't burst into flames."

He tried to control the shudder that ran through his body, hoping no one would notice. JoBeth squeezed his hand. He glanced at her, accepting her sympathy. She, of all people, understood how important it was for him to keep up a front. All his life he'd managed to conceal his feelings under laughter and teasing—he'd had to, to hide his own vulnerability. There were few who realized that he could be hurt just as easily as anyone else. JoBeth knew—even as a child she had recognized that hidden well of tenderness in him—and though he liked to think she'd forgotten, he knew she hadn't. Suddenly he wanted nothing more than to take her in his arms and tell her how much she'd been on his mind, how confused he'd been. He wanted to ask her if she'd been equally as troubled about their marriage. Had she married him just to become a part of his family? The questions preyed on his mind constantly. "I like the jungle decor," he whispered for her ears only. "Dare I ask what our bedroom looks like? I won't have to swing from a vine to get to the bed, will I?"

"Goddamn it, Brandon!" Lucas yelled. He was more exasperated with his brother than he'd been with Jo-

Beth earlier. If any two people deserved each other, these two did. "Will you quit gazing at your wife with your tongue hanging out. If you'd go on with your story we'd be out of your hair before you know it."

Brandon's cheeks flushed, and he shot a look at Lucas that told him he wasn't amused at being caught with his thoughts showing so clearly. Besides, he hadn't blushed since he was a teenager. The embarrassment hadn't set well then, either. "There's not a whole lot to tell. Bob and I, once we shoved away from the helicopter and watched it go under, lashed ourselves together with our neckties. We tried to stay close to where we crashed, hoping it would make it easier for any rescue attempt, but the current out there is surprisingly strong under that sluggish surface. It carried us farther and farther away. After exhausting attempts to keep our positions, we realized we were only using up strength and precious body heat, so we began floating along with the flow."

He leaned his head back, closed his eyes and squeezed hard on JoBeth's fingers, which were intertwined with his. "It was when the fish came that it really got to me. We must have floated into this school of them." He shuddered again, and this time it was visible to everyone in the room. "Both Bob and I lost our shoes, and the fish started nibbling on our bare feet. Bold little devils. We were afraid that if they bit hard enough to break the skin and bring blood we'd attract a whole different kind of trouble."

He opened his eyes and let everyone see his fear. "There were hard nudges against our legs and lower body, but whether or not they were made by sharks we didn't know." Brandon laughed suddenly, and everyone smiled, relieved that they no longer had to imagine themselves in his position.

"How did you pass the time?" JoBeth asked softly, wanting to cry out and scream for what he'd been through. Brandon had changed, subtly. There was a new seriousness in his gaze, a determination that made her heart pound. What if he'd decided that their marriage wasn't worth continuing? She'd heard stories of people facing death and living, only to change their entire life afterward.

"We talked, Bets." He turned more toward her and tightened his grip on her shoulders. "Bob told me all about his wife and two children, and I told him everything about this crazy woman I married."

Her eyes widened. "You didn't!" She'd forgotten the others. "Not everything!"

"Back to the first time I set eyes on you."

"Will you two stop it!" Matthew growled, but his smile couldn't be contained any longer. He grasped his cane and slowly climbed to his feet. "I think we've all worn out our welcome. It's time to leave the newlyweds alone." Everyone followed Matthew to the door except Kane. He'd caught Brandon's gaze and nod asking him to stay.

Shasta was the last to leave, and Brandon gave her an extra special hug. "I'll send him along in a minute. Wait for him downstairs in the Masters Security office." She was almost out the door, when his next question stopped her. "Hey, Shasta, have you seen Kane's new secretary yet?" He watched the big brown eyes narrow and the bouncy brown curls shake a negative answer. He chuckled wickedly, and before closing the door, he added with a mischievous twist of his lips. "You must meet her . . . soon."

"Brandon!" JoBeth gasped. "How could you?" He grinned and she realized his ordeal was beginning to wear off: the old Brandon was emerging a little more with each passing minute. "Why do you do things like that?"

He slung his arm around her waist and urged her down the hall. "Like what?"

"Start trouble, then back off and watch the sparks fly." She slipped her fingers into the back pocket of his jeans and pinched. He was forever stirring up a hornets' nest.

Brandon winced and moved his backside away from her questing fingers. "But, Bets, Shasta's sparks are so combustible and fun to watch. Besides, Kane can take care of himself."

"I know, but he's got enough trouble on his hands without you adding more." She tried to mask her guilty expression, but Brandon was always on to her tricks and knew she couldn't keep secrets.

"Give!" he said softly in her ear.

"Oh, well.... I guess Kane will find out soon enough." She told him quickly of Shasta's new acquisition and smiled when Brandon whistled long and low.

They were almost at the living room entrance, when he stopped. "Why don't you go on to bed. I want to have a few words with Kane, then I'll be along." She opened her mouth to protest, but he stopped her argument with a tender kiss that left them both a little breathless. "Go on." He patted her derriere lovingly. "I'll get rid of him fast."

Brandon watched her as she walked the long hall toward their bedroom. There was a throb in his loins, a radiating heat that demanded attention. He chuckled to himself. Facing death seemed to have increased his desire for his wife even more. It was all he could think about while he floated around in the Gulf. A cough from Kane brought his wandering attention back, and he stepped into the living room.

"I think you'd better put someone on our offshore operation, Kane. That damn helicopter was sabotaged just as surely as my name is Brandon DeSalva." His statement bought Kane to his feet as smoothly as a cat about to pounce on his prey.

"Tramble Baldwin, you think?"

"Possibly—probably." Brandon poured them a small amount of brandy. He held his snifter to the light and studied the brilliant flashing colors caught within the faceted crystal. "But I don't think this has anything to do with the stock takeover. Maybe he's just trying another one of his sick tricks to stop the computerized drilling experiment."

Kane stood tensely beside Brandon, watching him as he inspected the quality of the crystal. Their eyes met and locked in perfect understanding. If Tramble had anything to do with the crash, it wouldn't be long before his informants would find out about the stock manipulations. They were going to have to speed up their timetable. "How long before you're able to leave the supervision of the rig to your foreman?"

Brandon gave a tiny shake of his head, took a hefty slug of brandy and began to cough and choke. Swallowing saltwater, then throwing it up for hours had made his throat and stomach raw. He wiped his watering eyes and said, "Hell, Kane. I have to find out who I can trust before I turn it over to anyone."

"Understood. But how long? I want you to be free so we can move on our deal as soon as possible."

Brandon relieved Kane of his half-empty snifter, set it down and urged him toward the front door. JoBeth, soft and warm, was waiting for him, and he was impatient to be in her arms. He was in no mood to hear the problems Kane was about to heap on him. "We'll talk about this tomorrow. Right now, all I want to do is get some sleep in a bed that doesn't rock and roll," he lied.

"Sure, and pigs fly," Kane said with a knowing grin, but he stopped at the door, refusing to leave until he had one more answer. "Tell me how you knew the helicopter was sabotaged."

Brandon placed his arm on the frame, leaned forward and rubbed his forehead against his arm wearily. "When Bob and I bailed out and before the helicopter sank we had time to briefly swim around it. We found the remains of a small explosive charge and a timer at the base of the rotary blades, as well as some wires leading to the fuel line."

Kane still hesitated. "You're sure JoBeth hadn't talked to her uncle and leaked anything?"

Brandon slowly shook his head, suddenly sick of going over the same ground with Kane. "JoBeth knows how important this deal is to *all* of us. I've explained how ruthless Tramble is. Besides, she's never been very good at keeping secrets from me. If she'd talked, I'd know. Believe me, Kane! She would never do anything to hurt us. I trust her with my life."

"You may very well have done just that, my friend. Look where it got you, too...." Kane held up his hands and grinned. "Okay. I'm sorry. No more doubts. It's just that I have this feeling...."

Brandon all but pushed Kane out and almost managed to shut the door, but Kane grabbed it.

"I'll give Shasta the job of finding out who Tramble's informants and henchmen are on the rig." His grin began to spread with his new idea. "Hell, it will give her something to do with her spare time instead of driving me nuts."

"Fine. Good night." Brandon closed the door on Kane, then leaned against it with a sigh of relief. Home! He spun around, heading for the bedroom with an eager bounce in his step that had been missing for a long time. Facing death had done more for him than he'd ever thought possible. How, he wondered, did you thank fate for almost taking your life?

On his way down the hall he stripped off his T-shirt, kicked off his tennis shoes, and as he finally came to stand beside the bed, he shucked his jeans. She looked so innocent, he thought, with her face clean and shining and her hair tousled around her head like a halo. He squatted, bringing his face close to hers. When her father had first brought her to stay with them at the ranch right after her mother had died, he could remember hearing her cry out in the middle of the night. How many times had he stood at her bedside, looking down at her just as he was now? He touched her hand gently, and as she'd done in the past she grasped his fingers tightly. But this time he knew she was awake. "Open your eyes, Bets. I know you're not asleep. And if you've tied yourself to my side of the bed again, so help me..." He suddenly found himself drowning in misty gray eyes shimmering with tears. "Now why are you crying?"

She sniffed as a smile began to quiver around her lips. "I guess I'm happy you're home and in one piece."

"Thank you. So am I." He touched her shoulder, sliding the sheet down with his caressing hand. "Are you going to move over and let me in? Or have you really tied yourself to my side of the bed?''

JoBeth laughed and threw back the covers, allowing him full view of her naked body and enjoying the small catch in his breathing. She scooted over just enough to let him slide in beside her. He felt so good, warm and hard against her. She reached out and touched his hair, then ran her fingers down his cheek to the corner of his mouth. ''I never once doubted you'd come back, you know.''

''Of course not.''

''I would have known if something serious had happened.''

''I believe you.''

''I knew you were alive.'' Emotion caught in her throat, making her voice crack. ''I just didn't know if you were hurt or not.'' It was a strange conversation, she realized; each seemed to want to say things, yet held back. Once again there was the sting of tears behind her eyelids. She fought them back, knowing how much Brandon hated to see women cry. But all at once there was so much she wanted to tell him. What difference did it make if he didn't love her? JoBeth opened her mouth and lifted her eyes to his, only to have the words die on her lips as she saw desire burning brightly in the blue depths.

''Do you know what I thought of all the time I was floating in the water?''

''No,'' she whispered.

He rolled her over onto her stomach, lifted her hair off the back of her neck. ''I thought of this warm, fragrant spot just made for kissing.'' His lips caressed a small hollow at the base of her neck and she trembled.

His mouth traveled across her shoulders, nibbling a path of ice and fire. His hands stroked lower.

"What else did you think about . . . out there?" she said through her teeth. He was tasting the curve of her back, bringing goose bumps with each touch of his tongue. She grasped a handful of sheet and squeezed hard.

"This—" He gently bit at one firmly rounded buttock. "And this." His tongue played down the back of her thigh, stopping at the bend of her knee.

JoBeth moaned out loud, her breathing fast and shallow. "I'm afraid to ask what else you thought about."

Brandon chuckled, rolled her over onto her back and sat up, taking his fill of her beautiful body. He hadn't lied to her. He'd thought of little else while in the water. JoBeth meant more to him than he was willing to admit. He slid his hands up her sides, stopping only long enough to take each button nipple in his mouth. God, she tasted good. He hadn't known any woman that had ever pleased him as totally as his Bets did. His lips captured hers and he savored the depths of her mouth.

She was trembling, every muscle vibrating under his touch. Her fingers clasped his strong shoulders, slid down slowly over his back and then around to grasp the velvet length of him. She could wait no longer and guided him into her warm wetness with an eagerness that brought a wicked chuckle from the man above her.

"And what if I'm not ready?" he whispered in her ear.

"Tough," she growled back, and moved her hips in a fashion that made him gasp and groan. "I believe you are now," she said breathlessly.

Later, spent, shivering, JoBeth eased the covers up over herself and Brandon and thought how different this lovemaking had been from the past nights. There was an urgency in each of their bodies tonight, telling them things that words never could. Yet she knew she needed to hear those words, too. More than anything in the world she wanted him to say he loved her. She sighed, and Brandon moved beside her.

He touched her face in the dark, searching for a tell-tale trace of tears. "Listen, Miss Watering Pot, this has got to stop."

"It will. I promise." She hiccuped, and he laughed.

Brandon leaned up on one elbow and switched on the bedside lamp. He pulled out the drawer of the small table, retrieved a soggy velvet box and waved it under her nose. "Maybe this will make you feel better."

"What?" She sat up, letting the covers fall around her waist. Then, aware of his piercing gaze, she yanked up the sheet. Want him again she might, but a present from Brandon was something she couldn't pass up, even for sex. "Ugh! It's wet and cold, Brandon. What did you do to it?"

He fluffed his pillow and sat up beside her. "I'll have you know that box was in my breast pocket, protected by the lifejacket. It's a good thing, too. I lost everything else I had in my pockets. Go on, open it."

JoBeth snapped the top up so fast that the sodden velvet-lined box gave way and crumbled in her hands, making her dig for her prize. It didn't take long to find the emerald ring, and with a squeal she shoved it on her finger and held it out to the light. "My God! Brandon, it's beautiful." The big exquisite stone sat in a plain gold setting, catching the light and sparkling with green fire. She snatched her hand back, holding it close to her heart. "I told you once that emeralds were my favorite and that I wished my eyes were green instead of gray. You remembered."

"Did I?" Some of the happiness died in her eyes and he could have kicked himself. What would it have hurt to tell her the truth? "Do you like it?"

"Yes, of course," she said stiffly. "It's the most beautiful gift I've ever received." She held out her hand again, silently scolding herself for being such a fool. She should be happy he'd thought to take the time to buy her a present. Brandon grabbed her hand and she froze, knowing what was coming.

"Bets, where is your wedding ring?" He stared at her, noting the rising color in her cheeks, the way her eyelids dropped a little and the tightening of the corners of her mouth. He knew that look from old. "Okay, Bets, the truth. Where is your ring?"

She clasped the new ring back against her chest and gazed at him, her eyes a little dreamy, her brain working a million miles a second for a plausible story. Her first instinct was to lie. Then she knew she couldn't. "I don't know. Honestly, Brandon, I never took it off. It just disappeared."

He patted her arm comfortingly. "Think back to where you remember seeing it last, Bets." Before he was finished his sentence she was laughing. "What's so damn funny?" he grumbled, rolling her across his body with an unexpectedness that made her strangle on her own laughter. "Thought you'd be sneaky and get my side of the bed for once, didn't you?"

She grinned sleepily, turned off the lamp and snuggled up against him, her eyelids heavy with fulfillment and exhaustion from the release of the day's tension. As she yawned she thought that she ought to tell him what had happened to her today, then promised herself she'd tell him tomorrow. "One of these days," she murmured, "you're going to relent and let me have *my* side of the bed."

"Never." Her head was resting on his chest and he glanced down tenderly at her, then smoothed a wayward strand of silken hair that had caught in the stubble on his chin. He held her close, listening to her breathing change to the slow even cadence of slumber.

The room was pitch-dark, yet he kept staring at the ceiling as if he could distinguish every brush stroke the painter had recently applied. He'd had more than one serious shock today. At some point out there in the water, when he'd allowed himself to wonder if death was as close as it felt, he'd admitted that he loved JoBeth. It was a stunning revelation. Love was an overrated emotion as far as he was concerned. All his adult life he'd deliberately managed to avoid any permanent entanglements for that reason. He'd even been arrogant enough to think that marriage to JoBeth was in it's own way his salvation—a way to keep the husband hunters at bay. But much to his surprise his roving eye had stopped wandering as soon as he said "I do." He loved JoBeth! What a confusing, sobering thought. Now he faced a real dilemma. What were JoBeth's feelings for him? A bitter laugh escaped his lips at the unexpected turn of events. How long, he wondered, had he loved her? Years, probably!

In the privacy of the darkness, while he held her warm body next to his, he admitted his behavior since their wedding had been shameful. He hadn't been fair to her, and if they were going to build a life together he'd have to make a few concessions. His wife was a social animal—or was she? There'd been a few parties since he'd brought her home and she'd gone to only a couple of them. Now why was that, he mused, then realized he didn't know JoBeth Huntley DeSalva at all. He'd thought he knew her, but now he realized he'd been wrong. He didn't know her the way a man knows a woman before marriage.

The contradictions plagued him and he scowled fiercely. *Wait a damn minute,* he told himself. He'd grown up with her. She'd tagged around after him most of her childhood. He'd married her, for God's sake, and made love to her.

Still . . . there were intervening years he knew very little about. What they needed was some time to really get to know each other. He'd have to make an effort to be with her, to go to parties with her, *indulge* her. And he'd have to tell her the real reason behind the stock takeover of U.S.A. Oil. He couldn't continue to imitate Kane and lie to his wife. JoBeth deserved to know what she was getting into.

Brandon rolled over and pulled her farther into the curve of his body, smiled and sighed with contentment. He'd worked out his problems so easily. She'd love him. He'd see to that. Hadn't he always been able to manipulate her into doing what he wanted her to do?

CHAPTER TEN

THE MORNING SUNLIGHT KNIFED a path through a crack in the curtains, widening its beam as it spread across the bedroom. JoBeth ignored the ever-brightening room and the smell of fresh brewing coffee. Her body relaxed further as sleep once again tugged her deeper into her own darkness. Then Brandon roaring her name from less than five feet away brought her upright. Her eyes opened wide and the sharp retort on her lips died as she saw the reason that he was glaring at her.

"Where the bloody hell are my clothes?" He waved to the near-empty closet and its solitary occupant, a black three-piece suit. Jamming his fists on his hips violently, he had to grab for the towel around his waist, which had begun to slide toward the floor.

JoBeth tucked the sheet around her shoulders and propped her chin on her drawn-up knees. "I gave them away." She tried to keep a straight face as what she'd said sank in and he began to gobble like a hoarse turkey.

"Givenchy, Dior, Blass." He could have named a dozen more, but anger and confusion suddenly left him speechless. "You gave them away?" he mumbled, once he'd recovered his wits.

"Yes, dear." Her eyes shimmered with laughter as she met his look squarely.

Brandon took a step toward her, then stopped and ran a hand wildly through his hair. "Why?"

"You were becoming such an old fogy."

His eyebrows reached for his hairline, then thundered down into a fierce frown. "What in the name of hell am I supposed to wear? I have appointments this morning, Bets! Damn it, don't just sit there and laugh."

JoBeth grabbed her robe from the end of the bed, slipped it on and headed out the room. "Follow me." In a fast few steps she flung open the guest-bedroom door and waved him in as would a genie into Aladdin's cave of treasures. Shirts in a rainbow of colors spilled over open boxes onto the bed. There were new ties, socks, shoes, and a wide assortment of suits hung in the closet. She yanked up a pale blue T-shirt, and before he could stop her she'd slipped it over his head.

"Blue? JoBeth, what is all this?"

Like a magician she stripped him of his towel with a flourish, then held out the pants of a white linen Armani suit. "Step in."

"I can dress myself, thank you." He tried to grab the pants, but she was quicker and moved them out of his reach.

"Don't be a baby, sweet cheeks. Step in."

His fists clenched into tight balls of frustration. "Bets!"

"The Italians design such wonderful clothes. You can tell they love the human body, be it male or female, by the sensuality of their cuts and fabrics. Step," she ordered, and almost laughed as he shrugged and did as he was told.

"Bets, we have to talk."

"Yes, indeed." She worked the pants up to his waist.

"I mean it. There are things we have to straighten out. We have to be honest with each other."

"I agree." She took hold of the zipper, paused, looked him in the eye and said, "Like your going to the club and running into Carmen? She yanked up the zipper, inwardly laughing as Brandon sucked in a strangled breath. His face paled and she knew that his navel must have touched his backbone.

"My God, Bets. Are you trying to ruin me?" He let out a shaky breath, looking down to be sure he was intact.

She ignored the question, snatched up the white linen jacket and motioned for him to slip it on. "There, you look wonderful. Turn around." He looked better than wonderful. She wanted to grab him and haul him back to their bed. Maybe she wasn't as smart as she'd thought. If she found the new Brandon devastating, what would other women think?

"I look like a pimp!" He eyed his reflection with disgust, but after a few seconds the disgust turned to a questioning uncertainty, then to approval, and finally to vain admiration. But he wasn't about to let JoBeth know that he liked the new look, so he frowned at her.

"Oh, Brandon. You have no style. No adventure. No *guts*. And don't try to avoid the question of Carmen with a lot of double-talk and evasions."

He spun around and grabbed her by the shoulders. "Bets, I swear to you that meeting Carmen was an accident. Granted, I had no business going to the club like that, but . . ." What could he say? That he'd felt cornered by marriage all of a sudden and had rebelled the only way he knew how? "Carmen means nothing to me." He saw the anger and suspicion on her face and a smile twitched the corners of his mouth. "Jealous?"

"Of Carmen? Don't be silly." She turned her back on him and began digging through boxes, stopping when she came to a pair of white leather shoes. "Here, put these on. You can't wear that suit with your black loafers."

The shoes made him lose his train of thought. "Never! Never will I wear white shoes. Don't shrug like that and walk away from me. Bets, where are you going? Come back here. Damn it, woman!" He trailed behind her, more exasperated and frustrated with her than he'd ever been. "Okay, I'll wear the white shoes. Just stop and let's talk."

But JoBeth didn't want to talk. She was afraid of what he might say. "I have to get ready for work, Brandon." She headed for the bathroom with him following. "Do you mind?" She tried to close the door in his face, but Brandon wasn't having any of her high-handed tactics. Giving up, she let go of the door and began to wash her face and put on her makeup while he watched. Distraction was the best way to avoid a confrontation, so she started to chatter aimlessly until she finally hit on a subject that derailed his purpose. "Brandon, did you know that a man can get his pants hemmed while he waits, but a woman has to leave hers at least a week before they're ready? Why is that, do you think?"

Brandon looked down at the neatly hemmed pants and scowled. "How did you know the right length? And who did the tailoring? Never try to tell me you did it!" Then he began to laugh as the past reared its head once more. "Seems I remember getting a taste of your nimble-fingered work the first time I came home from college my freshman year. When I returned to the dorm with my nice clean laundry, which Mom had labored over all weekend, I found that someone had sewed all the flies together on my underwear. Very embarrassing that was, too."

As JoBeth applied mascara she chuckled, more at herself for having taken his mind off his questioning than at the story he was recalling. "Brandon, every tailor and men's store in town has your measurements."

That brought him out of his reminiscing with a jolt. "You know what we need, Bets?"

"Really, Brandon. I have to get ready, and if you don't leave I'll never make it."

"We need some time together so we can talk without interruptions."

"Sure. But not now." She rushed out of the bathroom, donned panty hose and underwear, slipped on a teal-blue silk dress, stepped into her black patent slingback pumps, picked up her purse and kissed him on the cheek. "You're going to be late, too, if you don't hurry." He opened his mouth and she stopped him with another kiss, on the lips this time. "We'll talk later. Bye." Spinning around, she was down the hall and out the front door before he could think of something to detain her. The dread of a cozy tête-à-tête pushed her every step a little faster. To her, talks with Brandon meant confessing to all sorts of things—like the lies she'd told. JoBeth corrected herself. She hadn't actually lied to him; she just hadn't told him *everything*. The best thing to do was to stay out of his way until he got over this strange urge for a serious discussion.

HIS WIFE WAS AVOIDING HIM. It had been two weeks since JoBeth had thrown out his suits, given him an exciting new wardrobe, then left him to his own devices. Brandon straightened the black bow tie, making sure the ends were flared properly. He glanced at the clock, swore for a few seconds, then yanked the black silk cummerbund from around his waist. Where was Jo-Beth?

He ran his fingers through his thick hair, leaving it a ruffled mess. What had she been up to these past couple of weeks? She said she'd been working hard, but those apologies were mumbled sleepily just before she dropped off to dreamland.

Slipping out of the tuxedo jacket, he pitched it across the back of a nearby chair and headed for the well-stocked bar. He'd have to hand it to her and her friends, though. Their company's aim to educate children and yuppies in etiquette had caught on like wildfire, capturing the eye and imagination of the public. JoBeth had appeared on no less than four local television shows, a couple of radio programs, and there were some serious negotiations going on with the producers of a well-known talk show in New York.

The new venture was more than a success—it was a phenomenon. And that increased his anxiety about intervening before it ripped them further apart. He shuddered. The limelight had always bothered him, even as a very young man. He'd seen the damage and pain that could result from the combination of wealth and notoriety.

His hand suddenly shook, making him spill a few drops of bourbon on his fingers. He yanked up a napkin, angrily wiped his hands, then tossed the wadded-up linen across the room. Damn! He didn't want JoBeth to become a national personality. He wanted her all to himself now that he'd faced his true feelings and, in his egotistical way, expected she'd reciprocate. Taking a hefty sip of his drink, he welcomed the brief pain of the fiery liquid. It was all well and good, he thought, to sit here and determine what he wanted, but what did Bets want?

Brandon shook his head slowly. He'd known her all his life. There were even times he could almost read her mind; certainly he could read her moods by her expressions. But lately she'd been hiding something from him and was doing a damn good job of covering up. That in itself was enough to make him suspicious. And there were several other things that added to his uneasiness. Phone calls that had gone dead when he'd answered. What was the old chiché? *If a man answers, hang up.* Well, there'd been plenty of those these past couple of days. Then there were the calls that she'd answered: the quick mumbled words, the even quicker goodbyes. What in the name of hell was going on? And the most poignant, the most disturbing thing of all was the loss of her wedding ring.

The telephone beside him rang and he jumped, determined that whoever it was was going to get a piece of his mind. "Now listen here—" he growled, then broke off. "Yeah, send him up." He set the instrument down with a curse. His wife was driving him a little nuts. With slow, reluctant steps, he walked to the front door, unlocking it just as the bell chimed.

"I understand your reasons for increasing security, but they questioned *me*." Kane's eyes flashed angrily then just as quickly simmered with laughter. "Masters Security is my wife's family company. Everyone knows me and yet they gave me the third degree. Shasta must have chewed out some rear ends for their slackness." He gave Brandon an unfathomable look. "She can be merciless when aroused. By the way, I'd like to thank you for telling her about Alice. She made a beeline to the office to check out my new secretary." Brandon couldn't restrain his laughter. "Go on, gloat, damn you. It didn't cost me very much. Shasta just handed me the bill for a new Lamborghini, that's all."

Brandon was laughing so hard his sides ached, and he was forced to sit down. He would have loved to be there to see the formidable Kane knuckle under once again to Shasta. No one ever got the better of his partner but his elflike wife. It was a long-standing joke among their friends. "What are you doing here?" Kane's expression immediately changed and Brandon sobered. "What happened?"

"Name it—it's happened." He helped himself to the stocked bar and filled a snifter half full. Then without asking, he poured one for Brandon and joined him on the couch. "Tex-Am's offices were broken into last night. No," he said, forestalling the question. "Nothing was taken, but it was different from the break-ins at the refinery. This was a professional job, done by a skilled burglar. Possibly a cat burglar, since he came from the top of the building to enter through a plate-glass window." He took a large gulp of brandy. "Of course this puts a whole new light on our problems. I don't think Tramble has the contacts to hire someone as professional as my office intruder. And if Tramble is the root of *your* problems with the computerized drilling rig, as we think, then we're in real trouble, because there's someone else out there trying to get to us."

"But Kane, with all these break-ins there's never been anything stolen."

Kane swore long and eloquently. "Don't you think that's been driving me crazy? What the hell do they want?"

Brandon thought for a few minutes. "Maybe just that—to drive you crazy."

"That's asinine, why would—" He broke off, his eyes narrowing a fraction as he stared off into space.

"Has Masters come up with anything?"

"No," he answered absently, still lost in thought.

Brandon watched as a strange expression crossed his friend's face: a mixture of suspicion and suppressed fury. "Kane?"

Kane shook his head quickly as if to clear his mind of the growing list of deductions and the obvious conclusion. Since he didn't want his new partner to guess his thoughts, he glanced up and smiled charmingly, scrutinizing Brandon's mode of dress for the first time. "Going somewhere?"

Brandon sighed, knowing full well what Kane was doing. Okay, he'd allow the man to work out his own problems, until those problems touched him then he would demand to know what was going on. "Bets and I were supposed to have dinner with the Fields, then go on to the ball for the British ambassador. But as you can see, my wife isn't home, and she hasn't even called." Brandon took a gulp of his drink. The mixture of bourbon and brandy on his empty stomach was making his head buzz.

"Oh, ho. The tables are turned, are they?"

"What the hell are you talking about?"

Kane stood, finished his drink and went to the bar. "You know very well what I mean." He fixed himself another brandy and sat down again.

Brandon looked glumly into his glass. "You're right, but it's different when the shoe is on the other foot."

"Naturally."

They were quiet for a few minutes, each deep in his own thoughts, trying to figure out the female race—their wives in particular. Finally Kane broke the silence.

"I want to start the takeover in about a week, Brandon. My inside sources tell me Tramble's starting to get suspicious with the movement of U.S.A. stock on the market. I've tried to buy in small amounts and spread out the purchases, but now I'm ready to call in the promised remainder from the other holders as soon as I can. The game is beginning to bore me and I want to get on with our *real* purpose."

"Fine by me."

The front door opened and both men became alert. Brandon, a little groggily, sat up straight, his eyes full of indignation. In silence he watched JoBeth walk toward him, accepted the warm kiss on the lips, then all but shouted like a fishwife.

"Where have you been? I've been waiting for you for hours. Did you forget we were supposed to have dinner with the Fields? Don't you know what a telephone is? You could have called me, for heaven's sake." Kane and JoBeth were laughing, and Brandon clamped his lips together, until he realized what he'd said and the way he'd said it. Then he joined in the laughter. After a few minutes he sobered and set the brandy snifter aside. "I don't believe I did that."

Still chuckling, Kane asked, "Have you heard anything further about the quarantine being lifted on the ship with our steel aboard?"

"What ship?" JoBeth asked. She eased her tired body onto the arm of Brandon's chair, listening carefully as both men talked at once, telling her of the German ship carrying their computer housing for the drilling rig, and how it was being held up on trumped-up charges. "Will the ship's release speed up the construction of the rig?" They gave her the "poor dumb blonde" look, and she gritted her teeth.

"It's all that's left to do on the rig, Bets."

"I see." She thought for a second, then stood and stepped over to the phone. Her first call was to the director of the health department. As she began to talk to her old friend, Kane and Brandon jerked upright in their chairs. "Yes, Robert," she said sweetly into the receiver, "I'll tell them, and thank you. Be sure to tell Sara hello." She hung up, giving them a sly glance. "The quarantine will be lifted immediately—seems the paperwork was misplaced by one of his new employees. Now," she asked with amused tolerance, as if she were speaking to two little boys, "what is the other problem? Oh, yes, the port authority. Let's see..." She tapped her fingernail against her front teeth, struggling hard to keep a straight face as two pairs of eyes, glazed with astonishment, stared at her. "Barbara Steston is an old friend, and I did her a lot of favors giving parties for port authorities and dignitaries. Hmm," she hummed, and dialed. No more than twenty minutes later she hung up, smiling hugely at both men as they slumped in their chairs. "They'll override their schedule and bring in your ship at first light tomorrow." She returned to sit on the arm of Brandon's chair. "Is there anything else you need help with?" she asked smugly, and dusted her hands together, gloating over the staggering jolt she'd given these two intelligent, wordly, helpless men.

Brandon, dumbfounded, gazed in awe at his wife. Kane rose, equally silent, and left the suite. All the years of throwing parties, doing favors and giving so unselfishly of herself had made her, he realized now, a rather powerful woman.

Brandon picked up the half-empty snifter, then set it down with a thump. He didn't need more alcohol. "Where have you been, Bets?" Leaning back, he covered her hands with his, stilling the nervous fingers that plucked at the silk pattern of her dress. Why was she so edgy all of a sudden? The brief thought that she might have just been with another man nagged painfully at him. "This isn't like you, Bets. Don't you want to tell me what's wrong?"

"Nothing's wrong, Brandon." She slid off the padded arm of his chair, wedged her body next to his and slipped her arm around his shoulders. "Our first class of children graduated today and the celebration lasted longer than expected."

Where had he heard that excuse before? Her words were basically the same ones he'd used on several occasions. "You could have called, Bets."

Her gaze dropped to the perfect bow tie. She had a wild impulse to yank its perfection apart. He was always so damn controlled, knowing what to say to make her feel like a heel. "The time just slipped by. I said I was sorry. I've been swamped with work, Brandon. Surely *you* can understand that?" She sat up stiffly, trying unsuccessfully to free herself from the chair and Brandon's restraining hold. "I work as hard as you do. Damn it, let me up," she snarled, her eyes flashing fire.

Was he to be haunted by his own words and excuses? Coming from JoBeth, he realized how lame and unconvincing they sounded. If only he'd taken the time to sit down and talk to her, tell her about his day and the problems he faced. Then maybe now she'd be willing to share her day with him. "Be still, please." He captured her hands once more and clasped them tightly in his. "You've been avoiding me, Bets. Why?"

"I have not! I've been working."

"Yes, and using work to stay away as much as possible."

JoBeth felt the lump in her throat grow. She was bone tired and mentally weary of fighting her problems by herself. There was a low throbbing behind her eyes and she wanted nothing more than to have a good cry. Instead of reaching out for the helping hand Brandon offered, pride made her shrug it away. "You forget, Brandon. I'm trying to get a business off the ground."

"No, that won't wash. You have so much help, and offers of more daily, that you could leave your company and nothing would change. Did you think I didn't care enough to keep advised as to how you're doing? But work is not the problem here, is it, Bets?" He released her hands and encircled her shoulders with his arm. "The problem you don't want to face is us, isn't it?"

"No!"

"No?"

She shook her head, her soft shining cap of hair swaying with the movement. There was a pain in her chest; her breathing was labored. Surely he could hear her heart pounding with fear, or see that all the blood had drained from her face, leaving the translucent skin as white as porcelain. She wanted to shut her eyes and close her ears to the words she knew were coming: he didn't want to be married to her any longer. She'd known it for weeks now. He'd changed. Always going out of his way to avoid an argument, always polite and caring. Even when she'd deliberately teased him and had done a few things that would normally have driven him crazy. But instead of shouting or laughing at her, he'd smiled. A silly, stupid smile that chilled her to the very marrow with its amused tolerance.

"Are you listening to me, Bets?" he asked testily.

"Yes, of course."

"You're pushing yourself, Bets. For what?"

She gazed at him, her gray eyes dark with confusion.

"You seem to have an obsession with your job, as if you're trying to prove your worth. It's not necessary, Bets. You've never had to prove anything to me."

Her vision blurred and the pounding of her heart thundered in her ears. What in the world was he saying? Where were the goodbyes and platitudes? Her life was falling apart in bits and pieces and he wanted to discuss her job! She blinked slowly, straining to catch his every word in case she missed something.

"I know I've teased you about your parties and the slothful way you used to live. But, Bets, I was only doing it to get a rise out of you. I never meant to hurt you."

Was that an apology? From Brandon?

"If this sudden ambition and obsession you have for your business is to show me that you're not the person I accused you of being, then don't bother. Stop this mad merry-go-round you're on before you ruin your health, my sanity and our marriage."

Her voice hung in the back of her throat and she had to swallow hard, then cough before the words finally came out. "You want to stay married?" she whispered hoarsely, holding her breath and waiting.

"You silly woman. What's been going on in that mixed-up head of yours? Of course I want to stay married. Who could make me laugh as much as you? Who would throw out an entire wardrobe and buy me an-

other? Who would turn my home into a jungle?'' He
wanted desperately to tell her that he loved her, but the
words wouldn't come. "Who knows me better than
you?'' His voice deepened, the timbre indicative of the
emotions he was holding back. "No one else could
make me feel the way you do. And most important,
who'd tell me I wasn't God's gift to women and keep
my ego intact?''

It wasn't exactly an admission of undying love, but
it was better than she'd expected. Somewhere in his explanation were the words *I love you*—she was sure of
that. The touch of his lips surprised her out of her
thoughts. She returned his kiss with a longing and passion she wasn't able to voice yet, either.

Brandon was the first to break away. With a sigh he
rested his forehead against hers. "Listen, Bets, could
you take a week off from work, starting tomorrow?''
He stopped the negative answer he knew was coming
with another kiss. "I know your company is important
to you, as it should be. And I'm not in any way trying
to take your achievements away from you, Bets. But if
we're to make this marriage work, we have to have some
time together. A belated honeymoon, maybe.''

The blood literally sang through her veins, making
the most beautiful vibrations in her ears. Like bells, she
thought. Happiness sounded like small tinkling bells.
"Where will we go?'' Perhaps the Caribbean, the Ba-
hamas, or maybe Mexico, since they were only taking a
week. But a place warm and humid with lush greenery
and a profusion of colorful flowers. As Brandon's eyes
darkened and his mouth took on that peculiar little twist
that meant he was up to something, the bells in her head
began to clang ominously. "Where?''

"How about the summer house in Galveston?''

The vision of a tropical paradise died a painful death. "Galveston? You conniving devil. Honeymoon, indeed. You plan to work." She struggled halfheartedly to free herself. "Damn you," she shouted, but the sting was gone from her voice. She couldn't be truly angry with him when he was smiling so charmingly at her, and the look in his eyes promised lazy nights and warm sand.

"I only have a few things to oversee on the rig." He chuckled at her useless attempts to scowl around her smile. "We can spend four or five days there, then go on to the ranch for the charity auction and ball. Ouch!" He laughed. "Don't pinch, Bets." He grabbed her hands and she stilled, staring at him with those soft gray eyes that never failed to touch some part of him. His fingers caressed the back of her hand in long strokes, stopping to play with the emerald ring. "You haven't found your wedding ring yet, I see." He wondered why the observation set her lips together in a grim line. "I know you always lose things, Bets. Don't worry. We'll buy another."

Her lips hardened further. "I don't lose things. Well . . . not my wedding ring, anyway."

He nibbled at the corners of her mouth until her lips softened. "It got up and walked away? Slid right off your finger and sprouted legs and ran off?"

"It must have, because I *did not* lose it."

"It will turn up." He kissed the column of her neck, working slowly up to her earlobe.

"Brandon," she breathed softly.

"Hmm?"

"What are we doing sitting here, when we could be nice and warm elsewhere? Take me to bed, Brandon."

He jumped up, pulling her with him. "Your wish is my command.".

She wished with all her heart that were true.

CHAPTER ELEVEN

SATIATED AND EXHAUSTED from a night of lovemaking, JoBeth slept most of the way to Galveston, waking only when they were on the long causeway that connected the island to the Texas coast. She yawned and stretched as far as the seat belt would allow, then looked over at Brandon.

He felt her stare and glanced at her, a pleased smile on his face. "Why so sleepy?"

She chuckled softly and sat up straight, trying to shake the lethargy that clung like a blanket. "Devil. You know very well why I'm so tired. And if you'd admit it, which you won't, you can hardly hold your eyes open yourself."

"Not me. I'm fresh as a daisy."

"Sure, and my name's Gertrude." She yawned hugely again, then inhaled deeply. Even in the air-conditioned confines of the Corvette she could smell the ocean, and she quickly rolled down her window, taking in huge gulps of the bracing breeze. Brandon switched off the cold air and opened his window, and she smiled her thanks. "Has the summer house changed much?" It had been at least seven years since she had stayed at the DeSalva beach house. She almost laughed out loud at the term *beach house*. Anyone who'd seen the old place knew that was a misnomer. Three Palms Mansion, named for the three huge palm trees that lined the drive, sat at the end of the island, it's wide stone facade facing sand dunes, beach and the endless waters of the Gulf of Mexico. The house had been built soon after the 1900 hurricane that nearly obliterated Galveston. Since its construction, Three Palms had withstood many attempts by nature and man to destroy it. "Is the county still trying to buy the property so they can build hotels and resorts?"

"They never stop with their offers...or their threats. Their last attempt to get their hands on the land was to try condemning the place. Granted, it's old and rundown a bit, but it's as solid as the DeSalva family that designed her."

Worriedly JoBeth chewed on her bottom lip. As a child, and later as a young girl, she'd come here often in the summer when the entire DeSalva family could get away. There were so many happy memories tied up in the old mansion that the thought of the place being ripped apart and knocked down was distressing. "You're fighting them, I hope?"

Brandon grinned at her, then returned his attention to the road ahead. "Have you ever known any DeSalva, past or present, to give up land willingly?"

Relaxing back into the leather seat, she sighed with contentment. "No. Letting go of an inch of land would be tantamount to cutting off an arm or a leg, wouldn't it?"

"You bet."

The wind picked up, rich with the scent of salt water, as they left the causeway and entered the island city's main street. Galveston was rife with history. Stories of smugglers and privateers like Jean Laffite abounded. The city was notorious for bootlegging in the 1920s and for the gambling, drinking and the red-light district on

Postoffice Street that flourished long after the rest of Texas had been cleaned up. Galveston was a tame kitten now compared to its wild past.

JoBeth brushed the hair from her forehead and shielded her eyes as she looked out over the seawall and the Gulf. The water was calm, as usual, a sluggish movement that could easily lull a person deep into his dreams. But appearances could be deceiving. During the hurricane season—September—the Gulf could be a wall of utter destruction, capable of taking lives, tearing apart brick, glass and steel and anything else that stood in its path. She shivered, remembering one such storm she and the DeSalva family had weathered. A sudden smile twitched at her lips as the memory of an incident caught and held.

"Do you remember the hurricane that trapped us here? The one where I saw that poor puppy trying to run down the beach in front of the house?"

Brandon snorted. "Of course I remember. It's one of the few times my father took his belt to me. You can laugh now, Bets. But if memory serves me correctly, you were in tears while I got a licking for something you talked me into."

"Me!"

"Don't play Miss Innocent. Yes, you. You saw that damnable dog and cried till I went out and rescued him. The problem was, Dad had forbidden us to go outside because of flying debris. So I got ten swats with his belt while you cried. Come to think of it, you got me into quite a lot of trouble with your tears."

"Is that why you hate women who cry?"

"Crying women don't bother me in the least." He took his attention off the road and looked at her pensively for a second. "It's *your* tears that always get to me, because I know that whenever you cry I'm more than likely the one who gets in trouble.''

"Not fair." She was laughing so hard tears filled her eyes, and the strong salt wind made them sting her cheeks. With the back of her hand she wiped them away, and was still giggling when Brandon turned the car into the lane leading to the back of the house and the big circular driveway. They passed the huge palms and she automatically made a wish, then laughed at the absurdity from her childhood.

"What did you wish for?"

Her head jerked around. "You remembered?"

"Of course. You had to complete your wish before you passed the last palm tree, or it wouldn't come true. God knows how many wishes through how many generations those palms have heard. Mother was the one who told me they were good luck, and I know she and Dad made a game out of it, too.''

JoBeth's attention returned to the house ahead and a flood of sweet memories washed over her. The pale brick, Greek Revival mansion stood two stories high, with twenty-four white Doric columns gracing all four sides. How many times had she tried to emulate Brandon and Lucas and scale those fat columns? And the mansion's high-hipped roof and four dormers were a favorite hiding place when she'd wanted to outsmart her tormentors.

A widow's walk wrapped around the entire second floor, and she remembered the times Catherine De-Salva had let them spread pallets on the wide porch and sleep under the cool breeze and blanket of stars. The few weeks here were better than anything she could remember because she usually had Brandon to herself, away from the girls at the ranch and school.

The car pulled to a stop, and she quickly opened the door and stepped out, anxious to slip back into the past. But there were changes that caught her attention. Subtle changes. Her eyes tracked the exterior of the house and her lips tightened. Crumbling brick, weathered steps, cracked and broken slabs of concrete on the walkway leading from the circular driveway to the house, peeling paint on the wood trim. "Brandon! This is terrible. How could you let the place become so run-down?"

Brandon swung a piece of luggage from the trunk and looked up. He followed her line of vision and grimaced. "I know, it's disgraceful, isn't it? It seems Three Palms has become relegated to painful memories." He wedged his suitcase under his arm and picked up Jo-Beth's, listing a little as he walked over to her and threw his other arm around her shoulders. "I think Dad, like everyone else, has very fond memories of this place. He doesn't want to come here, but he's not about to let it get out of the family, either." He guided her along the broken concrete walkway and up the sagging wooden steps to the back door. "Years of neglect have definitely taken their toll, haven't they?"

She dreaded seeing the inside if the outside was a testimony to the upkeep.

As if reading JoBeth's mind, Brandon dropped his arm from her shoulders and opened the door that led to the kitchen. "You'll be surprised how unchanged the interior is."

"I certainly hope so." The thought of having to spend her honeymoon—or any time, as far as that went—cleaning made her stomach turn. "Wait! Brandon, what about food? You'd better go to the store."

"I can't, Bets. The pilot is going to pick me up in about fifteen minutes." He glanced down at his watch, missing her expression of stunned disbelief and hurt.

"You what!"

"Have to get out to the oil rig. The helicopter is picking up the steel for the computer housing unit and transporting it from the port to the rig. Don't worry. I'll leave you the car and you can go to the store."

"Brandon DeSalva..." She moved away from him, fire sparking in her eyes as she jammed one fist on her hips. "What was all that talk about a honeymoon? It was all right for me to give up my work for a week, but not you."

"Now, Bets. I told you I had a little business to finish up. They're just going to bring in the steel, not assemble it. So I'll only be gone about three hours at the most."

"Oh." She relaxed her stance as her anger faded. Then a thought hit her and she groaned. "Do I have to go to the store? You know how I hate grocery shopping, Brandon." Faced with the reality of having to cook, she began looking around the big kitchen. "Where's the microwave? Don't tell me there's not one here?"

He was laughing as he dropped the luggage. Taking her arm, he led her to the far cabinet and pointed to the brand new microwave.

She was relieved and showed it, which brought more chuckles from him. "You're not trying to domesticate me, are you?"

"Can that be done at this late date?"

"Absolutely not!" She grinned at his expression and picked up a pencil and pad from the table. "Now what kind of frozen entrée do you want?'' She smiled, licked the end of the pencil and waited.

THE SUN FELT as if it might melt her bones. She snuggled down onto the beach towel and sighed with utter contentment. Not even the sound of an approaching helicopter disturbed her, but she listened with half an ear as it landed on the helipad behind the house. There was a flicker of her eyelids as the big rotary blades roared overhead again and the aircraft flew back out to sea. She smiled and wondered how long it would take Brandon to change his clothes and join her.

She heard him coming, the sound of bare feet being sucked into deep sand and the struggle to extract them. Opening one eye, she gazed at him when he was almost upon her. Naked except for a pair of denim cutoffs, he stepped gingerly around the thick, colorful morning glory vines that stabilized the dunes. Tall blades of sea oats tickled his bare legs and he stopped to brush them away.

''You should know better than to lay out here half-naked. My pilot almost crashed into the house.'' He stood next to the wide beach towel, dusted the sand off his feet, then dropped down to sit beside her. The long expanse of her bare back was beaded with perspiration, and the scant black bottom of her bikini sent a jolt of heat through his loins that had nothing to do with the sun overhead. The more he was around her, the more he wanted her. He stared pensively for a second, convincing himself that actions were better than words. He loved her dearly and he was showing her, wasn't he?

''People have seen as much of my back in some of the dresses I wear.'' Her voice was low, husky, and she noticed he immediately picked up on the tone of desire.

She wiggled her bottom as if she were getting more comfortable, and enjoyed watching his eyes follow the movement. It made her feel good to know she had this power over him. Then she corrected herself. It wasn't power; he loved her now. He *had* to love her if he was willing—no, eager—to stay married and suggest this time together. "Want to go for a swim?"

"I believe I'll pass, thanks. And I don't like the thought of your swimming alone, Bets. You know it's dangerous. What if you get a cramp?"

She ignored his question, rose up on her elbows and half turned, allowing him full view of her naked breasts. "You don't want to go swimming in the ocean because of your accident?"

"Right. I'll get over it in my own time. And I want you to promise you won't go swimming alone."

She flopped back down and sighed. "Brandon, you know very well I never go out beyond the shallow shelf. That's only waist deep, for goodness' sake."

He leaned over, brushed the damp hair from the base of her neck and kissed the warm hollow that never failed to tantalize him. Then, as if drawn like a magnet, his lips made a leisurely journey down her spine, tasting the damp, salty skin as if it were the most expensive champagne. "What did you say?" His fingers slowly outlined the V-shape of her bikini-clad bottom, then slid lightly down the backs of her legs.

She couldn't stand it any longer. She flipped over, and fingers flew to the waist of his shorts and unsnapped them before his hand wrapped around hers.

"Really, Bets, in broad daylight and on a public beach." His eyes were twin sapphires, twinkling with laughter and hunger.

"Have you ever made love on a beach before?" she whispered, and sat farther upright, her arms winding around his neck, her breast pressing against his chest. "Was it exciting?"

"Yes and yes. But never in the middle of the day. I'll have to hand it to you, Bets, my girl. You're unique." He yanked the side ties of her bathing suit bottom and quickly flung it away. "You did plan this, didn't you?"

"Yes I..." Her voice trailed off and she closed her eyes as his hand began to stroke teasingly up and down between her legs. "I, you see, have never made love on a beach, in broad daylight or in the dark." She sucked in a hard breath and opened up to him as his fingers found the moistness deep inside her.

Brandon removed his shorts as fast as he could, never missing a stroke. Once rid of the encumbrance of his clothes, he stretched out beside her. His arm slid under her head and gathered her close, bringing her face to his. The sound of the surf, the hot sun beating down on him, the sea gulls screaming overhead and the warmth of the sand were as strong an aphrodisiac as he'd ever encountered. "You feel so good," he murmured against her lips, and kissed her long and slow.

Leaning over, he gently gathered a pebble-hard nipple in his mouth and stroked it with his tongue until he heard her moan. His hand caressed her with a more determined stroke and she arched against his fingers. "You're not worried someone will come along and catch us, are you?"

Her eyes flew open and her head snapped first one way to gaze down the lonely beach, then the other.

Brandon moved, lightly resting his body over hers, smiling into the worried eyes now turned up to his. Desire, confusion and a shy curve of her mouth made him momentarily regret his teasing. "Think how exciting, how daring it will be if someone comes along and catches us."

"Devil," she moaned on a gulp of air as he slid into her.

He held her tighter as she wrapped her legs around his waist and began to move in a rhythm that sent his blood singing through his veins. "Wait! I think I hear someone coming." But she only laughed, moving with a stronger, surer thrust of her hips.

"I'll fix you for teasing me, sweet cheeks." And so saying she angled her body sideways, making him lose his balance.

Before Brandon knew what was happening he was lying on his back with JoBeth straddling him. The sight of her, her body slick with sweat, the feel of her skin warm and wet under his hands and the slow steady movement of her hips almost drove him over the edge. He gritted his teeth, grabbed her hips and thrust upward making her gasp and tremble before collapsing against his chest. "Never try to outmaneuver me."

She giggled into his damp shoulder and raised her head enough to gaze into his darkened eyes. "Ah, but I'm not through yet."

"Yes, you are," he said on his own gasp as he rolled her over and drove into her one last time. He shuddered in her arms, laughing and trying to talk at the same time. "You see, you are through, because I can't take anymore."

The sun beat down on them as they lay, side by side, in each other's arms, their breathing coming slow and easy in sleep. It was JoBeth who awakened first. She was hot; worse, she was burning up and soaking wet against Brandon. She moved away as carefully as possible so she wouldn't wake him, but their skin stuck together and pulled as she started to sit up.

"Come back here." He reached for her, grasped her arm, and she eased back down beside him. "Have I suddenly contracted the plague?"

"I'm hot, Brandon."

He opened his eyes and noticed her red, flushed face, and was immediately contrite. The sun and heat never bothered him and he sometimes forgot that others couldn't take too much of it. "Come on, let's go back to the house and take a cool shower." He then jumped to his feet and began to gather up the beach towel and their clothes. "You're not sunburned, are you?" The thought of his not being able to touch her made him even angrier with himself.

"No. Just incredibly hot and thirsty." JoBeth walked ahead of him and threw a look over her shoulder, smiling to herself at the way his eyes seemed to devour her nakedness. "Sex maniac. You're not concerned about me. You're just thinking about making love in the shower." She started to run across the beach, lightly stepping over the red and white morning glories that dotted the sand dunes.

"You crazy idiot! Don't run. Do you want to get sunstroke?" But he couldn't deny the appeal of her bouncing, naked bottom, and he started to run, too.

JOBETH AWAKENED to the scent of sun-dried linen under her nose and the smell of brewing coffee. She stretched, luxuriating in the feel of cool sheets next to her skin, then she hopped out of bed. Grabbing her robe, she shrugged into it as she bounced down curving stairs, then immediately came up on tiptoes when her bare feet touched the cold marble floor. She entered the big airy kitchen and shielded her eyes from the bright sunlight pouring in the open windows. She was starving, and the aroma of bacon frying brought her eyebrows up in surprise. "Good morning. I didn't know you could cook." She snitched a crisp strip of bacon from the platter, munching on it thoughtfully as she watched Brandon work over the spattering frying pan.

"Don't get your hopes up. Bacon and eggs are about the extent of my culinary accomplishments."

"Well, it's a start, isn't it? Who knows, with a little practice you could discover a hidden talent and become a famous chef."

He shot her an amused look. "You wish. And flattery won't get you anywhere this morning."

She sighed dramatically, plucked a coffee cup from a cabinet and filled it before she pulled out a chair from the table and sat down. "I'll have my eggs over easy, please."

Brandon began to chuckle. "You'll have them scrambled, Miss Astor, because it's the only way I know how to cook them."

"Yes, sir. Scrambled. Is there anything I can do to help?"

'Yes. Don't help.''

She eyed him over the rim of the cup, loving the way he was always at ease. Her gaze lingered on his short terry robe as she remembered the strong body beneath. She shivered suddenly, then told herself that *he* was turning her into a sex maniac. But yesterday and last night had been so right—so full of love, even if it was only physical. Brandon had been the perfect husband: attentive, giving. No woman could have asked for more. She frowned into her cup and wondered why she felt she needed more. Hadn't she promised herself that this week alone together would be ideal? And so far it had been. She shook her head, trying to force the doubts away. If she was accepting less than she had hoped for, then that was okay, as long as she was willing to face the problems ahead that might arise.

"You're not listening, Bets. Where are you?"

She forced a bright smile to her lips and looked up. "Back in bed—with you."

"Insatiable hussy. I have to go out to the rig."

"Oh, Brandon, no. Not this morning. I thought we'd go into the city and shop, then have lunch at one of those wonderful seafood restaurants."

He grabbed the platter of bacon and eggs and set it down on the table. With a few quick moves he put toast on her plate and sat opposite her. "Maybe tomorrow. But this is important. They're going to try to fit the housing unit in." Picking up his fork, he stopped in midair, then laid it down. "Listen, Bets, there's something I've been wanting to talk to you about before it becomes known. Up till now Kane has asked me to keep it quiet, but since you have a big stake in the new company I think you should know. But you'll have to promise not to tell anyone about this...not even Shasta."

With the mention of the company, his company, the reason for their marriage came rushing back. She flinched inwardly, feeling it was somehow sacrilegious to talk about it here in this house, especially after yesterday. Besides, it reminded her that the board meeting at U.S.A. Oil was rapidly approaching; also, that Tramble had suddenly become strangely quiet.

"Bets." He reached out and touched her chin, turning her head toward him. "What's the matter?"

"Nothing," she lied, trying to shake off an eerie sensation that trouble was just around the corner.

"I know you think Kane and I are odd bedfellows. But with Kane I've got a chance to build something on my own. To make *my* mark on the world. DeSalvas Corporation, with all its conglomerates and subsidiaries, was never mine. It was built decades ago and was handed down to Lucas and then me. It isn't my achievement, and I've never been a follower."

JoBeth picked up her fork, willing herself to listen to what she'd heard before. She wanted to be a part of Brandon's life, but she didn't want a constant reminder of how she had acquired her place beside him.

Brandon reached across the table and removed the fork from JoBeth's hand. "There's no synthetic fuel formula, Bets. It's all a sham, a cover."

"Do you mean that you didn't need my shares of U.S.A. Oil to develop and distribute the fuel?" Her heart began to beat with the hope that he had married her because he had wanted only her. But as she listened, her hopes were dashed.

"We needed the stock takeover and the merger of Tex-Am Oil and U.S.A. Oil to provide us with power—the kind of power only that joint venture could give us. Bets, Kane holds a terrible but important secret. Your uncle had Professor Melvin Kimble killed to keep the synthetic fuel formula from becoming a reality. But the formula was a ploy, a cover. Only Kimble and Kane knew the real secret that would some day make every oil and utility company tremble in mortal fear. The old professor had proved his theory in stabilizing and controlling fusion energy."

JoBeth frowned. She was aware of fusion energy and had heard about some of the problems surrounding it. "But Brandon, isn't fusion energy fueled by water?"

He threw back his head and laughed with delight. "Yes, by God."

"Then how can it benefit us if we bankrupt the oil companies?"

He'd caught the enthusiasm Kane emanated, regardless of the money to be made. "We'd still have our oil company and all its by-products, but the true benefit will come from the fact that we'll corner the fusion energy market. Also, we'll have the prestige of building the first fusion reactor. Then we'll build a few fusion plants—six, maybe—spread out strategically across the United States with the capability of lighting, heating and cooling each house and business in America for pennies. Listen, Bets." He leaned forward, eager to make her see its future. "The oil companies as they are today are useless old dinosaurs. The Middle East, with its wars and petty fighting, is going to ruin the oil business. If we are to survive as a nation we have to have a successful alternative. The big oil companies are unwilling to touch fusion energy because they don't want to let go of the billions they're making now—they don't want to see beyond the dollar sign. We'll be years ahead of them and give the public what they need—cheap fuel. The new Tex-Am Oil will control the process, development and building. We'll gain the profits." JoBeth frowned and he knew what she was thinking—that it was the same old story: big business reaping the profits while the little man pays and suffers.

"Bets, the utility companies fought nuclear power until research stumbled for lack of backing. Then they picked up the ball, financed research themselves, and when they proved it could work, *they* built the plants, controlled the construction, and the taxpayers paid through the nose. The petroleum industry financed research of shale oil extraction and when it proved a success they owned the process. But fusion is a whole new ball game that neither the oil companies nor the utility companies even want to contemplate. Their ventures have done nothing but put monstrous sums of money back in their pockets.''

"But the oil company, Brandon, and oil... Are you saying that oil is going to become obsolete?"

"Hell, no." He ran his fingers through his hair. "What I'm saying is there will always be a need for oil and its by-products, but fusion is a way to have cheap fuel and clean fuel. We'll eventually be able to clean up the environment."

She shook her head. It all sounded well and good, but the thought of removing oil from daily consumption was scary. All her life she'd been associated with the oil business.

"I know it's a little frightening, Bets, but trust me. Kane and I aren't going to dump the oil company. We're going to build on it, expand it and, in the process of making money, help consumers and improve the environment."

Seeing the eagerness in his expression and voice, she did trust him. Hadn't she always trusted him? Hadn't she given him her heart years ago?

JoBeth smiled and Brandon sighed with relief. The big clock on the wall caught his attention. "Damn, my pilot will be here in a few minutes. Think about what I've said, and when I get back I'll answer all of your questions." He heard the sound of a helicopter approaching and cocked his head. "I'd better go." Reluctant to leave her, he swore silently that today would be the last time for the next few days. After all, she deserved more from him. He stood, walked around the table and pulled her to her feet. "Don't I get a goodbye kiss like the rest of working America?"

She grinned into his gaze, her eyes sparkling like diamonds. "Just ordinary folks, right?" Winding her arms around his neck, she gave him something to remember her by, and if he seemed a little less eager to let go, she only smiled sweetly, the curve of her lips a mystery of promises. "You better go."

Squinting into the glare of the sun, she stood on the porch and watched as the helicopter rose and circled the house before it streaked out over the water, leaving behind only the sound of the surf as it gently touched the shore. But the peace was soon shattered by the sight of a fire-engine red Lamborghini racing up the driveway. With a screech of tires and flying gravel, the car came to an abrupt stop. Trouble had arrived driving a flashy car and sporting a mischievous smile. "Hello, Shasta."

"Where's Brandon? Was that his helicopter I saw taking off? Oh, damn."

JoBeth laughed. "When you're through swearing at the sky, come on in and tell me your troubles." She spun around and walked back into the house, slamming the screen door, knowing that as soon as her petite friend got control of her temper she'd follow. Sure enough, in a few minutes JoBeth heard the back door shut with a solid thud. "Would you like a cup of coffee?" She sat down, pushed away the cold untouched plate of bacon and eggs, cradled her chin on her folded hands and stared at Shasta.

Shasta eyed the coffeepot skeptically. "Who made it?" she asked with raised eyebrows, her eyes round and innocent and full of laughter.

"Brandon."

"Well—" she grabbed a cup from the cabinet and sat down "—if Brandon made it, I'll have some."

"Bitch," JoBeth grumbled good-naturedly, then frowned when she didn't even get a rise out of Shasta. "You've got that peculiar look on your face. What's the matter?"

Shasta jumped, a guilty expression streaking across her face before she could mask it. "Nothing's the matter. Should there be?"

"I don't know. You tell me. You're the one who came flying in here."

"Oh, that." Shasta waved, dismissing the statement. "What does 'B.O.I.' mean? I've been doing some work here on the island, asking some questions. But every time I think I've got someone who'll really talk to me they ask me if I'm B.O.I. I guess I look strange when they ask because they just suddenly clam up."

"The people on this island are cliquish. They don't ordinarily tell any of their business to outsiders. B.O.I. means 'born on the island,' and if you weren't, they aren't going to reveal much more than the bare facts about anything. What are you doing here, Shasta?"

Big, brown eyes as soft and warm as velvet gazed at JoBeth over the rim of a coffee cup. "I came to tell Brandon that I've found two men working for him who are paid employees of Tramble. From what I've been able to gather, one of these men was around the helicopter the day Brandon and his pilot had to ditch it in the Gulf. This man had the opportunity and the time to sabotage it."

"Sabotage!" JoBeth whispered.

"Yeah. You know, the bomb that forced them down."

"Bomb?"

"Sure. Brandon saw the remains of it before the helicopter sank. He and Kane asked me to look into it." Shasta hadn't been paying close attention to JoBeth's reaction, but when she noticed the shock on her friend's face her eyes grew even larger and her mouth tightened into a thin line. "No one told you?"

"No, damn it." JoBeth's knees started to tremble and she began to rub her thighs with hard strokes. "Sabotage."

"Aren't they real bastards? Never telling us anything. Always keeping their little secrets. Well, I'm sick and tired of their games, and I'm about to end them for good."

JoBeth's head snapped up and Shasta clamped her mouth shut as if she'd said too much already. "I have to go." Rising quickly, she was almost at the door, when she stopped. "Tell Brandon I've cleared his foreman and that I'll leave all I've found out with him. And JoBeth . . . while you're here by yourself be careful. I'll be keeping a watch on those two or someone from Masters will. But you never know, one of them could slip by us."

JoBeth didn't hear the roar of the powerful engine as her friend took off; she hadn't even paid close attention to Shasta's warning. All she could think of was that Brandon hadn't told her about the sabotage. What else could have happened that he hadn't told her about? Her cheeks flushed red-hot with anger, but immediately paled to a deadly white, as if a bucket of cold water had been dashed in her face. Who was she to get upset over a few secrets? Didn't she have a whole closetful? She poured herself another cup of coffee, trying to decide how she was going to chew Brandon out without feeling guilty herself. Worse still, if Tramble was behind the sabotage, then his strange quiet was more ominous than ever.

Taking a sip of hot coffee, JoBeth squeezed her eyes shut, realizing the danger her silence might have caused. She knew deep down, though she'd never admitted it, that her uncle was responsible for the things that had happened to her: the attempted hit-and-run and the aborted purse snatching. She had to tell Brandon. But how, after all these weeks of silence?

She was in real trouble now, she reflected as she stared into the empty cup.

CHAPTER TWELVE

Tthe sweltering day turned oppressive toward night. Scattered dark clouds rushed across the sky in a rolling, threatening motion. With the deep purple of dusk a veil of fog slithered in over the water, eating its way toward shore with each rush of the surf. The moon rose, a hazy yellow ball in the sky.

JoBeth stood at the wide bay window and looked down the slope to the sand dunes. This was the slowest part of the day, she thought. Although the light fought a losing battle with darkness, it repeated its struggle day after day. The Gulf was calmer than usual as the tides pulled the water back and forth in a game of give-and-take. Thin white patches of fog crept in around the dunes, snagging on the sea-oats grass and morning glories.

Guilt rode her every thought. Guilt and shame. Since Shasta's visit three days ago and her subsequent conversation with Brandon concerning the sabotage of his helicopter, she had felt like a worm, the lowest of low-life. No more secrets, he'd promised when she took him to task. No lies, no half-truths, complete honesty, he'd sworn. She had spent three days listening to him apologize. The more contrite he was, the quieter she became. The more he fretted over her silence, the more she felt like a bug under his heel. By not telling him about the attacks and her conversations with Tramble, she had

as good as lied to him. At least, that's the way he would
see it. Her situation was like a two-headed monster. But
she didn't want to ruin what remained of their honeymoon, and there just never seemed to be a good time to
confess to him. They were going to leave early tomorrow morning, drive to Houston to pick up some clothes,
then start for the ranch.

She was damned if she didn't tell him what had been
going on and damned if she did. There was absolutely
no doubt whatsoever that once he found out he was
going to be furious. She would not only ruin their time
together, but more than likely everyone at the ranch
would be dragged into the fight. Yet sooner or later, she
told herself, she was going to have to tell him, because
things were becoming dangerous. If she did, though,
what would happen to the new closeness they'd found?

"Such deep thoughts. Where are you, Bets?" He
touched her shoulder lightly and she turned, accepting
the crystal snifter of brandy.

"I was just thinking how I'll hate to leave tomorrow."

"Me, too. It's been fun, just the two of us alone. And
I've even managed to oversee and complete the instal-
lation of the housing unit on the oil rig." He stood by
her side, silently contemplating the setting sun, then he
put down his glass. "I have to make a couple of phone
calls to Lucas and Kane, then I'm going to take a long
hot shower." He turned his head, his gaze resting on her
pale profile. "Why don't you join me?"

Setting her own untouched brandy on the low win-
dowsill, she said, "I think I'll go for a swim."

Brandon scowled, worry and disapproval making
deep grooves between his eyes. "Not alone. Wait till I'm
off the phone and I'll go with you." He kissed her on

the cheek, and before she could answer, he took off up
the curving staircase, his mind on the calls he was about
to make.

JoBeth watched him taking the steps two at a time as
he headed for the bedroom and the only working telephone in the house. When he reached the landing and
turned out of sight her shoulders slumped in defeat. She
wanted nothing more now than to be alone, and the
thought of the vast quiet waters soothing her ragged
nerves seduced her into action. Maybe out there,
wrapped in the dark, warm water, she could figure out
what she was going to do.

In a matter of seconds she had shucked her white
shorts and shirt, kicked off her sandals and quickly
stepped out of her underwear. She grabbed a beach
towel and eased open the door. A damp breeze touched
her skin. She shuddered and almost changed her mind.
But the thought of warm waves caressing her body sent
her running over the deep sand dunes and the hard-
packed beach to the edge of the water. She took a deep,
excited breath and plunged into the rolling surf, letting
it lap at her feet a few seconds before she ventured farther in. When the waves reached her thighs she dived
under, luxuriating as the water curled over her naked
body.

Silence surrounded her, and with it a kind of peace.
Reluctantly she rose to the surface and began a slow
steady stroke parallel with the shore. When her muscles were pleasantly tired she stopped, trod water and
looked back at the house. The only light on was in their
bedroom, and she wondered if Brandon had missed her
yet. Then it happened.

Something hard and alien clamped around her ankle
and yanked her under. But before the dark water swal-

lowed her completely, instinct made her gulp in a huge breath of air. The hold on her tightened, pulling her off the shallow shelf into deeper water.

She kicked wildly at the band around her ankle with her other foot, hitting it with her heel, and finally managed to break free. Shooting to the surface, she sucked in great quantities of air, too stunned even to contemplate the danger she was in. A voice in her head screamed for her to move, get away, swim for shore and Brandon. But before she could swing her arm up to begin a single stroke, something grabbed her other ankle, and she had no doubt that it was a human hand.

As the water closed over her head again she lashed out in fury. Bending the knee of the leg her captive held, she angled her other foot so that when she struck out it would land with a stunning blow to her assailant's shoulder or head. She kicked with all her might again and again until her lungs felt as if they would explode from the lack of air. Adrenaline raced through her, giving her the strength for one last mighty kick. Suddenly she was free and clawing upward.

The surface broke over her head; sweet air filled her lungs, and in total panic now she struck out for shore, her strokes erratic. When her feet touched bottom, she stood and began to run, swearing and crying as the water seemed determined not to give up its hold on her. Finally she reached dry sand, and she paused a second, throwing a quick scared look over her shoulder, wondering if it was her imagination, or as a patch of fog parted, did she really catch a glimpse of a head bobbing in the water? She didn't stay to investigate, but began running as she had never run before, until her heart felt it would burst in her chest. She sobbed and stumbled, realizing for the first time as her hand touched the doorknob that someone had just tried to drown her.

Tears blurred her vision, making it difficult to see the steps of the curved stairway, and she slipped down on one knee. The pain acted like a shot of pure energy. She grabbed the polished wood railing with a shaking hand, rose quickly and ran, sobbing wildly up the last few steps and into the bedroom. A loud hiccup escaped her lips and Brandon jerked around with the phone receiver dangling from his hand.

"Brandon," she pleaded, standing across the room, naked and dripping wet. She felt as though she'd been fighting for her life for hours, but now she realized she'd actually only been gone a short time.

"My God, Bets, what's wrong?" He hung up the telephone and gathered her into his arms. "You're all wet. Damn it, I told you not to—" He broke off as she hiccuped again.

"Never mind all that. Brandon, someone tried to kill me, to drown me." She shuddered in his arms and began to tell him as coherently as possible what had happened.

"Now, Bets, maybe you just got your foot tangled in something."

She pushed out of his embrace and sat down on the end of the bed. Holding out her legs, she pointed to the bruised ankles. "Do those marks look like I got tangled up in seaweed? I tell you, someone tried to drown me!" She flopped back, pulled the covers around her and continued to shiver.

Brandon squatted and lightly traced the red marks that wrapped around both ankles like fingers. "This is totally crazy, Bets. Who would want to hurt you?"

"My uncle."

He sprang to his feet, staring down at her with hard eyes.

She hiccuped on a deep sob and watched a frown gather across his brow. "Oh, Brandon! You're going to be so angry with me."

"Why?" he asked softly, an ominous ring of dread in his voice. "Just why would Tramble have this done to you? He knows nothing. Right, Bets?"

She shook her head and hiccuped.

"What have you done?"

"You must promise you won't hate me." She immediately reverted to a childhood statement when she was in deep trouble.

"Bets."

"Promise."

"JoBeth!"

She squeezed her eyes shut so she wouldn't witness his disgust when she told him. "I told Uncle Tram that I had given you voting rights over my stock in U.S.A. Oil." She cringed at his bellow of outrage and rushed on. "But I didn't tell him that I'd sold you half my shares. Honestly, Brandon, I didn't."

"What else?"

She sat up and opened her eyes, a little relieved by his calm tone, but the minute she saw his face she closed her eyes again. He was going to kill her for sure. Prolonging the inevitable, she began to tell him about everything, from her conversations with her uncle to the attempted hit-and-run to the purse snatching in the parking lot. He listened, never stopping her or questioning her. When she finished and opened her eyes, she wished she hadn't.

"Of all the stupid things to do! Do you realize that you put us all in danger? Your big mouth could have gotten me and my pilot killed. How could you lie to me?''

''I never lied,'' she said stoutly. ''I just didn't tell you.''

''And that makes it okay?''

''No.''

''Damn right.'' He lost his temper and started shouting. ''Why did you do it, Bets, when I begged you not to have any contact with your uncle?''

''I couldn't help it, Brandon. He got me so mad I blurted it out, thinking it would make him leave me alone. Please say you forgive me.''

''You jeopardized us all by letting your anger overcome common sense, and you never once tried to tell me.''

''That's not true. I did try, but something always interfered. As time went on it got harder and harder to tell you. Then we came here and I didn't want to ruin what we had together.''

''I see. I could have been killed, but you didn't want to ruin what we had together. Do you realize just how crazy that sounds?''

''I know, but it's true. Please forgive me.''

Brandon wasn't so easily appeased, and walked to the bedroom door. ''You could have gotten us all killed,'' he mumbled, ''yourself included. Do you think your uncle is going to relinquish any portion of U.S.A. Oil without fighting the dirtiest way he knows how? That's considerable, Bets.''

''Where are you going?''

''Outside to check if anyone is still hanging around, then I have to call Kane and tell him what's happened.... I may be gone a while.''

He walked out, leaving her in a miserable heap on the bed. She waited an hour, and when he didn't return, she rose, bathed, then huddled down in a cold empty bed.

Rain spattered on the roof, the steady rhythm easing the tension of the day. Propped against the headboard with the covers pulled tight across her bare breast, JoBeth waited for Brandon's return. Another half-hour passed before she heard his footsteps on the stairs.

He stopped in the doorway, studying her for a long moment before he spoke. "I'm going to take a shower."

"Brandon," she called softly as he headed for the bathroom. But he didn't turn, and she sighed, deeply disturbed by his silence. "I'm sorry." Now was the time to tell him just how much she loved him. The words were on the tip of her tongue, when she realized how wrong that would be. He would only think it was a play for forgiveness.

"You should be asleep. It's late."

That he'd talk to her at all gave her hope. "Brandon, please listen to me."

"After my shower, Bets." At the bathroom door he swung around and faced her. "There was no one out there, so you can rest a little easier. If you want to talk, how about making me a sandwich. I sat downstairs drinking brandy and I need something to soak up the alcohol so I can concentrate."

No sooner had the door closed than she was reaching for her robe and flying down the stairs. A sandwich she could manage. Twenty minutes later she carried the loaded tray back up the stairs, wincing as the edge touched the bandage on the finger she'd cut.

As she entered the bedroom, Brandon covered the receiver and asked, "What time did Shasta leave here the other day?"

Setting the tray at the foot of the bed, she dropped her robe, crawled between the covers and reached for a sandwich, the bowl of chips and one of the Cokes. "I don't remember, but it was about fifteen minutes after you left that morning. Why?"

Brandon raised his hand to stop any further questions and continued his murmured conversation with Kane. When he hung up he chuckled, but the sound had a worried edge to it. "It seems Kane has misplaced his wife." He picked up a sandwich, peeking between the two slices of bread before he bit into it.

"I don't think Kane and Shasta are getting along. I bet she went off somewhere to think. She's done it before, Brandon."

"Maybe." But they both fell into a worried silence.

She let him finish eating while she sipped on her cold drink. When he sat the empty tray on the floor and turned toward her she swallowed visibly. This was going to be more difficult than she'd envisioned. "I'm sorry. No, don't say anything. Let me finish. I don't think, even with all your warnings about my uncle, that I truly believed a member of my family could be as evil as you said. I was wrong not to tell you what I had done, wrong to go against what you had asked of me, knowing you were doing it in part for my safety. What else can I say or do?"

"Bets, for three days I've felt like a dog because I didn't tell you about the sabotage and you found out from Shasta. You let me go on feeling bad about that knowing what you'd done! How could you?"

Her chin dropped a fraction and she looked at him from under her eyelashes. "I don't know. But if it will make you feel better, I felt like a worm."

"That helps a little. You might go on feeling that way for a couple of days, though." He grinned at her, then his expression sobered. "I promised you then, no secrets, no lies, no half-truths. It's time you made the same promises."

She threw herself into his arms, kissing his face all over as she said each promise like a vow. "Am I forgiven?"

Brandon settled her more comfortably in his arms. "I'll give it some serious thought." He gazed at her with speculation and desire. How was it, he wondered, that he never stopped wanting her, even when he felt like strangling her? "You could speed up this feeling of forgiveness a little by appeasing another demanding appetite."

THEY AWAKENED to a watery morning, the streets slick from the previous night's thunderstorm. As they drove back to Houston, JoBeth slumped in her seat and tried to think of something to break the silence that had arisen between them. Even though Brandon had finally forgiven her there was still a tension in their relationship that hadn't been there before last night. Not irreparable, but a small tear in the fabric of their life that would take some time to mend properly.

The sight of the DeSalvas Building raised her spirits some as she realized they would soon be on their way to the ranch. Surely Brandon would be more willing to come around while in the loving lap of his family.

He pulled the Corvette into the underground parking lot and climbed out. "Why don't you go on up? I'll get the luggage and collect the mail from Frank and follow in a few minutes."

Without a word JoBeth did as he asked, but a frown puckered her brow. He just might be pushing her a little. After all, she was trying to make up; so could he. The suite smelled musty, unused, even though it was cool from the air conditioner. Rushing around, she gathered the clothes she needed for the ball and the stay at the ranch. She was about to shut the suitcase, then remembered she'd neglected to pack a nightgown. She pulled out the lingerie drawer of the dresser. There, lying on top, was the exquisite gown Brandon had given her. Puzzled at its return, she wondered if the maid *had* sent it to the cleaners. But she didn't have time to ponder the mystery further as she heard the front door close. "Brandon," she called out, "don't forget to get your patent leather evening pumps from the closet in the guest room." When no acknowledgment came she snapped the locks on her suitcase, swung it to the floor and carried it out of the bedroom.

She saw him standing in the entry hall, stock-still and as pale as a ghost, staring at a large brown envelope in his hand. Something was terribly wrong. "Bad news?" She set down the suitcase and walked toward him.

He looked up, contempt clear and bright in his eyes. "Bad news?" He repeated her question. "You could say that, my sweet."

Brandon held out his hand as if to give her something. She automatically held out hers. Something round and gold was dropped into her palm. "My wedding ring! Where did you get it?"

"From your lover, my dear, cheating whore of a wife," he said with a world of loathing and revulsion in his voice.

The words were like a slap in the face and she staggered under the blow. "What are you talking about?"

Still too stunned from his attack to fully comprehend what he'd said, she just stood there as he turned a handful of 8 x 10 black-and-white photographs so she could see.

"Is this something else you conveniently forgot to tell me about?" He fanned the photos in his hand.

She gasped as the contents of the pictures were revealed. They were of her and a man, in various poses, in various stages of undress. She was speechless as the lewdness of them caught her attention. "I know that man!"

"Well, my dear, I should certainly hope so," he said with a sneer. "It would seem he knows you very intimately if these pictures are any indication."

"No!" she yelled. "You don't understand. I told you about him."

"I'm afraid not. I don't think I'd forget if you told me something like this."

"No, no, no. Rod—the man in the photos—is the man who saved me from the purse snatching in the parking lot."

Brandon shuffled through the pictures. "Sure, just a newfound friend, right?" He selected one and held it up for her inspection. When she reached out to take it from him, he snatched it back. "Do you normally sit in an outdoor café making eyes at your savior and holding hands? Or are you going to tell me that's how you lost your wedding ring? That this man who supposedly rescued you slipped it off your finger and neglected to return it? Or were you so enthralled you left it on the nightstand in the hotel room?" He pulled out another picture. "Is it your usual custom to allow men to embrace you and kiss you passionately in a public parking lot? I suppose you want me to believe that the kiss was just a sign of your gratitude? For what, I wonder?''

''Please listen to me, Brandon. This is all some crazy mixed-up plan.'' Tears filled her eyes as she saw her words were met only with disgust.

''Goddamn you, don't you dare start crying.''

She wished he would yell and scream at her, but this soft-voiced stranger with contempt in his diamond-bright eyes scared her. ''Let me see those.'' Again she reached for the photos. She managed to grasp one, but Brandon twitched it from her fingers, ripping it in half. For some crazy reason, she wadded up the glossy paper and stuffed it into her bra. ''Why won't you let me see them?''

''Because, dear Bets, this is divorce evidence, and I'm going to make damn sure you don't destroy it.''

''Divorce? Oh, God, no! Brandon, you can't believe those!''

He held them out so she could examine them one by one. ''Is that you, Bets?''

She stared at each, appalled and sickened at the pornographic poses. ''Yes—I mean, no. The woman looks like me.''

''No, Bets, she is you. And by your own admission you know the man, correct?''

She felt as though she were in a court of law. Her heart beat erratically and her mouth went dry. ''Yes, I know him, but I only met him that once.''

''That's all it took for these to be made, baby. Just once.''

He showed her another and another, over and over again, until she pressed her hand to her mouth in panic, frantically wondering if he had observed what she'd just noticed. His next words confirmed her worst nightmare.

"The nightgown? It's one of a kind. Would you like to tell me how this woman, who is not you, could be wearing your clothes?"

"The gown must have been stolen, Brandon." He looked at her as if she were dirt, and she wanted to run and hide. But she was innocent. He had to believe her. She had to make him see she would never be involved in anything so disgusting.

"The gown was stolen from this suite?"

"Yes, from here." She knew the minute she'd said it, that she'd all but buried herself. There was no way he was going to belive her theory. "Brandon, the men who delivered the plants that I didn't order must have done it."

"They stole the gown? Went into our bedroom, riffled through your lingerie, picked an expensive one-of-a-kind gown and took it? If that's true, then why didn't you say anything to me?"

She shrugged, adding another nail to he coffin and wanting to die on the spot.

"I see," he said. "Would I get the same answer if I asked about the times I came home to the smell of cigar smoke, or the times the telephone rang and when I answered they hung up?"

"I don't know anything about those calls. But the cigar smoke had to be Tramble's."

"I might accept that. Even that the phone calls were the wrong numbers. What I won't accept is your lie about the nightgown. I saw it in your drawer just before we left for Galveston."

She closed her eyes, at a total loss as to what to say. She hadn't seen the gown there. Hell, she'd never even opened the damn drawer, because she wasn't about to pack a nightgown for her honeymoon. "Brandon, please believe me. I never had an affair with that man. I never cheated on you. As for the nightgown, I just don't know. It was missing for days, then suddenly turned up again. Someone must have broken in to put it back."

"Stop! Just stop right there. No more of your lies, for God's sake. This entire building is secure, the penthouse suite even more so." He reached out and grabbed her by the shoulders. "Damn your lying mouth."

He let her go and she stumbled backward up against the wall, so shocked and stunned by his violent words that she was speechless.

"I should have known. All your life you've had a legion of men hanging around you. Always teasing them with your body and looks."

Outrage made her spine straighten. "Shut up!" she yelled. "How dare you say that to me. You who have bedded any woman who would spread her legs for you. At least I didn't go to bed with every man I looked at. How dare you talk that way to me! Whether you like it or not, I'm your wife."

"Not for long," he mumbled, and began stuffing the photographs back into the envelope.

"You've known me all my life. How *could* you think I was capable of doing the things in those pictures? Why would you believe them, Brandon?" She waited for an answer, and when he only looked at her with a blank expression, she picked up her suitcase and headed down the hall.

"Where do you think you're going?"

She turned around, tears streaming down her face, tears she didn't bother to hide. "I'm going to pack the rest of my clothes and leave here."

"Over my dead body." He caught up with her and took hold of her suitcase. "We're going to the ranch even if I have to carry you out of here kicking and screaming...and believe me, I will. The family is expecting us, and we'll be there. Then, when we get back to Houston, we'll start divorce proceedings."

CHAPTER THIRTEEN

THE SMALL CAR WAS WORSE than a tomb. They had argued off and on most of the way to the ranch, trading biting remarks, digging up petty grievances from the past, yet skirting the subject that had set everything off like fireworks. But for the past fifty miles only silence filled the confines of the car.

Anger radiated from Brandon like heat from a red-hot stove. She touched the tissue to her nose and sniffed. How could Brandon believe she would have an affair with another man? His initial anger she could understand, but his total acceptance of those damn pictures hurt worse than anything she'd ever endured.

What nagged at her most were the pictures themselves. They were fakes, clever fakes, taken, arranged and retouched by someone who hated her so much they didn't care who else they ruined. That was another point—the photos were indeed aimed at both her and Brandon. They were meant to do exactly what they had done, to destroy their marriage.

Only one person would benefit from destroying her life: her uncle. After all that had happened and with what Brandon had told her, she had no doubts whatsoever that Tramble was the instigator of the whole plot. Brandon should immediately have realized this, too, but his ego was so wounded that he believed what was in the photos.

"I guess I should have expected it of you," he growled, his eyes never leaving the road. "You always wanted the best of both worlds. Maybe I should be grateful you showed your true colors so early in our marriage. God help you if we'd had children."

"Why you arrogant, single-minded...alley cat," she hissed, then clamped her mouth shut, refusing to sling mud any longer and say things that would never be forgotten or forgiven. Somehow she had to prove to him that the pictures were fakes and she was being framed.

She turned her gaze on the passing scenery, hoping the serenity of the velvet-green rolling hills of South Texas would soothe her shattered nerves. The wildflowers were in bloom—blue bonnets, Indian paintbrush and others she'd long forgotten the names of blanketed the side of the road and open fields with a collage of blues, reds, yellow, orange and white. She always loved to return home to the country at this time of year, but today the beauty was marred by the blur of tears that filled her eyes. She sniffed again and began to talk softly to herself. "Of all the nerve," she mumbled, "thinking I'd jump in bed with another man. When did I have the time, for God's sake?"

"You can stop that sniffling and crying, too. It doesn't faze me in the least."

JoBeth's head snapped around. "Crying!" she yelled and glared at him with hot, dry eyes. "Don't flatter yourself that you're worth my tears. But, then, your ego's big enough..." She trailed off as he spun the Corvette up the long driveway to the DeSalva ranch house. Squeezing her eyes shut, she frantically wondered what she was going to tell Lucas and Matthew. How was she going to explain those damn pictures? More important, what was Brandon going to tell them?

The car had no sooner come to a stop before the mammoth double doors than she was unbuckled and out, her hurried steps carrying her as far away from Brandon as possible.

"JoBeth," he roared.

She would have ignored the summons, but his use of her given name warned her of the dangers that lurked beneath each loud, drawn-out syllable. "What?" she snapped.

He pointed to her side of the car and the gaping door. "Shut the Goddamn door."

While he turned his back on her and began to drag out the luggage, she shot him a dirty, killing glance laced with revenge. Straightening her shoulders, she marched around the front of the car, grabbed hold of the handle, then swung with all her might. The car rocked with a satisfying squeak of springs. Over the top of the still-moving vintage Corvette, Brandon's pride and joy, she met his look of shock and white-hot fury. Her lips curved up at the corners into a spiteful smile.

The very air around them seemed to crackle with their anger, as if all other sounds had been sucked into the vortex of their emotions, leaving a strange silence.

She'd gone too far. Brandon loved his car with what she considered an unnatural affection. But, then, she wasn't a man, and would never understand men's slavish devotion to steel and bolts and screws. Figuring a quick exit was her only salvation, she sprinted for the front door, stumbling a little in her determination to get as far away from her husband as possible. Suddenly the door swung open, and she found herself in the understanding embrace of Brandon's brother. "Lucas." she hiccuped, then bit her lip.

"I know you can't have missed me this much, Jo-Beth. Careful, honey, don't squeeze so hard." He held her at arm's length and smiled. His warm greeting died as he took in JoBeth's white face and the shimmer of tears in her red-rimmed eyes. Lucas sighed. "What's he done this time?"

"He's going to divorce me, and I say good riddance."

"Please, God." Lucas closed his eyes, tilted his face toward heaven and groaned. "Not another one."

JoBeth stiffened in his hold. "What do you mean? Another—" But a female shriek from the depths of the house made her glance around Lucas's broad shoulders.

With a long-legged stride, Samantha Grey made a beeline for her. Tall, slim and with a classical beauty that was marred only by a mass of freckles and a flowing mane of outrageous poppy-red hair, Samantha was, unbelievably, a famous artist, wife of international celebrity-singer, Boston Grey, and the mother of five very small chidlren.

"I could just shake you until your teeth rattle," Samantha yelled, still halfway down the tiled hall. "You disappear for a year and not *one* word from you. Some friend you turned out to be." The sting of her words was immediately dispelled by a warm embrace. "It's good to see you. You look terrible." The sculptured lips quirked up at each corner. "Married life wearing you down?"

Lucas coughed loudly, drawing the women's attention from each other. They all turned and silently watched a grim, uncommunicative Brandon as he stomped past them without a word of greeting to either his brother or Samantha.

Samantha's red eyebrows arched higher in amusement as her eyes followed Brandon's stiff-legged retreat. "A lover's tiff?"

JoBeth slumped against the wall. "We're getting a divorce."

"What, you too?" Samantha pulled her away from the wood paneling, slung a careless arm around her dejected shoulders and led her down the hall. "I've left Boston. Shasta's left Kane. Now you." She tossed back her head and laughed. "Jennifer's the party pooper. She and Lucas are disgustingly happy." She threw a forgiving smile at the man who was following them and chuckling with every step. "So, my dear JoBeth, come join the party. Lucas has deemed this day the women's, and he's promised us we can talk and drink and eat to our heart's content without any bother or interference. Our kind-hearted knight will defend us to the end. Right, Lucas?"

"Right. Don't look so puzzled, JoBeth. Samantha and Shasta have been hitting the wine since noon." He shook his head in mock disgust.

Samantha tapped JoBeth's gaping mouth shut. "So unladylike."

JoBeth was led into the living room, where Samantha announced loudly that she and Brandon were divorcing. Then Samantha closed the door and left JoBeth leaning against it while she joined Jennifer and Shasta at the big, round oak game table. "What's going on here?" JoBeth finally managed as three pair of eyes were trained on her. "Shasta, how long have you been here? You were in Galveston just four days ago."

"Yesterday," she snapped, "I received an urgent phone call from a special friend, and thought it prudent to skip town before Kane could find me."

JoBeth frowned. This wasn't making any sense.

"Don't try to figure it out," Samantha said. "We've tried but Shasta's been exasperatingly closemouthed."

"I have not," Shasta denied, her owlish gaze on Samantha. "You arrived first and should tell us why you've left Boston."

JoBeth's gaze shifted back and forth between the women as they sniped good-naturedly. "Jennifer, do you know what's going on?"

"Sure, you're *all* crazy! Samantha comes driving in here day before yesterday, chauffeured by two red-headed giants she introduces as her brothers. She says she's left Boston, then proceeds to laugh at all of us when we demand to know what's happened." She shook her head, sending the long, blond hair flying around her face. "Yesterday at dawn Shasta shows up on our doorstep. We still don't know how she arrived or why, just that she's left Kane and that if we don't wish to see murder done we won't reveal her whereabouts. I thought I'd heard it all, till you show up and Samantha tells us that you and Brandon are getting a divorce." She paused a second for a strangled breath of air. "I wish someone would explain to me what's going on. Damn it, JoBeth, quit holding up the door and come sit down."

JoBeth grinned, met two pairs of wide eyes and began to laugh. "Poor Jennifer. Always the peace-maker." She pushed away from the door, letting her eyes search out every corner of the room for changes. There were none. Massive oak beams crisscrossed the ceiling, and above the rough wood mantel hung the an-tique collection of *retablos*. The butter-colored stone floor was covered with Persian rugs. The high reading loft had been her secret haven for years. She didn't think she could face seeing her childhood memories rearranged or packed away. Not now, after what she'd been through. Slowly she made her way to the big round table, and for the first time noted the lazy Susan loaded with cheeses, breads and sliced meats. Each woman had a tall wineglass in front of her and the remnants of a meal on her plate.

"Red or white?" Jennifer asked.

"White, I guess." She slid into one of the unoccupied chairs, leaned back, closed her eyes and let out a shaky breath.

"Jennifer," Shasta said plaintively, "I want a martini. This wine's for women."

Her statement struck everyone as funny and they all laughed.

Samantha quickly reached out, picked up a slice of cheese, a piece of meat and slapped them between two pieces of party-size rye bread. She leaned sideways and stuffed the small sandwich in Shasta's mouth. "You need a martini like you need another hole in your head. Eat! Maybe it will soak up some of that wine you've been throwing down." She pulled the sandwich out. "What did you say?"

Shasta sputtered, "Go to hell." Her next words were cut off as Samantha replaced the sandwich with added force.

When JoBeth quit laughing and caught her breath, she took a hefty sip of wine and eyed each woman carefully. Something was terribly wrong here. Where were their tears? Neither woman appeared brokenhearted or even concerned over the prospect of leaving her spouse. "Samantha, where are the children?"

"With Boston."

"You mean you left Boston *and* the children? How could you leave your babies?"

"Easy." She sent the lazy Susan spinning, grabbed the bottle of wine as it passed, filled her glass, then replaced the bottle in exactly the same spot.

For some reason JoBeth couldn't discern, this act sent Shasta and Jennifer into hysterics.

Samantha studied her glass a moment, then looked up. "Well, I guess now that we're all together I'll tell you the whole story."

They all sat up straighter except Shasta, who slid downward a little. JoBeth, out of curiosity, glanced under the table to see if her petite friend's feet touched the floor. They didn't, and she knew if Shasta consumed much more alcohol she would slide out of the chair and onto the floor.

"It all started while I was trying to finish both paintings for the auction. Boston got it into his head that he needed to do another music video and that it had to be done *immediately*."

JoBeth's brow crinkled in confusion, until she remembered that Samantha had worked for a big-time New York advertising agency and produced television commercials. It was during one of those filmings that she met Boston.

"He knew I couldn't leave the children and stop work on the paintings to run off with him to California and produce a video—and I told him so. Well, he promptly said he never asked me in the first place and proceeded to blow that famous temper of his till the real truth emerged. He's jealous of his own children and the time I spend with them." She held up both hands when all three women were about to speak at once. "I know, I know. I have a housekeeper and four maids to help, but

Pearl and the young girls can just do so much. I tried to tell Boston that the babies need *us*. He disagreed, though I knew he was lying and so did he. He just wanted me to himself. So he forced the issue. I let him go off to Los Angeles and do his damn video. Then when he came home I told him I wanted a divorce and left. Now he'll have a taste of what it's like to be a mother, and he'll see just how much spare time he has." She began to chuckle at the open mouths around her. "Of course, he never dreamed that Pearl would follow me to my parents' house, or that three of the four maids would suddenly become ill."

"Do you mean to tell us," asked JoBeth, wiping the tears from her eyes, "that you left him to care for a four-year-old girl and four two-year-old boys?"

"And three dogs, two cats and one mynah bird that talks like a sailor who's been denied shore leave for two years. The children's pets, you know."

When JoBeth could get enough breath to talk, she asked, "Then you really don't plan to divorce him?"

"Are you mad? Of course not. But he doesn't know that." She reached for a wine bottle, motioned for each woman to place her glass on the lazy Susan, then turned it slowly as she refilled their glasses and returned them to their proper places. "I went to Dad's house and waited. Though I must admit I was impressed with Boston's determination. It took him two days of dealing with five kids before he broke down and called. Of course he panicked when my brother, Mark, answered the phone and told him I wasn't there and he didn't know where I was. You could hear the yelling and pleading in the next room." She chuckled wickedly, her aquamarine eyes bright with laughter. "That, ladies, was four days ago. I would imagine that by now—if he's

still among the sane—he's ready to take back all the
nasty, hateful, selfish things he said to me.... He's on
his knees.'' She picked up a small wedge of Brie and
began to nibble, enjoying the awed silence that met her
tale. ''Nothing like a good dose of motherhood to put
everything back into perspective, is there?''

Abruptly, out of the momentary calm, came the
sounds of doors slamming, squeals and childish giggles. Samantha went still, her wineglass suspended in
midair, and cocked her head. A huge smile bloomed on
her lips and she shoved her chair back, rising quickly to
her feet. ''I believe I hear the voices of my little angels.''
Another ear-splitting squeal was followed by a deep
baritone growl. Samantha's smile grew, her eyes shimmering with amusement. ''And I think I hear the rather
strained voice of that world-famous singer, husband
and father.'' Stepping over to the picture window, she
began to chuckle. ''Yes, indeed. Come see how the
mighty fall, girls.''

They nearly tripped over each other as they jockeyed
for a good position in front of the window. JoBeth took
in the sight and was forced to bite her hand to keep from
cracking up. Boston Grey—sex symbol, celebrity, powerful, temperamental and always immaculate in his appearance—was standing in front of the porch, a dazed
look on his face as the cabdriver hastily threw out luggage and raced back down the driveway. His once clean
and neatly pressed suit hung in a mass of wrinkles. The
thick coal-black hair that was always perfectly brushed
seemed to be standing straight up on one side of his
head like a rooster's tail.

''Oh, my,'' Samantha said, choking on the words.
''There seems to be something very sticky in his hair. I
warned him of the hazards of giving the boys candy

without strict supervision and plenty of wet towels. Poor dear. I imagine his fame, sex appeal and good looks weren't enough to induce the airline stewardesses to take on my wild bunch.''

"What's wrong with him, Samantha?'' JoBeth asked. "He's just standing there, holding Rebecca's hand, while one of the boys is clinging like a monkey to his leg.''

"Battle fatigue, I think they call it,'' Shasta added helpfully.

"There,'' JoBeth whispered. "There...see, he moved. He is alive, after all. He's trying to shake the child off his leg.'' They all laughed at the sight of Boston's halfhearted attempts to loosen the boy and at the same time give orders to the other three, who were now running around him like Indians on the warpath. "Which boy is which, and who is the little limpet?''

"Our timid and third-born of the quads, Robert.'' She got misty-eyed for a second. "Look at my darling daughter. Isn't she a little beauty? Thank heavens she has her father's looks and coloring. The boys will make it through life with chestnut hair—they'll fight anyone who dares to call it red—but my sweet Becky wouldn't be that tough. She'd come home in tears and it would be her daddy who'd have to knock heads together.'' She sighed, then remembered JoBeth's request to put names to the rest of her boys. "The one Becky has under control now is Elijah, number two. Kane, an unlikely namesake and number four, is the one sitting on the luggage with his nose buried in a picture book. Now where's Boston, Jr.? Ah, there's the firstborn.'' She turned to Jennifer. "I hope you don't mind him watering your lovely geraniums?'' When she could be heard over the strangled laughter, she went on. "My little watering pot. At least I broke him of aiding the house-plants."

By the time Samantha finished, Shasta was sitting on the floor, wiping her eyes with her soaked napkin, Jennifer was leaning helplessly against the cool window, her forehead pressed onto the glass, and JoBeth was doubled over holding her side.

Samantha grabbed Shasta's arm and hauled her up. "Lucas is outside greeting them. He'll be in here soon. Quick, everyone back to the table."

Sure enough, in less than five minutes the door swung open. Boston stood there, red-eyed, wrinkled, a wreck of a man and surrounded by five sniffling, clinging children. Lucas was behind him in the doorway. Boston managed to disengage himself from his children, and shot across the room to embrace his wife before his brood came to life and followed.

"Sparky," the beautiful, world-famous voice cried hoarsely, with a pleading note that had never been there before, "don't every leave me again. I beg you! I'll do anything—anything!"

JoBeth watched and grinned through the blur of tears brought on by the touching picture of Samantha in the loving embrace of her husband and children. She sniffed. It didn't look as if she were ever going to have a chance at a similar life.

Lucas ushered the reunited family out of the living room, leaving JoBeth, Shasta and Jennifer alone. The door suddenly flew open again and Samantha stood there with hands jammed on her hips. "Don't any of you dare say anything important. As soon as I settle the children and Boston I'll be back." She began to pull the door shut and winked. "I know what you're all thinking, but Boston is so exhausted he only wants to take a nap."

Like a ship without the wind in her sails, the room calmed and everyone settled down to wait. JoBeth reached out and quickly gathered the makings for a double-decker sandwich. Her head was already spinning from the wine and she had a feeling their partying wasn't over yet. She took a bite, savoring the combination of rich, dark rye bread, Swiss cheese and corned beef sliced paper-thin.

"Jennifer, whatever happened to that rotten sister of yours who threw her lot in with that mad Frenchman, Jean-Paul?" JoBeth asked. "Did Lucas and Brandon ever determine how much they stole from the De-Salvas?"

Shasta and Jennifer exchanged glances, then Shasta nodded.

"Have I asked something I'm not supposed to know about?"

The door flew open. "Stop right there. I said no talking till I got back. Now—" Samantha settled in her chair "—repeat everything that was said."

JoBeth quickly filled her in and they all turned to Jennifer.

"The last word Masters had on Susan was that she was making her home in Switzerland." She stopped and gazed off into the distance, remembering all her stepsister had put her through. "Kane finally had to tell Lucas that there was no way to get her back in the continental limits of the United States short of kidnapping. But Kane came up with a clever idea to relieve Susan of some of DeSalvas' money. It seems Kane knows a con man, a European gigolo who's notorious for swindling money from women. He's sent him to

Switzerland to meet Susan and guarantees that this man will take her for at least half of what she has.''

"That's my husband, ladies," Shasta said sarcastically. "Always willing to do for others what he won't do for his wife." She clamped her lips together and stared remorsefully into her empty glass.

"Okay, Shasta Stone. I've watched you drink yourself silly and feel sorry for yourself ever since I got here. What's happened between you and Kane that makes you think he wants a divorce?" JoBeth took another bite of her sandwich and, like the rest, waited.

"Come on, Shasta, give," Jennifer demanded. "I've never known Kane to be angry with you—frustrated, yes—but never truly angry."

Samantha held up her hand to stop Jennifer. "I think you'd better know something, Shasta. When I was putting Boston to bed I heard Lucas talking to Kane. From what I gathered your husband was using the car phone, and Lucas kept looking out the window and down the lane as if he expected to see Kane's car drive up at any minute. After he hung up Lucas told me that Kane had asked if there was a big enough tree on the ranch to hang you from.''

Shasta paled. "I told you!" she shouted at Jennifer. "He wants to kill me, then divorce me."

"Shasta, Shasta." JoBeth stopped her friend from reaching for the wine bottle. "Tell us what's happened."

The elfin face screwed up into a terrible grimace. Her big, round, brown eyes touched on each woman before she dropped her chin to her chest. "You know all those break-ins at Tex-Am Oil's office and refinery? I'm responsible."

"What!" They all shouted at once.

Shasta grabbed her head. "Please, *ladies*."

"You robbed your own husband's business?" Samantha asked, her mouth half-open in astonishment.

"Rob? Whoever said anything about stealing? I merely showed them that any cat burglar worth his salt could play havoc with their ultrasophisticated security system. Besides, it drove Masters and Kane bananas."

"How could you, Shasta?" Jennifer demanded as a frown played across her forehead, only to disappear when brown eyes as big and innocent as a doe's were turned on her. She knew the lie of that particular look.

"Well, hell! What was I supposed to do?" she cried passionately. "He ignored me, told me to buy a station wagon, has kept secrets about the business from me and hired a new secretary who has the face of an angel and boobs out to here." She stretched her arms out in front of herself in an exaggerated gesture. "I tell you, Kane Stone is not the man I married."

A roar from the depths of the house instantly silenced everyone's laughter and forced what little color there was from Shasta's face. "It's been nice." She reached down, picked up her purse and snatched her wineglass from the table. "I'll call one of you when I get to a safe country."

"Sit down, Shasta." JoBeth surprised everyone, including herself, with the order. "He's not going to hurt you, not with all of us here." She looked doubtfully around the table for help.

"Right."

"Of course not."

"We'll punch his lights out."

They all fell silent as another roar rumbled through the house. Then without warning the double doors were shoved open and bounced against the wall.

Shasta, like poured liquid, slid from the chair and
under the table in one smooth movement. The effect
was marred only by her outstretched hand clutching a
full wineglass.

Kane Stone, in all his decadent beauty, stormed into
the room, his silver eyes ablaze. "Shasta Masterson
Stone, how could you?" The hushed quiet met his
question and he spun around to face Lucas and Brandon. "I thought you said she was here." He caught a
movement out of the corner of his eye, swung back
around and leaned down. Wide brown eyes, huge with
uncertainty and anger, glared at him from a pale face
surrounded by a cloud of delicate brown curls. How
could a person stay mad at a ruffled kitten? Except this
cat had claws. "Come out from under that table this
instant."

JoBeth leaned down, smiled and whispered, "Don't
do it, Shasta."

Kane's piercing steel gaze turned on her. "I wouldn't
be giving advice to anyone with the mess you're in," he
growled, then turned back to his wife. "Come out." She
shook her head, sending the fluffy curls dancing.
"Okay, if you want to wash our dirty laundry in front
of our friends, so be it." He moved a little closer to the
table, then to the astonishment of the others sat down.
"Why, Mouse?"

Hearing her old nickname, one he hadn't used in
months, sent her anger soaring. "Damn you, because
after your father died and left you Tex-Am oil you never
even bothered to ask me if I wanted to come back to
Houston and settle down. Then when we got here you
started working eighteen hours a day." Her bottom lip
began to tremble and she glared harder at him, furious
at herself for weakening. "You never asked me what I

wanted. You just went ahead and did what pleased you." She took a huge breath and let it out slowly. "I want a divorce."

"Oh, Mouse." He moaned softly and ran his hands through his hair. His shoulders slumped. "I started the stock takeover proceedings today and it should all be over within a couple of days. Just bear with me."

"You never even asked!" She crawled out from under the table and over to where he sat. "Will you tell me everything that's been going on?"

"Yes."

Everyone watched, fascinated, as this small woman wound the hardened, worldly Kane around her little finger once more.

"You'll stop working till all hours?"

"Yes."

"You'll get rid of the Baby Jane with the humongous knockers?"

There was a long pause, meant to irritate his wife. "Her name is Alice, and yes, she goes to another department. Now come here." He pulled her roughly into his arms and despite the audience kissed her passionately. "Do you have any idea how humiliating it was for your grandfather and me to be told after an extensive and expensive investigation that the only one who could have caused the break-ins was his own granddaughter and my wife? Quit squirming. The investigator—your cousin Harry, by the way—informed us that there were only three known cat burglars who could have committed the crimes. One is in an Italian prison, the other is somewhere on the French Riviera and the third was *you*. After the shock and the cussing we did manage to have a good laugh, but it wasn't funny at the time, I can tell you." He hauled her to her feet, put his arm around her waist and was about to guide her from the room for a more private discussion, when Lucas clamped a hand on his shoulder.

"Sorry, old friend, but I promised the ladies this day was theirs. Men are definitely de trop."

"You're kidding." Kane dug in his heels. "I want to talk to my wife. There're a few other things we need to get straightened out now."

"Tough. There'll be plenty of time tomorrow. Come help me keep my brother from drinking himself into oblivion."

Shasta was prized from her husband's side and sent back to her chair, where she began to whistle, pouring herself another glass of wine. "Anyone need a refill?" she asked cheerfully and, miraculously, completely sober now. "My, isn't it nice to have an understanding and forgiving husband?"

"Luck, Shasta," Samantha told her. "Luck of the elves."

JoBeth let the laughter and talk wash over her as she stared at the closed doors. Brandon had stood there, leaning against the frame, totally ignoring her. Her spirits plummeted. Maybe she should have stayed in Houston instead of coming to the ranch. Her problems seemed a thousand times more impossible here, where she'd grown up. There never had been a time, no matter what she'd done in the past, when Brandon hadn't forgiven her... until now.

He couldn't even look at her. She pushed a few crumbs around on her plate, then absently tapped the remaining pitted black olive before she jabbed the tip of her finger in the hole. How could he hate her so much for something she hadn't done? She brought the olive, stuck on her finger, almost to her mouth before she froze, her gaze on the three pairs of eyes staring at her. Staring back warily, she popped the olive in her mouth and waited for her friends to pounce on her.

"Okay, JoBeth," Samantha said, grinning, "It's your turn. Tell us why Brandon is drinking himself into a stupor and threatening divorce."

CHAPTER FOURTEEN

"IT'S NO THREAT, Brandon is deadly serious." She didn't know if she wanted to tell them everything that had happened. She'd made such an ass of herself and had done so many dumb things...she didn't want them to laugh at her and agree that she was a complete idiot.

"Come on, JoBeth," Shasta urged, "out with it. And don't try to convince us that Brandon wants a divorce. He's too in love with you."

It was JoBeth's turn to laugh, but instead her voice cracked and she shook her head sadly. "You all promise you won't laugh?" She waited until they agreed, then took a deep breath. "Let me tell you a story." She started at the beginning, when Brandon found her at the Santana Dude Ranch in West Texas. When she got to the part about the stock deal and how she'd forced Brandon into marriage, she faltered, then stopped talking. Her so-called friends were laughing uproariously! "So much for promises!" She took a gulp of wine and waited until they got control of themselves. "Just what's so damn funny?"

"My dear," Samantha began, but was interrupted by Jennifer.

"Really, JoBeth. How can one woman be so blind and dumb at the same time? Have you ever known *anyone* to force Brandon into doing anything he didn't want to? He married you because he loves you."

"But you don't know how badly he wanted my stock."

"Cow patties." Shasta chortled, then came out with an unladylike snort that broke everyone up again. "You two deserve each other—you're both crazy. If Brandon just wanted those shares he didn't have to marry you to get them. He'd have found another way."

"Yes, indeed," Jennifer added. "In all your life have you ever denied him anything he wanted from you?"

She didn't want to answer that question, and continued to scowl at her friends.

"Oh, forget it. You're as thickheaded as he is." Shasta waved her half-empty glass at her. "Go on with the story."

At first JoBeth was afraid she wouldn't tell it right or that she'd leave out how Brandon had reacted to some of the things she'd done. But as her friends' expressions ran a gamut of emotions, she deemed her explanation suitable and forged on. Yet when she got to the mugging in Houston and the attempted murder in Galveston she received only blank looks, as if she'd suddenly lost what little mind they'd given her credit for. She kicked off her sandals, pulled up her jean pant legs and thumped her feet on the table. "Do you think Brandon made these bruises? I'm telling you, a very strong man tried to drown me while I was swimming." She met each of her friends' gazes one by one. "Someone really tried to kill me."

Shasta's eyes narrowed into dark slits. "Did you finally tell Brandon then about everything that had happened to you?"

"Oh, yes, and he was so angry he practically went through the ceiling."

"As he should have been. How could you, Jo-Beth?" Shasta shouted. "He warned you and warned you to stay away from your uncle." She stopped and glared. "You *do* realize that Tramble is behind all this, don't you?" She didn't give JoBeth time to answer. "Of all the empty-headed, featherbrained, stupid—"

"Shut up, Shasta," snapped Samantha. "There's more, so let her finish."

JoBeth shot Shasta a dirty look. "Don't call me 'stupid.' If everyone had leveled with me in the first place... I was winging this whole mess, you know. And it's all your fault and Kane's. He's the very one who got Brandon in on this takeover scheme."

Shasta rose angrily to her feet. "Now just one minute! My husband had nothing to do with your marrying Brandon."

"Children, children," Jennifer scolded, then began to giggle at their startled faces. Suddenly they were all laughing.

"Go on, JoBeth," Samantha urged. "What you've told us thus far isn't enough to cause Brandon to demand a divorce. What else happened?"

A strangled laugh escaped her lips. "You're not going to believe this. When we returned to Houston to pack for the trip here, there was an envelope waiting, addressed to Brandon." She paused and closed her eyes for a brief second, and the hurt and pain intensified as she remembered his expression when he saw those ugly pictures. She told her stunned audience everything. "I swear that woman wasn't me! I've never cheated on Brandon. I wouldn't," she choked out. "I couldn't." No one said a word and she shouted desperately, "Don't you believe me?"

"Yes, of course. But—" Jennifer started.

"Damn it, you're all supposed to be my friends. There should be no buts about it."

"Don't curse, JoBeth," Samantha ordered absently, her frown matching the others'. "Jennifer didn't mean that she doubted you. It's just the strangest story we've ever heard. Did you keep the pictures? I'd like to see them."

"Keep them? Brandon wouldn't let me touch them. Evidence, he said, that a divorce lawyer would savor—" She broke off, remembering her frantic grab for the offending pictures and where she'd placed the torn piece. "Wait a minute." A shaky hand slipped into the top of her blouse to pull out a wad of black-and-white photo that she'd stuck in her bra. With trembling fingers she laid the moist, crumpled paper on the table and stroked it flat. The picture had been ripped across the middle, giving a clear view of the couple from the waist up. She stared at the strangers. No, they weren't strangers. She knew the man and there was no mistaking the woman: it was her. Her face, her hair, her silly smile and half-closed eyes. There was no misjudging the nightgown, either. Brandon had given it to her and it was a one of a kind.

"The nightgown was missing from the time the florist delivered all those plants. But when I told Brandon that it was gone, it was back in the drawer." She looked up at her friends. "Someone stole the gown from the penthouse and then returned it." Shaking her head, frustrated and confused, she returned her bewildered gaze to the picture in front of her. A moment later Shasta began to swear, loudly and eloquently, and JoBeth's numbness receded enough for her to glance up.

Shasta held the limp piece of paper between her hands, almost jumping with anger. "This man...I know this man."

"His name is Rod Sharp. He's the one I just told you about. The one who helped me the day I was attacked in the Saks parking lot."

"Poor JoBeth. Your uncle is really running scared. Here's our proof of his perfidy. My girl, this so-called charming gentleman is Cal Randal. He and a little ferret-faced weasel by the name of Willy tried some of their tricks on Kane and me a couple of years ago. They're two of your uncle's most unsavory henchmen and have worked for him for years." She circled the table, picked up a newly opened bottle of wine and filled everyone's glass as her statement was absorbed.

"There's one other thing. Cal—or Rod, or whatever he's calling himself these days—was in Galveston while you and Brandon were there. More than likely he's the very one who tried to drown you. As for those photos, they're fakes, masterfully done, mind you, but fakes nonetheless."

She held the piece of paper up between the tips of her fingers for all to see. "They somehow took pictures of you, possibly while this Cal, or Rod, saved your life in that mock attack. They stole your nightgown, something expensive and identifiable as yours. What better item for a husband to recognize than a sexy nightgown? It just so happened they lucked out and that particular gown was one of a kind. Anyway—" she paused, picked up her glass and took a sip of wine, allowing the suspense to stretch to the breaking point "—they found a woman with a figure as close to yours as possible, superimposed the head and reshot the pictures."

The room fell earachingly quiet as everyone but JoBeth gave the waiting Shasta an awed and respectful moment for her deductions.

JoBeth's shoulders dropped. "I knew it wasn't me, and I was close to figuring it all out." She eyed her friends with a wry smile. "Well, I *was* close! After all, if it wasn't me, then it had to be someone else—right?"

"Don't give her any more wine." Jennifer reached across Samantha and removed JoBeth's glass from her hand. "And none for me for a while. I'm starting to understand her."

Slumping in her chair, JoBeth said softly, "Brandon doesn't think it's someone else, though. He's sure that woman is me...I..." She thumped her chest. "Jo-Beth DeSalva."

"There's one way to rid him of that belief." Shasta rose, and Samantha and Jennifer followed suit. "We'll just go tell him what *I've* figured out. I'm sure that after Kane sees the picture he'll confirm my theory."

They were almost to the door before JoBeth stopped them. "No!" The dizziness she'd been feeling disappeared at the thought of her friends gallantly trying to clear her with Brandon. "Come back here." She stood, walked over to the side table and poured herself a cup of coffee. "I don't want you to say a word to Brandon." How was she going to explain the hurt she was feeling? How could he believe she would do something so ugly? She couldn't begin to tell them how much pain his distrust caused her.

"This is something Brandon and I have to work out for ourselves." She could see the arguments coming and headed them off. "Don't you see?" she pleaded. "He has to realize on his own that it's not me. For some reason Brandon doesn't trust me. He has to learn to now, or this marriage is truly over." She sat down, taking a large sip of the hot coffee. "I just don't know what I've ever done to make him think I'm the type of woman who'd cheat on her husband."

Samantha patted JoBeth's hand reassuringly. "Have you ever considered that Brandon just might love you so much that he's blind to the truth?"

"Not him." JoBeth's gaze dropped to the cup clutched in her hands and she murmured to herself, "I wish I knew what I've done to make him think so little of me."

No one could give her an answer to ease her pain. After a few minutes the strained atmosphere was broken by a scuffling noise beyond the doors. Male voices rose and rumbled in argument, then quieted. The women turned their attention to the opening door.

Brandon stood there, and JoBeth felt her heart slam against her ribs. That he'd come to realize the photos were fakes, she had no doubt. He'd gone to a great deal of trouble to please her. He'd dressed in the white linen slacks and turquoise T-shirt she'd bought him. He'd even worn the white canvas shoes, sans socks. She drank in the sight of him while she toyed with the idea of strangulation. He ran a hand through his damp hair, and she wondered who had stuffed him under a cold shower long enough to sober him up. A cool smile touched her mouth. And who had helped him see the error of his ways? The silence was obviously making him nervous; he was tapping the rolled-up pictures against his thigh.

"Bets." He took a few steps, then stopped. Never had he felt so helpless, so ashamed. By God, he was a lawyer with a supposedly logical mind. He never jumped to conclusions but always withheld judgment until all the evidence was in. Yet he'd judged, condemned and convicted JoBeth in the short time it took for one quick look at those pictures. Now he could only plead his case and hope for forgiveness. "I was wrong, Bets. Please forgive me."

"Are you drunk?"

Before he answered too quickly he gave her question a second of serious thought. "I wish to heaven I were. I wish I'd been blind drunk this morning. Then maybe I wouldn't have hurt you the way I did." A noise from behind him made him lose track of the speech he'd planned. He spun around to see his brother, Boston and Kane slipping like thieves into the room. He resigned himself to having an audience witness his downfall and humiliation. But then, he thought cynically, he'd deserve it if she made him crawl. He raised the fist that clutched the pictures. "The woman in these is not you. It took me a while to see that. Will—"

"And who pointed that out to you?"

He frowned and clamped his mouth shut. He was trying to be humble, but it was damn hard when all he wanted to do was pull her into his arms and make her see that she didn't need to extract her pound of flesh. "No one had to point it out to me. As a matter of fact, no one has seen these but me." She raised a disbelieving eyebrow, and he took a few quick steps and came to stand directly in front of her. "I've done a lot of things lately that were wrong, but, Bets, I've never lied to you."

With a lump in her throat the size of an apple, she nodded. "How did you know it wasn't me?" she whispered.

Brandon laid the rolled up pictures on the table and smoothed them flat. Suddenly everyone was crowded around, each snatching a picture from the stack. Brandon ignored the comments and jeers, yanked the one he'd been looking for from Kane's hands, and shoved it under JoBeth's nose. "See that?" The tip of his finger tapped the woman's bare breast. "She's smaller than you."

JoBeth's cheeks flushed a bright red. "Hush."

"You don't have a mole there, either." His finger moved a fraction of an inch. "And look at that." He tried to get closer to her, but everyone was packed around them. Looking over his shoulder, he said sarcastically, "Do you mind? I'm trying to save my marriage here and you voyeurs are interfering." Laughingly they drifted away and he went on. "You see, Bets, after I took the time to look at those pictures closely I realized the woman wasn't you." She gave him another of her cool looks and he swallowed. "You must understand the state I was in when I first saw them, honey." He heard a chuckle behind him and threw a killing glance at Boston, who was now stretched out on the couch with his head comfortably resting in his wife's lap.

Brandon's hand clamped around her arm. "Let's go somewhere we can discuss this in private. I've been ribbed about this all afternoon and I don't need it while I'm trying to explain my feelings." But before he could get to the door it was barred by Kane and Lucas. "What's this?"

Kane chuckled. "Oh, no, my friend. We were all forced to crawl before an audience. What makes you think you're exempt? Besides, we're all busybodies like our wives and want to know how you could possibly mistake that woman for JoBeth. Hell, I could see at a mere glance that it wasn't her." He shot Brandon and JoBeth a wolfish grin and sauntered away.

Brandon looked pleadingly at his brother.

Lucas shrugged in sympathy but remained blocking the door. "Kane and Boston would skin me alive if I let you go. They're not too thrilled that I've not joined them in the doghouse."

Brandon guided his mute and smiling wife to the love seat, sat down and glared at the six pairs of eyes that stared at him. He turned his head and corrected the figure—seven—as he met JoBeth's dark gray eyes. "I don't know what you want to hear."

She sighed loudly and slumped back against the soft, persimmon-colored leather, her eyes now bright with anger.

"You're not making this any easier," he said piously.

"No. Put yourself in my place and see how you feel."

He thought a second and nodded. "Right. But I'll be honest with you, Bets. I don't know how to put into words what I felt when I saw those pictures. I don't think you can totally blame me for jumping to conclusions, either." He gave her a knowing look that only brought a thundering frown. "Only a few hours before I had found out that you'd lied—"

"I never lied," she snapped. "I just never saw fit to tell you everything."

"And almost got yourself killed in the process," Lucas added gruffly, then shut up when he met his brother's stony stare.

"If I have to do this in front of everyone, the least you could do is *butt out*. I don't need you adding your two cents every two minutes." Everyone was laughing at him and his anger mounted. "All right, Bets, I'll concede that you didn't actually lie to me. *Omitted* is a more appropriate word. But everything else! Damn it, you talked to Tramble behind my back when I repeatedly asked you not to. You told him things, let slip information that you shouldn't have. Don't shake your head. I know you. You can't keep a secret."

"Stop yelling at me."

"I'm not yelling. I'm just speaking distinctly."

The room erupted in laughter and then as quickly died.

"Surely you can see the state I was in? You were nearly killed—twice—then out of fear you unloaded all that had been happening. After that we returned to Houston and I saw those damn pictures. And you, as bold as brass, admitted you knew the man. Of course I went berserk and yelled and ranted and said things I didn't mean. I wasn't a sane man at the time." He touched her for the first time, letting his hand encircle the back of her neck as his fingers stroked the soft downy spot he'd come to love. "I don't know any other way to say I'm sorry other than to just say it. I'm truly sorry that I thought the woman was you."

Tears filled her eyes and she nodded. Suddenly she was being smothered in his embrace. She understood his explanation and accepted it, but deep down there was a coldness in her, a hurt that was yet unmended. That he would believe she was a wanton, promiscuous woman who would sleep around after marriage made the knot of pain grow until she thought it would strangle her.

She wanted desperately to get away by herself, but knew that if she tried to slip away now he would follow her. Leaning back into his arms, she smiled, accepted the cup of coffee Jennifer handed her, then turned her attention to the others. Brandon's lips touched the delicate curve of her ear and she shivered at his whispered words.

"We'll talk later when we're alone."

She brought the hot coffee to her lips and drank deeply of the scalding liquid, hoping the burning would ease the deeper pain.

Kane was sprawled on the floor, with Shasta settled between his legs, using his chest as a backrest. Boston and Samantha were on the couch, Boston stretched out, explaining his need for rest after five nonstop days of being both father and mother. No one disagreed. Lucas was slouched in the wide peach leather chair, with Jennifer sitting cross-legged at his feet. As always, he was touching his wife, his hand resting on Jennifer's shoulder. The conversation caught her attention and she looked up as Samantha let out a loud laugh.

"Beasties! You used to call the children your 'little angels.'"

"Yes, my dear Sparky, but that was before you left me to the mercies of those five." Boston reached up and patted her cheek. "That's all right. I'll forgive you. But the next time you want me to play connect the dots with your freckles it will take a powerful inducement."

Kane choked on his drink and Shasta laughingly threw back her head at the sudden image of Boston leaning laboriously over Samantha's long, freckled, naked body with a pen.

Boston sat up a little and lazily eyed them all. His jet gaze came to rest on Kane. "At least I'm not henpecked like you."

Kane thought for a second, then said with a smile, "Well, henpecked is a damn sight better than being a widower. If I hadn't brought my formidable wife home from Europe she'd have had every dope dealer and crook either in jail, dead, or after her."

Brandon and Lucas sat up, alert to Kane's slip of the tongue.

"So," Brandon drawled, "you now admit both of you worked for the government."

"I do not!" Kane's frozen smile didn't invite any further speculation. "And I wouldn't laugh too loud, Lucas DeSalva. Never have I seen such a change in one man as in you. Why, you actually know how to smile."

The men began to trade good-natured insults, stopping only when the women demanded explanations. JoBeth knew she could slip away now without anyone noticing or missing her. She leaned over and whispered in Brandon's ear, "I'll be back in a minute," then slowly eased off the love seat when he nodded absently, patting her arm and mumbling to hurry back.

She shut the double doors behind her and leaned against the hardwood for a second. She needed some time alone to think, but where? Pushing away, she started down the central hall, then stopped, removed her leather-soled sandals to keep them from clacking against the polished Mexican-tile floor and giving her escape away. She had always loved this house with all its antiques and history, but there was one room in particular that for some odd reason brought her a kind of serenity.

Huge, brass carriage lamps dimly lighted guided her to the dining room. A warm glow from the lamps threw shadows across the high, vaulted brick ceiling and the long, gleaming oak dining table. Crystal and china neatly arranged in built-in cabinets winked with opulent laziness. But it was the row of tall, arched windows and the scene beyond that beckoned.

She pulled a chair from the head of the table, turned it around and sat down. A three-quarter moon hung heavily in the sky, shining brightly on the rolling front lawn. The smooth carpet of green velvet was marred only by the darker pools of shadows cast by the mammoth trees.

JoBeth sighed, rested her head against the carved back of the chair and closed her eyes. A little more than a mile away was what used to be her "part-time" home. The place her father had built for his bride, where JoBeth was born and her mother had died. A home that wasn't truly a home at all. A home divided in more ways than one. She'd grown up here with the DeSalvas as her father's business took him farther away and for longer periods of time. Matthew was her second father; Catherine and Elizabeth, her mother and sister until their deaths; Lucas, her brother; and Brandon, her... JoBeth's eyes snapped open as she mentally clamped down on her thoughts, fighting off the pain of too-recent memories.

Out of the darkness a hand touched her shoulder, but her scream came out soft and strangled as she twisted around and saw Brandon's father grinning down at her. "Oh, Matthew, you scared the life out of me." She pressed her hand to her heart, feeling the pounding. "To say nothing of almost giving me a heart attack. I didn't hear you come in." Glancing at the cane gripped tightly in the old man's veined hand, she realized she'd been so lost in thought a bomb could have gone off behind her and she'd never have heard it.

"This was Catherine's favorite place when she was troubled." He turned stiffly, pulled a chair from the table and sat down slowly beside her. "I'd catch her here and join her. Sometimes we'd talk. Sometimes we'd just sit and stare out those very windows." He thumped his cane with a soft thud on the Persian rug. "You want to talk out your problems or just sit?"

She smiled tenderly into the green eyes still sharp and bright despite the years of emotional and physical pain. "Just sit quietly, thanks."

But Matthew wouldn't leave it at that. "For some reason unknown to me, my youngest son seems determined to make a fool of himself. I can't understand where he gets that thickheaded stubbornness." He shot her a twinkling look. "Do you know it took Catherine only two weeks of chasing me before I finally caught her?" He gave her a sly glance and JoBeth chuckled. "Mind you, once I came to my senses and caught her I couldn't see any reason we should be conventional. Her family kept dithering about a wedding date till it drove me crazy. So I kidnapped her from her strict father and brother and brought her here. Two days and nights alone with me were enough for her family to speed up the wedding." He grinned at JoBeth's giggles, then reached over and picked up her cold hand. "Look what happened to Lucas, how Jennifer totally knocked him over. Did you ever see him act so strangely in your life? No! I tell you, JoBeth, just be patient and Brandon will come around. We DeSalvas never do things the ordinary way. Just give him some more time."

She didn't know how much time she could give without some sign of how he really felt about her. Her fingers curled around the bony warm hand and years of lovely memories rushed back. Fat tears slipped from under her eyelids and rolled down her cheeks. She didn't want to cry, knowing if she started she might never stop. With her free hand, she quickly scrubbed at her wet cheeks. A change of subject was in order, and she bit her lip and managed to speak around the lump in her throat. "I like your new cologne. What is it, eau de baby powder?"

A rich, deep chuckle met her question. "I've been in the nursery with my grandchildren." He chuckled again. "I'll tell you, I thought the twins were a rare handful, but those five little Greys!" He clucked his tongue.

She sat there for a long time, half listening to him talk and holding his hand, letting the darkness and the sound of his voice soothe her frayed nerves. Finally, as if she were jerked from a deep slumber, she twisted in her chair and faced him. "Is my old house closed up?"

"No. Lucas plans to use it as a guest house for the people staying over tomorrow night after the ball. Why?"

"I want to go home—now."

"Now?" He increased the pressure on her hand. "This is your home, JoBeth. It always has been and always will be."

"I know, Matthew. But I must see it tonight."

He tried to read his watch in the darkness, then gave up, grumbling about old age and not having his glasses with him.

"Is there some way I could leave here without anyone hearing or seeing me?"

He thought for a moment, then smiled conspiratorially. "In ten minutes open that window and head for the patio. Use the west gate. I'll have my Jeep there, waiting. But don't start it. From the west side of the house you can coast down the lane to the highway, then start it up." He rose slowly, a gleam of pure mischief shining from his eyes. "The boys thought I didn't know that was how they used to sneak out to meet some girl.

Young fools! I used that very same incline when I was that age." He squeezed her shoulder as he rose.

Excitedly she listened to his slow gait, the step, tap, step receding as he made his way down the tiled hall. What was it that was pulling her back to her old home? It was a place of beginnings, a place that had nothing to do with now. Or did it? She glanced at her watch and stood. Whatever the reason, she knew that she needed desperately to go home and try to heal the pain and coldness in her heart.

CHAPTER FIFTEEN

MOONLIGHT EMBRACED the landscape, illuminating the straight, crushed-shell lane, making it look like a silver ribbon ablaze in the night. A moist, dew-laden breeze caressed JoBeth's skin. She shivered in the open Jeep and eased it out of gear. Slowly at first, the vehicle began to move. Then, as the incline steepened, the Jeep picked up momentum, and suddenly was flying down the lane. The speed, the cool wind blowing her hair into a tangle around her face, the mingled scents of pine, cedar and freshly mowed grass were so exhilarating she abandoned her troubles for a few seconds, throwing back her head and laughing into the night.

Memories flooded back. Sweet memories of when she was twelve and the entire DeSalva clan had gone to the Texas State Fair. She recalled a double Ferris wheel and Brandon's saying that he was going to unlatch the safety bar and throw her out if she didn't stop teasing him about his girlfriends.

The Jeep lurched to the side of the lane. JoBeth jerked the wheel hard before the tires could catch in the soft ground and send her careering into a huge oak tree. The near accident stopped the kaleidoscope of pictures and brought her attention back to the road ahead. The high wrought-iron entrance to the Mariposa appeared sooner than she'd expected and she was forced to jam on the brakes, sending crushed shell flying everywhere as she came to a halt before the highway crossing. With a quick glance in both directions she sent the vehicle speeding across the road and onto the opposite lane that led to her old home.

She looked neither right nor left as she drove the long, winding road, but kept her eyes straight ahead, waiting for that first glimpse of the stone house that her father had built for his bride. Of course, as the years added to his wealth, the additions to the house multiplied, until it resembled a hotel or dude ranch of sorts. Wings took off in all directions; porches wrapped and wound around the outside like a serpent seeking shade. And yet, for all its ugliness, there was a charm to the sprawling monster with its natural-stone exterior and rough cedar beams.

She pulled the Jeep to a stop before the front entrance and turned off the engine. The cessation of noise hurt her ears. Then, suddenly, the night creatures that had been scared by her arrival began to resume their chorus of calling to one another. She listened, strangely reluctant to leave the Jeep, knowing that any movement would bring on the quiet again. A lump formed in her throat and she felt the heaviness of her heart in her chest. Windows, blank and dark, stared back at her with an unwelcoming bleakness. Why had she come here? This was no home to her. Then why the pull to return? She searched her mind for an answer, and when nothing came other than just an urge to retrieve an item from her past, she squared her shoulders and jumped out of the Jeep.

Her hand touched the doorknob, and even though Matthew had warned her that the house was going to be used as guest quarters tomorrow night, she was unprepared for the easiness with which the heavy cedar door swung open. The scent of lemon oil and fresh flowers assaulted her senses. The shining surfaces of polished furniture met her eyes in the gloomy entrance hall. The moonlight that filtered in made shadows dance across the walls, and she began to move faster through the house, uneasy with its emptiness.

JoBeth was surprised that there was no urgency to stop, gaze in each room and recall the past. Then she realized the awful fact that she really had no past here to remember. All her memories were tied up with the big hacienda across the highway. Relieved that no ghosts were going to jump out at her, she rushed down the long hall, the slapping of her leather sandals the only noise to announce her presence.

At the end of the hall JoBeth stopped. She reached up on tiptoes and touched a short chain, swearing when it eluded her fingers. Finally, with it secured in her grasp, she yanked, stepping back to watch as a series of wooden steps neatly unfolded. The entrance to the attic yawned like a black hole, and the smell of dust and decay made her heart pound harder against her ribs. But she steeled herself to face the past that awaited and set her foot on the first step. Once at the top she found the light switch and blinked as an eerie yellow glow bathed the attic. Dark shadows of every size and shape hugged the walls, leaving a strange open space in the center of the room.

As her eyes adjusted, she quickly amended her observation. There was a large cedar chest sitting in the middle of the floor, the very chest she'd come to inspect. A hard shiver slipped over her skin as if a cold wind had entered the airtight attic. Had someone anticipated her desire to come here and...? She immediately shook away the thought. Who could know what she was after? She'd only decided a while ago herself. Still, it was weird that the very chest she was seeking among the hundreds of packed boxes in the room would be so conveniently set before her.

Fingers that trembled slightly touched the cold, unyielding wood, tracing the engraved name "Huntley." With a little more courage, she traced the intricate carving in the bowed top and dropped to her knees, then spread both hands across the cool surface, caressing it lovingly before she opened the heavy lid.

The blood drained from her face as she gazed at the lone, handwritten sheet of paper resting atop the neatly arranged items in the chest.

She lifted it to the light and read:

Daughter,

I've gathered together a few items I thought you might want to keep. Your mother's wedding dress, the first diamond brooch I was able to give her, her family Bible (I lost mine years ago in the oil fields). There are other treasures here that I'll leave for you to discover. Your diaries are here also, pumpkin, and please forgive me, but I read them.

How I wish I'd known the pain you suffered from being apart from me most of your life. I only wanted to give you the world as I had wanted to give to your mother. Always remember, next to her I loved you most of all.

Forgive me, JoBeth, for what I'm about to do, and know it's more than a failing business that makes me take God's work in my own hands. I'm tired and lonely and just ready to go before my time.

Your loving father

P.S. If you love Brandon as you say you do, then
don't let anything stop you from getting him. Hold
on to love, child. It's the only thing worth the effort in this life.

Tears streamed down her face and the taste of them
was as bitter as gall. Not until this very moment did she
realize how much she'd hated her father for taking his
life. How, in some way, she had felt responsible. But
now all the pain, self-doubt and sorrow washed away as
she finally understood he had simply been an old man
who longed to join his wife.

JoBeth wiped the wetness from her cheeks and
blinked the blur from her eyes as she reached for one of
her diaries. The worn leather felt familiar, and she held
it to her chest in a childish gesture of longing. Her life
was spread out in the ten bound books. From the age of
eight until she was seventeen, she'd kept track of the
important events and passions of her days. She glanced
at the one in her hand and set it on the floor.

Carefully, as if each were a precious jewel, she laid
the books out in chronological order. For a long while
she just sat, staring at her life before her, marveling that
she had actually kept those neat records of her
thoughts, her dreams. As eager as an eight-year-old she
picked up the earliest one, pressed the catch on the lock
and gasped at the first line. *I love Brandon DeSalva!!!*

The bold statement from a little girl and the childish
exclamation marks made her struggle for air. She hadn't
remembered ever putting her feelings for Brandon into
those exact words. Quickly she flipped through the
book, astounded at the many times she'd repeated the
declaration. On the last day of the year and the last page
she'd written, *I still love Brandon DeSalva*. And thus it

was for each book. The beginnings, the endings, all with the same words. For ten years she'd declared her love on paper for only herself to see. She couldn't remember why she'd stopped keeping the diaries when she reached seventeen. In a way it was a sad tribute to what she felt now. After today she was numb to any feelings of love.

Brandon, in a few seconds, had sent her world spiraling in a crazy whirl of jumbled emotions. That he would believe, after knowing her all her life, that she was capable of adultery was unfathomable. The mere word made her flinch. It was ugly, and the torment of his belief was a wound she didn't think would ever heal. Keeping aside three diaries, she gathered the rest and replaced them in the chest.

A deep-seated sorrow washed over her as she realized that the reason Brandon could believe those pictures was that he'd never really known her at all. After years and years together, he still didn't know the *real* JoBeth. Anger began to stir deep inside her. Brandon was a man with a strong sense of honor, and as a child he'd known her to be equally as honest and honorable. Why now would he think her honor less than his? Whose standards had he judged her by?

After hours of holding it all in, the strain of the day burst loose and she laid her head on her folded arms and began to cry, great racking sobs, for Brandon, herself and everything she'd lost this day. She even felt she'd lost a part of her innocence. Then a jarring thought, one she'd had many times lately, came back to plague her, and this time she said the words aloud and faced the truth. "I've given my heart, but maybe my heart is too much."

The words, though spoken in a hush, seemed to echo softly around the room. Shadows swayed as if in protest to the loneliness and grief in her voice. She realized she felt emotionally defiled by what Brandon believed of her. As if she were an immoral degenerate not to be trusted.

The worry and sorrow she'd been feeling turned abruptly to icy anger. She stuffed the three diaries into a woven straw bag she pulled off a nearby crate and stood. This was one time she wasn't going to be beguiled into forgiving so easily. Brandon would have to prove to *her* that he trusted and cared enough to make the marriage work. It was his move.

DARKNESS GATHERED AROUND HIM like a blanket and he welcomed the obscurity, hoping that in the vacuum he could figure out how he was going to handle the situation with JoBeth. Nervously he shifted his weight on the hard marble bench. How many times in his life had he come to this very spot when he was troubled? A hundred? A thousand? The heavy scents of honeysuckle and gardenia were all too familiar. They brought back visions of his mother on her knees, talking softly to him as she planted the white gardenia she loved so much. Of course, his father had argued that the mingled scents of the two plants would be overpowering, but as always, he'd given in to her wishes.

Brandon inhaled deeply. His father had been wrong. The merging of the two delicate scents resulted in a tantalizing fragrance. The coldness of the marble bench bit into his backside and he shifted once again. The sound of tinkling water reached him and he smiled tenderly. The big fountain with its goldfish pond was a favorite of his, too. He turned his head, his gaze traveling over the polished patio tiles brought from Spain by an ancestor, to the big marble fountain, also carted from Spain by another long-dead DeSalva.

How many times had he dared JoBeth to stick her hand in the lily-thick pond and hold it there for three minutes? Of course, she never lasted that long, as a big goldfish would swim up, take a taste of her fingers and send her jumping away, screaming.

He laughed softly to himself as he remembered her childish squeal. Resting his elbows on his knees, he let the sweet sounds of water rushing from the stone lion's mouth wash over him. But unlike years ago, there was no solace here. Tonight the water's melody only seemed to increase his discontent.

Why, he berated himself, had he not seen that the woman in those pictures wasn't JoBeth? All it would have taken was a little time. But, no! Like some great bellowing bull, he'd charged off half-cocked. He cringed as he remembered the accusations he'd made, the names he'd put to those pictures.

Brandon dropped his face in his hands and laughed at the irony of it all. Here he sat, waiting for JoBeth to return so he could reinforce his apologies and make her forgive him, and he couldn't even forgive himself. He laughed again, the sound a crude travesty to the turmoil of emotions he was feeling. That he was willing— no, eager—to beg forgiveness came as a further shock.

All his life he'd managed to laugh and tease his way through rocky times in relationships. But JoBeth had always been different, he conceded. He was forever pulling her out of trouble and she had the irritating ability to make him lose his temper where others merely made him laugh. He loved her, but didn't know how to tell her. That was the worst agony of all. The words wouldn't pass his lips.

He was disgusted with himself. Three little words and anyone would think they were part of a national secret. Damn it, she needed to hear how he felt—she deserved to know. Yet deep inside a tiny voice bedeviled him with a warning of possible rejection and pain if he laid his feelings at her feet and she stepped on them. What if she only cared for him like a friend or an old dog? He shivered, revulsion crawling all over him. What if her words of love were only words of gratitude? The old fear rose like bile in his throat. After all, hadn't she always wanted to be a part of the DeSalva family—a true member?

Headlights suddenly split the darkness, reaching out in the night and creeping across the honeysuckle-covered brick wall that surrounded the patio. He rose eagerly, only to sit back down heavily. The situation would have to be handled with care or he could blow more than his marriage: he could ruin the rest of his life. As he listened to the engine being turned off and the crunch of her footsteps on the shell driveway, he frantically rehearsed what he'd planned to say.

The wrought-iron gate to the patio opened and quickly closed. Brandon stood and turned. "Bets."

She hadn't expected to see Brandon waiting here for her, and gasped as she spun around. The moonlight seemed to gleam in his black hair like stars and his sapphire-blue eyes glimmered with determination. Oh, she'd seen that look before and steeled herself. She was tired, emotionally spent, and she didn't think she could go another round with him tonight. Afraid that if he persisted she would give in, she said, "Good night, Brandon," and started past him without another word.

Brandon reached out and clasped her arm gently, swung her around and gazed down into her red-rimmed eyes and a nose that reminded him of a clown's. "Oh, Bets," he whispered tenderly.

She turned her head away and tried to shrug off his hands. "I'm tired. Please, Brandon. Whatever it is you want to say to me can wait till tomorrow." She eyed him coldly.

"No, Bets, it won't wait."

An awkward silence fell between them and for the first time in his life he was at a loss as to what to do. Like a madman he searched his mind, but his pretty speech had vanished. Now all he was left with was the truth, and yet he couldn't say the words. Anything, he reasoned, would be better than this utter silence. *I love you* might be the simplest words in the world, but he was so afraid of rejection they weighed a ton on his tongue. "I'm a fool."

"Yes."

"But you must forgive me, Bets. There are other reasons I acted the way I did."

"What?"

He smiled his most endearing smile. "Come on, Bets, you've always forgiven me." If he could have reached his backside he would have kicked himself—hard.

"Let's forget it, Brandon."

"You know that's not possible." His arms wound around her and he was relieved that she didn't pull away, but rested against him so easily. "I want you to try to look at it from my side. I acted like an idiot, but you'll have to remember I've seen—" He never finished, instead he began to swear eloquently as the patio doors were thrown open.

"Here they are," Boston called over his shoulder.

Suddenly the romantic scene was ablaze with lights and music as everyone moved from the house in a great

horde, carrying ice buckets and glasses. Shasta came
through the doorway carefully, the portable compact-
disk player in her arms, a stack of disks piled high on
top, secured by her chin.

"Music to soothe the savage beast," she mumbled
stiffly, then almost tripped.

Everyone was a little blurry eyed.

Kane glided over, removed the straw bag from Jo-
Beth's grip and handed it to Brandon. "Hold this, old
man. I want to dance with your wife. Mine's all feet tonight for some reason."

"Am not!" Shasta dropped the few remaining disks
she had in her hands and glared at Kane.

"Go dance with her, Brandon, before she gets it into
her head to show all of you her antics as a *once* cat
burglar *extraordinaire*."

Brandon glanced at Lucas, his expression bitter.
"Thanks!" But there was nothing left to do or say. His
friends were determined to have a party. Shrugging, resigned to his fate, he accepted the drink Samantha held
out to him.

"Drink up, Brandon. The night has just begun."

And Brandon groaned out loud.

HE GROANED AGAIN as the morning sunlight stabbed a
path through his brain like a red-hot poker. He squeezed
his eyes shut, rolled over and buried his face in the curve
of JoBeth's neck, but the pounding in his head only
seemed to intensify. "Bets? Make your heart stop beating just for a few seconds." Her rude answer and abrupt
movement sent him sprawling over onto his back. The
pounding grew louder. He raised his head and, glassy
eyed, squinted at the door. "Stop that infernal racket,"

he yelled, then let his head drop back to the soft pillow.

"Get up, you two." Lucas hammered on the door once more. "The governor and the vice president will be here in about two hours. Besides, breakfast is ready—hot coffee, brother, gallons of it."

Brandon groaned again, swung his feet to the floor and broke out in a cold sweat as his stomach flipped over. He let the nausea pass, then glanced over his shoulder at his slumbering wife. She looked entirely too comfortable. His hand smacked her backside, and he grinned as she sat straight up and glared at him. "Good morning. How do you feel?"

JoBeth pulled the sheet to cover her naked breasts from the cool air. "Fine," she lied. "I didn't try to drink everything in sight last night, nor did I try catching the goldfish with my bare hands."

Brandon chuckled into his hands as he rubbed his stubbled chin. "Would you believe it? Kane and Boston trying to climb the oak tree and hang from the limbs like possums. It's so out of character for them. What the hell brought that on, anyway?"

"Shasta!" they both said, and smiled at each other.

"The pixie was in rare form last night," Brandon added.

JoBeth's eyes darkened and gleamed wickedly as she looked at Brandon's pale face. "Talking about rare form...what happened to the man determined to make love the instant we got into bed?"

Brandon had the grace to blush. "We'd better get ready and go down to breakfast. I'm sure there are a million things to do today before everyone starts to arrive."

"Chicken. You didn't answer my question, Brandon."

He was halfway to the bathroom and stopped. "Shut up, Bets," he growled, but he was laughing as he turned on the shower.

THE ONLY SOUNDS in the dining room were those of soft moans, dishes being quietly set down and the careful steps of the young Mexican maids as they served the traditional Mexican breakfast. No one at the table even spoke till they were fortified with a couple of glasses of ice-cold orange juice laced liberally with champagne. Then, one by one, forks were picked up and napkins unfolded. After a while, there was a great collective sigh of appeasement.

Lucas tapped a knife against his crystal glass, received a few winces for the noise and rose. "Another two years have passed." He dropped his hand on Jennifer's shoulder and gazed down at her lovingly. "We've added to our ranks... Jennifer, my son and daughter, Boston and Samantha's quadruplets, and though Jo-Beth has always been a part of our circle, she's now officially a family member, thanks to the wisdom of my brother."

Brandon flinched inwardly at the reference to Jo-Beth's long attachment with the family. He had enough fears without his brother's reminder.

"Maybe in two more years they'll have their own children to add to our little collection of friends and family." He paused and swung his gaze to Shasta and Kane. "The patter of little feet isn't as bad as some people think."

Shasta shook her head sharply in quick denial, then made the mistake of looking at Kane. Her eyes widened at his serious contemplation of the matter. She paled, picked up her glass and drained it quickly. "Surely not," she mumbled.

"Let's raise our glasses in hopes that everything goes off as planned today and that we raise a bundle of money for the cancer wing of the Children's Hospital." Lucas leaned over, kissed Jennifer's cheek and said, "Let's not forget my wife's efforts to pull this thing together by herself."

"Here—here," they chorused, and toasted once more.

Lucas reached under the table and pulled out an early-morning edition of a Houston newspaper. "I've saved this for last." He flipped the front page around for everyone to see. The headline was bold and they all smiled. Texas/American Oil Pulls Off the Stock Takeover of the Year on U.S.A. Oil. "It's official."

Kane and Brandon literally snatched the paper from Lucas's hands. Suddenly everyone was crowded around, trying to read over their shoulders.

JoBeth sighed and closed her eyes, thankful that at last it was over. She was about to ask about her uncle and his reaction, when she found everyone looking at her. "What...what did I do?"

"It says that a spokesman for Kane Stone and Brandon DeSalva, co-owners, has already announced one appointment." Boston cleared his throat importantly before going on. "JoBeth Huntley DeSalva, a major stockholder, has been named vice president of public relations."

"Oh." Her mouth formed a perfect circle as she gazed at Kane, then Brandon, then back and forth several times. "You didn't tell me," she accused dumbly. Tears filled her eyes as she realized the enormity of the offer. They didn't really think she was an empty-headed butterfly, after all. "Oh! Hell! I don't know what to say."

Brandon slung his arm around her waist and pulled her close to his side.

"My business? What will become of it?"

"You'll have to decide if you want to keep Etiquette, Inc., or find a way to delegate some of your work and authority. That is, if you want to take the job with Tex/Am. But, Bets, before you decide, I want you to know that I'd like to have you with me."

She was going to blubber like a baby, and grabbed her napkin, burying her face in it until she could compose herself. She managed to nod her acceptance. Damn! Here she was, prepared to be cool, distant and righteously angry at Brandon, and he pulls this on her. Everyone was talking around her, and only the sound of her uncle's name brought her thoughts back to the present.

"How's security around here, Lucas?" Brandon asked, his hold on JoBeth automatically tightening.

Lucas chuckled. "What do you think, with the governor and vice president coming?"

Brandon's gaze was deadly serious. "I don't have to tell you that until the board meeting day after tomorrow, the takeover isn't official. Tramble could still try one last-ditch effort to retake possession. The biggest block of U.S.A. Oil is owned by me and Bets. With her out of the way, her shares would revert back to Tramble, leaving him with controlling interest. Need I remind you her life could be in danger?"

"Yours, too, Brandon," Kane put in.

"Oh, God." JoBeth closed her eyes and slumped in Brandon's arms. "Will it ever be over?" Her eyes snapped open. "Surely he wouldn't try anything here. He's not invited, and if he showed up he'd be recognized in a second."

Shasta shook her head and clucked her tongue. "For an intelligent woman, you are incredibly naive sometimes, JoBeth. A man like Tramble doesn't dirty his hands. Surely after what you've been through lately you know that."

Brandon hushed Shasta with a look. "We don't know what he'll pull. I know after his attempts to call in another company for financial help failed, he telephoned the president for assistance. Kane talked to the vice president yesterday and was told the president informed Tramble he couldn't jeopardize his public standing and interfere. So he's desperate, alone and as hungry as a shark." He turned to JoBeth, taking her shoulders in his hands. "Please, please be careful. Tramble's silence is ominous. Promise me you won't go off alone, no dark corners, and don't trust anyone but those you know. Have someone with you at all times."

A chill crawled over her.

"Promise, Bets."

"Only if you'll do the same."

They both nodded, then Brandon kissed her tenderly. "No more games."

A flush of heat rose in her cheeks. She said softly and sarcastically, "No games. I'll leave that to those with experience." She shrugged off his hands, reminding herself once again that he truly didn't trust her or love her. He only cared about her damn shares and his own dreams. "Now we've all got work to do," she snapped, and tucking the tail of her pink-and-white Western shirt into her jeans, she whirled and stomped off. Everyone followed, and she threw a mischievous look over her shoulder as their hard-heeled boots made a horrendous noise on the tile floor. The racket brought her further joy as she caught the expression of excruciating pain on each of their faces. She pushed open the back door and everyone piled out behind her.

Brandon, always the clown, dramatically dug in his heels and covered his eyes with both hands. "Oh, God. The sun's a harbinger of hell sent to welcome me!"

They split up, each with a specific duty to perform. JoBeth grinned as she watched them take off reluctantly. It was one thing to sit in an air-conditioned house and plan the day; it was another to step out into the bright sun with a hangover. She started off down the walk, stopped and swung around, looking back at the vivid white hacienda with its red tile roof and wrought-iron balconies. She'd stood thus years ago with Catherine by her side. That woman had been the wisest, most loving person she'd ever known, and though she'd been dead years now, a lump still formed in JoBeth's throat when she thought of her.

The morning heat simmered around her, and she quickly unsnapped the first few closings on her shirt and walked on. If there was one thing Catherine had taught her, it was never to try to outdress the guests at these gatherings. People always showed up in the most outlandish outfits, and on a hot afternoon, in three or four hours they would be wilted like flowers. With her sensible cotton Western shirt and jeans she could outlast any of them.

"The house is beautiful, isn't it? Like a bright jewel nestled in green velvet." Shasta had turned back from the others, feeling an urgent need to stay with JoBeth. She never ignored one of her premonitions. "I talked Kane into doing my work today. I'll help you check on

what the caterer has set up for the ball tonight." She ran
a little to match steps with JoBeth, then grabbed her
arm and pulled her to a stop. "Why do my boots feel as
if they weigh a ton this morning? Couldn't be because
of all those drinks last night, could it?"

"Come on, you." JoBeth laughed and took off
across the grass. "Another clown I don't need." She
found the golf cart assigned to her and climbed in behind the wheel. Overhead a Lear jet circled the De-
Salva airstrip, lining up with the runway for a landing.
"That should be the governor and vice president." She
started the cart and headed over the thick grass to the
paddock, where a huge, black-and-white striped tent
had just been erected. She felt Shasta watching her
closely, gauging the emotions that showed all too clearly
on her face.

"Are you jealous of Jennifer now that she's running
all this for the DeSalvas? After all, you did it for years."

"Has Kane truly forgiven you for the break-ins you
committed?"

Shasta sighed loudly. "Okay, so I'm sticking my nose
in your business again. And no, Kane says he's not
through with me yet." Her lower lip stuck out and
JoBeth chuckled. "You're not jealous, are you?"

JoBeth laughed. Shasta had a knack of getting what
she wanted, one way or another. "Of course I'm en-
vious." She took one hand off the steering wheel and
waved it to indicate the workmen as busy as ants, the
trucks coming and going, the miles of wire, the tents
and the stacks of wood that'd soon be transformed into
a beautiful, highly polished floor for the main tent.
There were huge fans set to one side and air conditioners ready to be mounted in the four corners of the tent.

You couldn't have hundreds of the socially prominent elite in formal wear sweltering on a hot night.

"It's a heady feeling to control all this, even just for a while. But there's really not much to it anymore, except hours of supervision. We've used the same caterers for years. They have this routine down to a fine art." She smiled to herself as Shasta shook her head in amazement.

A noise caught JoBeth's attention and she raised her hand to shield her eyes from the sun. Far to the east in a pasture another tent was going up, not as elegant as the one she was near, but bigger. There two hundred guests would dance to a country and western band, bid on the livestock and art that would be auctioned off, eat a barbecued lunch served by genuine cowboys—ranch hands of the DeSalvas—and vie with one another for the attention of the few society columnists who were invited.

But it was the evening events that JoBeth eagerly anticipated. There was always an indescribable ambience that resulted from the fusing of elegance and nature in these surroundings. "Do you know, when I was a child I used to hide down by the lane and watch the big limousines arrive, or sneak down to the airstrip and count the planes and helicopters that landed. Brandon used to catch me there, and sometimes, depending on his mood, he'd sit with me for a while, then walk me back to the house and tuck me in." She gave Shasta an embarrassed look and stopped the golf cart before the tent. "Well, it looks like they've got everything up, and it's always been a tradition with me to be here when they hang the DeSalvas' two Waterford crystal chandeliers." She smiled and punched Shasta's limp body. "Perk up, you've only got about sixteen hours left before you can go to bed. Believe me, it's going to be an enjoyable day, but oh, Shasta, the night . . .'' There was the promise of a young girl's dreams come true in her voice.

CHAPTER SIXTEEN

A SHOWER OF BRILLIANT COLORS, sharp and clear as a rainbow, flashed from the crystal chandelier hanging over the elegantly dressed guests. The canvas sides of the spacious tent had been rolled up, the air conditioners were turned up full force and the huge fans sent the crystal prisms tinkling softly.

In the tent where the buffet dinner had just been completed, guests sated with Maine lobster, Alaskan king crab and fat Gulf shrimp and oysters meandered graciously, accepting glasses of champagne from traditionally dressed cowhands carrying silver trays. There'd been prime rib and steaks three inches thick from the DeSalva ranch. And for those who preferred a more delicate flavor for their finicky palates, there was tender veal. Four white-garbed chefs in tall hats made fettuccine and linguine. There were tables piled high with fresh vegetables, desserts and exotic fruits, all artfully arranged among luscious flowers and greenery. A feast for a kingdom, JoBeth thought, and smiled as she nodded to an elderly couple whose name she couldn't recall.

There was a heady scent of mingling perfumes in the breeze, as well as the anticipation of the auction to come. Unlike the afternoon auction, this one was not for charity but strictly for those with enough money to claim a prize bull, quarter horse, or a much sought-after piece of art. The evening events were the icing on the cake of the DeSalva party.

JoBeth heard the commotion around the auction arena and began to make her way through the sea of women dressed in haute couture, dripping with fabulous jewels, and the men who, no matter how elegant, still reminded her of penguins, in their black ties, white shirts and tails.

BRANDON SPOTTED HER AND STARED, his breath suspended painfully in his chest. Black lace provided a beautiful contrast to her creamy skin. He swallowed visibly, then quickly glanced around to see if she had the same effect on others as she had on him. There were a few lustful looks that brought his eyebrows down in a thunderous frown. The strapless dress seemed to be hanging precariously on the tips of her breasts and the fitted lace bodice reminded him of one of those old-fashioned corsets.

He tore his gaze away from luminous skin and tantalizing cleavage and continued his hungry inspection. A wide band of silky material was gathered low on her hips where the tight-fitting bodice ended and the straight floor-length skirt began. When she walked his heart skipped a beat as the fine material parted, revealing a fascinating length of thigh and calf. He raised his glass automatically to his lips, caught himself and set it down on the nearest table. He'd be damned if tonight his desire would be just empty words. He wanted her with a ferocity that stunned him, and it took all his willpower to keep his passion from becoming obvious.

He started making his way through the crowd toward JoBeth, thinking that for the first time since this morning he was relaxed. His concern about Tramble faded with the passing of each uneventful hour. Surely if the old bastard were going to try something, he would have made his move by now. Brandon was almost upon her and he grimaced as she shot him a cool, polite little smile, totally lacking in welcome. He definitely had his job cut out for him. Reaching out, he grabbed her arm and gently pulled her to his side. "You look good enough to eat tonight, my love." She bared her teeth at him, and he couldn't help the chuckle that escaped his lips. "I wonder what our friends and the guests would think if I threw you over my shoulder and carried you out of here." He glanced around, as if seriously considering the idea.

JoBeth stiffened. Brandon had that dangerous gleam in his eyes and there was no telling what he would do in one of these moods. "You wouldn't dare." And despite herself, her pulse quickened at the tantalizing prospect.

"No?" He raised his hand and let his fingers glide across her shoulder and collarbone before they quickly skimmed the tops of her bare breasts. "I must say, Bets, that dress is the most wicked thing I've ever seen." He lowered his voice. "It just begs to be torn off."

"Behave!" she commanded, and swatted his hand away, glancing around to see if they were being observed. "The auction has started and I want to watch." Sexy devil! Always playing on her emotions. She willed her knees to stop their foolish trembling.

"We'll watch together." He slipped his arm around her shoulders and turned her back to him. "Though I'd much prefer looking at you."

What the hell was he up to? His arm slid down her back and his hand guided her through the crowd, then the gallant pressure was replaced by his caressing touch on her derriere. Angrily she slapped his hand away. "Stop that this instant! People are looking." She bit her lip to keep the smile from edging away her righteous indignation.

"So let them. All they'll see is a man who can't keep his hands off his bride." He was walking behind her and leaned down to plant a butterfly kiss on the delectable curve of her neck.

JoBeth whirled around. "This isn't like you, Brandon. What is it you want?" She wished she hadn't asked. The bright gleam in his eyes told her he was going to answer despite the frantic looks she threw at him.

"You, my love. All soft and warm and naked in my arms."

"For heaven's sake, shut up," she choked out, and swung back around with a silly smile plastered on her face. She was going to kill him... slowly.

Brandon resumed his walking behind her, clucking his tongue and whispering outrageous suggestions in her ear, until her cheeks glowed bright red with embarrassment.

She came to an abrupt stop before the arena and turned her head. "Hush, damn you."

"Yes, my love, anything you desire."

"Brandon!" Her heart hammered against her ribs. That was the second time he'd used the endearment "my love," and she wondered if he was even aware of the slip. But one thing was sure, he was being entirely too loving. She just wished she knew what he was up to. There was no doubt that Brandon had some devious plan hatched and he was just waiting for her to fall into his trap. But why? "What's up, Brandon?"

Brandon wrapped his arms around her waist, pulled her backward against his chest and grinned into her soft fragrant hair. "Such a suspicious mind. I simply want my old Bets back, not this chilly stranger who glares at me every chance she gets."

"I don't glare."

"You're going to have to forgive me, Bets. We can't go on like this."

"You mean *you* can't go on like this. Maybe we shouldn't—go on, I mean." She held her breath at the momentary silence that met her words.

"You don't mean that, do you? Listen, I flew off the handle like a crazy man because—"

"Has anyone seen my wife?" Kane asked, scanning the crowds.

Relieved at the interruption, JoBeth said, "The last time I saw Shasta was at the buffet table. Then she got a funny look on her face and said something about spotting a ferret-faced weasel. She put her plate down and took off."

They were amazed at Kane's stunned expression and the way his face drained of all color. But before they could even show their concern or ask a question he was gone.

"Trouble, do you think?"

Brandon chuckled. "Have you ever known Shasta to get involved in anything *but* trouble?" He began to laugh and wave his finger before her eyes. "There. See. You forgot to be angry and those beautiful gray eyes are just brimming with lust for me."

JoBeth twisted away, biting down hard on her lip. "You're crazy."

"Just about you, Bets. I tell you, yesterday was the worst day—" He got no further as a heavy hand clamped down on his shoulder.

"Have you seen Jennifer, Brandon?"

The muscles along Brandon's jaw began to bunch. "What is this?" he growled in exasperation. "Why does everyone think I know where his wife is? Go away Lucas—now."

"Touchy bastard, isn't he?" Lucas grinned at Jo-Beth and walked away.

"Is there a conspiracy going on around here to harass me so I can't talk to you?"

It was hard to stay angry with that poor, hangdog look, but she only had to remind herself of those pictures to stiffen her spine.

"Bets, a man can just take so much."

"Oh, yes—a woman, too, *dear*."

"Will you please listen to me?" Who the hell would have thought he'd have such a difficult time with one stubborn woman? He plunged in before she could answer. "There are mitigating circumstances to my reaction."

He'd planned this carefully, damn it! Knowing her to be a lady in public—she would never contemplate causing a scene by walking away, raising her voice or throwing a temper fit—his tactics had been to place her in a position where she had to listen to his explanation. But, damnation, he never expected all this interference.

"I hope you're satisfied. You've made me miss the cattle and horse auction."

"Damn the four-footed beasts."

Kane crept up behind them as soundlessly as a cat on the prowl and touched Brandon's shoulder. "Shasta's gone." Brandon gritted his teeth.

"Gone?" questioned JoBeth, puzzled at the anxiety in Kane's voice. "You mean she's left the party?"

"No! I mean she's gone—disappeared."

"This is ridiculous," Brandon almost shouted.

"I'm serious. She's vanished. I've checked everywhere I know, but I need your help now." He grabbed Brandon by the lapel and practically dragged him away.

A deep frown creased JoBeth's brow, yet at the same time she wanted to laugh at her husband's obvious reluctance to be hauled away and Kane's determination that he go with him.

Forty minutes later Brandon was back, his expression foreboding and determined.

JoBeth automatically accepted the cold glass of champagne extended to her and asked, "Did you find Shasta?"

Brandon threw back the amber liquid as if it were water. "Yes."

After a long pause she could see he wasn't going to add anymore without prodding. "Well?"

Brandon didn't want to tell her what they had found. He and Kane had frantically searched all the secret little places only someone familiar with the ranch could know about. They were just about to give up, when Brandon remembered the pump house and they drove down a lonely strip of back road. Unexpectedly their headlights had picked up Shasta, an extremely angry Shasta, marching down the dirt road, resembling a small furious kitten who had been pulled through the bushes. In fact, she had been—gagged, trussed up and dumped in the huge azalea bushes along the lane leading to the service road. He and Kane had taken her, wildly swearing and threatening murder, back to the ranch house, where Kane fussed over her as she changed her torn gown. After they had calmed her down enough to pry out her story, Brandon had felt a chill right to the bone. Shasta had found her old adversary, Willy, sneaking around the party. When Brandon learned that this Willy was an employee of Tramble's and about as unsavory a character as they come, his chill had turned to a deep sense of icy dread. They had immediately alerted the police to pick up her assailant. Now all they had to do was wait until he was caught and made to explain what he was doing sniffing around the DeSalva party.

"Brandon! Where was Shasta? Is she all right?"

"Oh, she's fine," he said chuckling. "She was just checking out the local flora and fauna." His expression immediately sobered. "I don't want to discuss Shasta, though. I want to talk about us. Bets, you have to understand why I was so devastated over those pictures and misjudged you so."

"Look, Brandon. They're bringing out one of Samantha's paintings to auction off."

He ground his teeth, grumbling flowery obscenities under his breath.

"I wonder where she is." Her gaze shifted through the crowd and was drawn instantly to the bright red hair towering over many of the male heads. "You know, only Lucas and Jennifer have seen the painting, and from what Jennifer let slip it's a real eyepopper."

There was a collective gasp as the two cowboys carrying the big oil painting flipped back the covering. Silence fell over one hundred people, then out of the hush came a loud indignant roar of disbelief and embarrassment. There was no mistaking the identity behind the voice. Boston Grey, world-famous singer, half Indian, proud and fiercely protective of his private life, had been painted in the briefest breechcloth, with long flowing hair decorated with feathers and beads.

JoBeth felt for her friend, but had to secretly admit the portrait was magnificent. It captured the sensuous, earthy side of the man as no camera had ever been able to. This must be how other women dreamed of him: the savage with the piercing, jet eyes, high cheekbones, lips that looked as if they were chiseled from stone. And that body! She gulped, as taken with the image as every other woman in the room. And by the silence, the men were not as unaffected as they would have preferred— envy and admiration were expressed in their stares.

The crowd came alive and went wild. The laughter and wolf whistles were suddenly overridden by the roar of applause as everyone turned to Samantha at the opposite end of the room and paid tribute to a masterpiece in oil. But Boston was having no part of the excitement, and as the auctioneer opened the bidding he was the first taker.

For the next twenty minutes JoBeth and Brandon laughed until their sides ached. So frantic was Boston to obtain the portrait there were times when he even bid against himself. Finally the crowd of friends and admirers relented, stopped driving the price up and let Boston acquire the painting.

"Looks like Boston's fight with Samantha cost him more than five days alone with his children. I believe that last bid he made was one hundred and seventy-five thousand dollars." Brandon whistled in amazement. "I'd hate to see what she would do if she really got angry with him."

Out of the chaos around them a hush once again began to fall, but this time there was a difference, an undercurrent. Quiet rode the night in a great wave, washing over the people. One by one they ceased their conversations and laughter as they realized that Boston Gray was about to sing. Awed and full of anticipation, they watched him position the tall stool before the microphone, then pick up a guitar.

A soft sigh gathered upon the fragrant night air as the rich voice sang a love song so sweet, so full of hope and promises, that even the most hardened, world-weary man reached for the soft curves of the woman he'd brought, remembering what it was to be in love. After four songs, Boston laid down the guitar, and though the audience applauded, there was no shouting for an encore. Boston Grey never sang before a live audience anymore, and everyone knew they had been treated to a show of friendship and love for his family and friends.

JoBeth sniffed and rubbed her cheek against the soft velvet of Brandon's lapel. "I understand the reasons he stopped doing concerts, what with the threats of the crazies in this world, and his records and videos are fabulous, but nothing, nothing can compare with a live performance."

The orchestra that had been patiently waiting during the auction struck up a tune. Brandon turned JoBeth in his arms. "Come dance with me." He didn't give her a chance to answer but swept her onto the cleared area with the rest of the couples.

While Boston had been singing the ranch hands had eased down the tent top, so that all that stood between the guests and the sky was the tent's frame, and that had been laced with tiny lights. The luminous glow of the chandelier and the stars above added to the enchantment. The night was pure fantasy. JoBeth snuggled into Brandon's arms, forgetting to be hurt or angry, just loving being held close, feeling the steady rhythm of his heart hammering under her hand.

"Bets."

"Hmm."

"About yesterday..." He held his breath, then let it out slowly when she didn't pull away or bite his head of. "It was as you thought —" A firm hand on his shoulder put an end to his patience. Brandon set JoBeth aside and spun around, ready to deck the intruder, no matter who.

Kane, as fast as a snake striking, grabbed the fist aimed at his jaw. "Hey! Hold on there *friend* and watch who you're swinging at." He ignored the sapphire-blue eyes that damned him. "The governor and the vice president want a meeting with us."

"Tonight? For God's sake, Kane. I'm trying to put my life and marriage back together here. Damn the vice president."

Kane grinned, then shifted his eyes between the men on each side of him. "When the president sends his number-one man, you don't say, 'thank you, but no, thank you. My wife is angry with me.' Move, Brandon, or these two will do it for you."

JoBeth watched him go, wanting to laugh, except she felt too much like crying. In her weakness she had been ready to listen to his reasons and excuses—and believe them, too. It was just as well that Kane had come and taken him away. She wasn't really ready to forgive and forget, at least not until Brandon could do better than he'd done so far. She chuckled. He hadn't had much luck tonight, and if she had anything to do with it she would be even less available tomorrow.

But damn, she argued with herself, he looked so sorry, so sad and unhappy.... Like a dog that had lost his favorite bone before he'd gotten through with it, she reminded herself. And she was the bone here and had to remember that. Hadn't she always forgiven him for all the things he'd done to her in the past? She swallowed the frog in her throat. He seemed truly sorry for what he'd done and said, for distrusting her. But, then, he'd always been able to sweet-talk her whenever he wanted to. She wasn't about to stay with a man who didn't love her, and obviously he didn't if he could believe those damn photographs.

She stopped a passing ranch hand, plucked a glass of champagne from the silver tray and took a sip. She closed her eyes for a brief second, as if the cold liquid had quenched a terrible thirst. But in reality the hurt and pain of the day had washed over her, leaving an ache so deep she didn't think she would ever feel normal again. Tomorrow she'd find some way to stay away from Brandon and give her bruised emotions some time to heal. She opened her eyes, a new resolve shining in the gray depths. Tomorrow she'd decide what she was going to do about their marriage.

THE WORLD WAS AGAINST HIM!

Brandon lay on his back, his arms crossed behind his head, staring at the ceiling with bloodshot eyes. Dawn crept into the bedroom through the open-curtained balcony doors and he followed the shaft of light as it crawled across the room. When the sun reached the opposite wall, he told himself, he was going to wake Bets.

She sighed beside him and he turned his head, the frown that had distorted his features instantly replaced with a grin as she snuggled up against his side for warmth. He studied her for a second, enjoying the sweet serenity of her face. The lashes that lay like shadowed crescents on pale skin, the dark blond eyebrows that, when she was awake, framed misty gray eyes. Those eyebrows, another barometer of her moods, suddenly wiggled up and down. He chuckled, then caught himself before the noise woke her. Her lips moved like a whispered invitation, all pink and soft. She had a remarkable face, really. So expressive. Yet it could also be totally devoid of her feelings, cold and unyielding. He sometimes thought she'd turned to stone. What amazed him was that even as a child she'd had the ability to hide behind that expressionless mask whenever she wanted to. And though what usually went through that pretty head showed on her face, he'd learned over the years that her "stone face" was used only to hide a deep hurt. In the past twenty-four hours all he'd seen was pale skin, stormy gray eyes and a face as blank of emotions as a statue. The hurt was all his fault.

Careful not to awaken her, he began to pull the covers up over her bare shoulders, then paused. Her warm flesh was another invitation that couldn't be resisted, and he allowed himself a light caress before he tucked the sheet up around her neck. Then, reluctantly, he eased out of bed, knowing that if he didn't leave her, he'd make love to her whether she wanted it or not. Damn! He wanted his wife.

Shrugging into his terry robe, he walked over to the balcony doors, quietly opened them and stepped outside. The morning air was clear and dry, promising a scorching day ahead. The faint sounds of men's voices and trucks starting up floated on the breeze, and he knew the caterers, workmen and ranch hands were busy cleaning up after yesterday's events. During the next few days horse trailers and cattle trucks would roll in and out, picking up their owners' new purchases.

There was the smell of animals and fresh hay in the air and he inhaled deeply, letting his mind drift back over the years. How many times had he sat on the corral fence and watched the loading of prime stock? And as he grew older, how many times did *he* get stepped on, kicked and generally trampled on? He smiled as his memories wandered farther back. He remembered unloading a particular sorrel pony that JoBeth's father had bought her and shipped to the DeSalva ranch. Of course, the old man hadn't accompanied the gift, and it was left up to the DeSalvas to teach the eager seven-year-old how to ride.

Brandon's smile grew. That task had fallen on Lucas's shoulders because he was the eldest. Brandon had sat on the fence rail, watching and giving instructions, sometimes laughing at the determination of the little girl who threatened to outride him someday. But he had laughed one time too many at her mistakes. With a cynical twist to his young lips he'd watched her jump off her pony, tears filling her eyes as she marched right up to him. He remembered, too, that little stone-face staring up at him, her pigtails coming loose, her lips a tight line, her cheeks red from frustration and anger. Then suddenly he'd found himself cartwheeling backward into the water trough. He began to chuckle to himself as he remembered her childish giggles. It seemed years since he'd heard her free and easy laughter. Was he responsible for that, too?

Brandon shivered, his thoughts returning to the present with the intrusion of sounds from below. The kitchen staff were busy preparing for breakfast, and a loud horn sounded near the paddock. He stepped into the bedroom, leaving the past behind. The future was more important now.

As he closed the balcony doors, JoBeth murmured his name, reached out and touched the empty space. Her hand balled into a fist as if in protest to the lack of warmth, then her fingers opened wide as she stretched and turned over, dragging the sheet with her, managing to tangle it around her legs, leaving her totally exposed to his hungry eyes.

Like a man hypnotized, he stepped to the bed, stopping only when he whacked his shins against the edge of the mattress. His blood raced thick and hot in his veins, there was a heaviness in his groin and the pounding in his ears was almost deafening. Clenching his hands, he barely stopped himself from reaching out for her warm flesh. He wasn't about to make love to her here. Not with his luck lately for interruptions. He cleared his throat and spoke. "Bets, wake up."

She moved, stretched, a lazy unwinding of her naked body, and he thought he might choke to death from the lack of breath. "Come on, Bets. We're going home."

Sleepy eyes, as gray and smoky as the morning mist, slowly opened. "Good morning." She smiled, then her lips froze in place as she remembered how he'd left the party for a short meeting only, never to return. Her gaze narrowed and shifted to the pillow beside her, surprised to see the signs of use. She hadn't even been aware when he'd come to bed.

"Up, Bets. Now! We're going back to Houston. Come on, get your pretty butt out of that bed." He began moving around the room, gathering their clothes, stuffing them into suitcases as he talked. "There's a conspiracy going on here—everyone is in cahoots to keep me from talking to you. They think it's hilarious that I'm in deep trouble and can't extract myself with my old finesse.''

"Brandon! Don't you dare wad my dress up like that. And we were going to stay another couple of days. I don't..." She trailed off as he swung around and stared at her. There was that look that said, "You do it my way. There's no debating, arguing or yelling." One way or another, she was going to have to do as he wanted. Brandon wasn't against using a little force when he thought he was in the right. Obviously there was no doubt in his mind this morning. A mulish expression stole over her features. She was tired of doing as he wished. Hadn't she given up her valuable time with her company just to have a few days with him? *And look what happened,* a little voice reminded her.

"You needn't give me that look, Bets. We're going."

She sighed, knowing she was defeated. "We're alone now if you want to talk. Though God knows what you could possibly have to say of any importance this morning."

"Sarcasm won't do you a bit of good, either. We're leaving. As for being alone...yes, we are, but the way my luck has been going lately, I'd no sooner get the first words out before—"

A knock sounded on the door and Lucas's voice rang out. "Breakfast in thirty minutes. Hurry up, you two. We need to get through so the staff can set up the brunch for the governor and vice president, as well as some other guests."

Furious, Brandon threw the evening gown he held in his fist onto the floor and yelled, "See! They've bugged our bedroom. I know they have."

"Nonsense. For years we've had our breakfast this early." She propped herself up against the pillows, pulled the sheet to her neck and tucked her chin in the folds of the material to hide her smile. "I don't want to leave today, Brandon."

"Tough." He glared, his sapphire-blue eyes darkening with turmoil and frustration, his mouth a grim line of determination. "We're leaving, Bets, make no mistake—even if I have to dump you in the car seat stark naked."

She opened her mouth to protest, but quickly changed her mind when her red-and-white silk blouse suddenly covered her head. Before she could regroup and yank off the blouse, her navy slacks followed, then underwear. She just managed to uncover one eye when she saw him picking up her white huaraches. "Don't you dare," she snapped, struggling her way from under the mound of clothes and bedding. At the bathroom door she turned. "This is crazy, Brandon. We don't need to go home just to talk. We could go for a ride in the car or on horseback . . . a walk, anything."

"No! I don't trust them." He tried to glare at her once more, but his eyes seemed to have a mind of their own and were feasting on every naked curve. "Go get dressed, Bets," he said gruffly.

JoBeth slammed the bathroom door with feeling, then leaned against the smooth cool wood. Sometime during the night she'd made up her mind that she was going to find out once and for all how Brandon felt about her. She couldn't go on this way. She knew he was right and they needed to get clear of family and friends to discuss their problems. Yet she couldn't help the token resistance just to aggravate him. A hoarse laugh escaped her lips as she stepped under the shower. Who was she kidding? She dreaded learning the truth, yet anticipated it, too.

But she had to know. *Then what?* a little voice asked. *What will you do if he doesn't love you? If he comes right out and tells you that what he feels isn't love—not the kind of love you want?* She closed her eyes in anguish. If he didn't love her, she couldn't and wouldn't stay with him and her marriage would be over. Maybe she'd been a fool to listen to everyone who told her Brandon loved her. Maybe she'd been an even bigger fool to listen to her heart. She rested her forehead against the wet tile, letting the hot water beat down on her like tiny stabbing needles. Today she'd know, one way or the other, what the rest of her life was to be: heaven or hell.

CHAPTER SEVENTEEN

SAYING GOODBYE WAS ALWAYS PAINFUL, no matter the circumstances. JoBeth had kissed everyone quickly and retreated to the car, waiting while Brandon made his long farewells. The sun hung like a ball of fire in the azure sky, making the confines of the Corvette a small oven. Frantically fanning herself, she frowned at Brandon's long-windedness. His "just a few seconds, Bets" was taking forever. Finally he broke away from the three couples, giving them one last wave over his shoulder as he headed for the car.

"Sorry." Brandon fished in his pocket, struggling with the skintight jeans a few seconds before they surrendered the car keys. "You look a little hot under the collar."

"Funny man." She leaned forward, waved goodbye once more to everyone and said between her teeth, "May we go now?" Brandon chuckled, and she turned her head away from his sparkling eyes and pretended she was studying the paddock off in the distance. Suddenly something caught her eye. "Brandon, the gate to the mares—"

"Oh, hell!" he growled. "I forgot to tell Kane something important."

"Brandon, the gate is open."

He mumbled under his breath, unfastened his seat belt, yanked on the door handle and swung out of the car. "I'll be right back."

"Wait! Damn it, leave me the keys." He was a few feet from the car and pitched the keys, giving her a grinning thumbs-up as they landed on the driver's seat. "Smart ass. Tell Lucas that Dancer's Son is going to get into Paddock Three with the mares if the gate isn't shut." She waited a second for some sign that he'd heard, and when none came she snapped, "Men. Do they ever listen? Hell, no." Fumbling with the key ring, she searched for the right one, then shoved it into the ignition and started the engine.

Her silk blouse felt as if it were glued to her back. She leaned forward, switched the air-conditioning on, rolled up the windows and sighed as a gush of cool air fanned her face. For a few seconds her only concern was the temperature, but as Brandon's conversation lengthened, her gaze wandered out over the rolling green pastures and Dancer's Son caught her attention. That black devil of a stallion was heading directly for the open gate and the mares. If someone didn't do something he'd be in his own version of horse heaven.

EVERYONE HAD STARTED BACK to the house, all eager to return to the cool darkness, when Brandon called Kane's name.

"Kane, wait up," he yelled again, and began to jog toward them. A movement from the back of the house caught his eye and he smiled, but the smile immediately turned to a scowl as he watched his father hurrying down the steps, waving his cane. Old fool, he thought, he wasn't supposed to run. And what was he yelling?

Suddenly Brandon couldn't breathe. The very air around him had been sucked from the earth. He watched as if outside himself as everyone spun around, looking with horror beyond him. Then like a rag doll his arms were flung out wide, and it felt as if a giant hand shoved him in the center of his back, sending him stumbling forward. In a fraction of a second the sound of an explosion rent the air with its violence, and was immediately followed by heat and flames that stretched toward the sky.

Righting himself, Brandon whirled in time to witness another explosion turn his car into a raging inferno. Bits of searing white-hot metal began to pelt the ground, catching dry grass aflame. The enormity of what had just happened hit him like a sledgehammer in the gut. "Bets!" he screamed. Then he was screaming her name over and over while Lucas and Kane held him back, keeping him from charging into the flames.

Boston grabbed Samantha and Jennifer, turning their faces into his chest, shielding them from the carnage. Shasta ran for Matthew, catching him before he fell to the pavement, and held the old man close as he mumbled and cried in her arms.

"Brandon. For God's sake, man, you can't do anything," Kane said. "It's too late." They dragged him, struggling, away from the intense heat radiating from the burning car.

"Bets," he whispered, his voice a hoarse rasp, raw from screaming her name. Tears ran like silver rivers down his cheeks and he went limp between the two men. "Bets," he whispered again, and sagged to the walkway, burying his face in his hands. "What have I done?"

Hysteria and pandemonium broke out around him. secret-service men prowled the ranch as others urged the vice president to leave immediately. Ranch hands with hoses and fire extinguishers worked uselessly to put out the flames. When the fire truck finally arrived the men's efforts took on a feverish, almost crazed urgency. What use now? Brandon thought. Too late, too late. Too damn late!

Shasta, having turned Matthew over to Jennifer's care, eased down beside Brandon, wrapped her arms around him and pulled his unresisting body close to her, allowing him to cry into her shoulder.

"I never told her I loved her, Shasta. I never had the guts."

"She knew," Shasta lied. After all, what harm would it do now?

Never had he hurt so much, not even when he'd lost his mother and sister. JoBeth had touched him, reaching down deep inside where he didn't want to feel. What a bastard he'd been not to tell her he loved her. Even worse, a coward.

There was a yell and the activity around him seemed to freeze. He flinched, realizing they must have been able to reach and release her body from the twisted, melted car. A deep moan of anguish escaped his lips and he slumped in Shasta's arms.

"Come into the house with everyone else, Brandon. This isn't going to do you any good."

The only sounds he could hear were the hot crackling of burning grass and his own breathing against Shasta's blouse. Then there was a strange stillness and he went stiff, listening. Lucas's cry of amazement and the chorus of other voices joining his brother's brought him upright, alert. Every muscle cramped with the sounds around him. The sudden hope was a torment.

He was on his feet. Then he was running. The air scorched his lungs it was so pungent with the odors of burning gas, metal and grass. A group of men crowded around the hood of his car, which was at least fifty feet from the Corvette. As he came closer a muffled moan reached him, a voice he'd recognize in his sleep. His pulse leaped to a frenzied beat of excitement and he prayed it wasn't his imagination playing cruel tricks. He prayed again with each step. The men parted, making room for him as the black, burned metal hood was lifted.

His heart surged to his throat, choking him. Then suddenly he was breathing air, fresh and sweet. She was there. Bruised, dirty, lying like a broken porcelain doll, but alive, by God.

Brandon dropped to his knees beside her. "Bets. Bets, speak to me." What inane words, he thought wildly, but he wanted to yell, sing and dance around like a crazy man.

"Don't touch her, Brandon." Lucas's hand clamped firmly on his shoulder. "We don't know how badly she's been hurt. You wouldn't want to cause more damage."

"She is alive! You heard her moan, didn't you?"

"She's alive."

"Where's that damn doctor? Has someone called the guest house and told them it's an emergency? For God's sake tell him to hurry." He couldn't take his eyes off her white face and the dark discolorations across her forehead and cheek. He flinched when he thought that those patches might be burns and that she might be suffering.

Once more Brandon turned to his brother for reassurance, and Lucas was forced to swallow the huge lump that had lodged in his throat. How many years had it been since he'd seen that look on Brandon's face?

"She'll be all right, won't she, Lucas?"

"Sure." He turned away from the worry in the sapphire-blue eyes so like their mother's. "Boston," he yelled, "what in hell is keeping Dr. Randall?"

"She's so still." Tentatively Brandon reached out and touched her hand. "She's cold, Lucas." His voice caught and cracked and the men hovering around them backed away, embarrassed at the show of so much emotion from another man.

"Here, Brandon." Kane handed him a blanket and stepped out of the way as he saw a man running toward them, carrying a black bag.

"Come on, Brandon." Lucas touched his brother's shoulder. "Move and let Doc Randall see to her."

"She's going to be all right, Lucas."

PAIN WAS THE FIRST THING she was conscious of. Her head hurt like the very devil, and when she tried to roll it from side to side experimentally she whimpered from her efforts. Slowly she became aware of the rest of her body's aches. Moving each muscle with care, she tested the depth of her pain, but when she tried to move her left hand it refused to budge. The thought that she might be seriously injured startled her. Again she tried to wiggle her fingers, only increasing the pressure around them. Then, out of the blue, she remembered some of what had happened as fragments of pictures flashed behind her closed eyes. JoBeth groaned out loud.

"Hush, Bets." Brandon gently squeezed her left hand. "Everything is going to be okay now. You'll see. We'll make it work. Just speak to me."

What was he babbling about? So unlike him, losing control, and the desperation she heard in his voice made her want to comfort him. "Brandon," she said, her own voice only a raspy whisper, like the wind blowing across dry leaves. Then panic struck as she realized that darkness surrounded her, swallowing her up, suffocating her with its blackness. "Brandon, I can't see." Hysteria edged her words and she grabbed at the hand holding hers and wailed. "What's wrong?"

"Open your eyes, Bets. Nothing is wrong with you but numerous bumps and bruises."

She did as she was told, and sighed with relief. "Why is it so dim, Brandon? What's happening? Please tell me."

"Calm down." He rose from the chair next to the bed, settled down beside her and stroked the hair back off her forehead. "It's dark in here because it's dusk. You've been in and out of consciousness all day." He reached out and turned on the lamp.

The blast of brightness hurt her eyes and made her head pound. Her eyelids squeezed shut and she flinched, turning her head away from the light until Brandon flicked the lamp to its lowest setting.

"We were ready to fly you to the hospital in San Antonio, but the doctors said it wasn't necessary, that you have a mild concussion and all we needed to do was watch you carefully."

Mutely she listened with half a mind to him talk, while the other half tried frantically to untangle the mystery of what had actually happened. She shook her head in puzzlement, then wished she hadn't as a thousand sharp knives stabbed through her brain. "What happened?"

Brandon brought her hand to his lips, turned it over and gently kissed her palm. "We almost lost you, Bets. A temperature bomb—a wedding gift from Tramble."

"Temperature?" She closed her eyes. It hurt to think.

"Don't try to talk. Just let me explain." He chuckled softly. "My poor Bets. You look like you've been through a war and lost."

JoBeth's eyes widened, then she scowled, but the movement hurt too badly and she immediately relaxed her facial muscles. There was a knocking on the bedroom door and she yelped at the sound.

"We have a lot of talking to do, but first, let me take care of this tiny problem."

With a few long, angry strides he yanked open the door, and she was forced to smile, just a tiny curve of the corners of her lips. Kane, Shasta, Samantha, Boston, Lucas, Jennifer and Matthew were all vying for a position in the doorway to see her. She only had time to raise her hand and waggle her fingers before Brandon shut the door firmly, then wedged a chair under the knob. She raised a questioning eyebrow and winced as real pain shot through that side of her head.

"Just in case someone decides to interfere in my life again." He quickly sat down beside her and grabbed her hand as she tried to touch the knot over her eye. "You have a bump there the size of a goose egg. As a matter of fact, you have three good-sized lumps on your head, my sweet."

"I want a mirror."

Once again Brandon pulled her hand away from her face. "No you don't. It's nothing serious, but you have a real dilly of a black eye." He pointed to her right eye.

"There're a couple of scrapes and bruises—here and here and here." He touched each place lightly. "And under that nightgown your body is a little black and blue, but no broken bones. Other than that, how do you feel?" He grinned down at her, his eyes bright with relief and laughter.

JoBeth caught the shine in his eyes and wondered for a moment if it was the shimmer of tears. "I hurt all over. What hit me, by the way?" She smiled wearily.

He returned her smile, and for the first time in hours he felt truly happy. "The hood of my car." She looked at him blankly and he went on. "Why don't we start with you? And just why did you get out of the Corvette?"

"Dancer's Son was about to get in with the mares. I tried to tell you, but you didn't hear me. I had to close the gate, and was about halfway there—" She broke off, frowning a little. "That's all I remember. What's this about a bomb and my uncle?" She studied him for the first time and noticed the ravages of the day on his face. "Brandon. Oh! Brandon, what has been happening?" Her hand stroked his cheek, loving the feel of his face against her fingers and the way he turned his lips and caressed her palm.

"We thought for so long that you were dead, my love. No one saw you get out of the car." He paused and swallowed painfully, his eyes dark as he remembered the devastation he'd felt. "It was a good while before the men found you under the hood of the car. It must have blown off and caught you, knocking you down, but it also protected you." He didn't know how he was going to begin to tell her all the things he wanted to, but he had to now, knowing what he'd gone through when he thought he'd lost her for good. But first he had another unpleasant task to perform.

He picked up her hands, holding them clasped between his. "Bets, Tramble is dead. He tried to kill us both, and when he found out that his plan failed and that he'd been implicated in the planning, he had a heart attack and died."

She flinched, closed her eyes and moaned, but this time the pain was not physical.

Brandon winced at the anguish he'd caused. No matter what Tramble had done, he was still the last of her blood relatives, and now she'd have to live with the memory that he'd tried to kill her.

"Please go on, Brandon. Tell me everything. I have to know it all."

He hurriedly told her about Shasta's run-in with Willy at the party. "We didn't want you to know. It would have ruined the night for you. Besides, we—"

"And just who is 'we'?"

"Shasta and Kane. Anyway, the police arrested this Willy character in San Antonio and he sang like a bird once he realized that he was going to take the rap for murder when the bomb went off. So Willy turned state's evidence and implicated your uncle. And to make matters worse, Tramble came to San Antonio to be close when the news of our deaths was announced. The minute the police had Willy's confession they called the ranch. Dad had just received that call and was on his way to warn us, when the bomb went off. It was designed to detonate when the engine reached a certain temperature. You activated it sooner by turning on the air conditioner, forcing the temperature to rise rapidly. Under normal circumstances, we would have been on the highway when the explosion occurred. That would

have suited the old bastard just fine. I'm sorry, Bets."
He plucked a tissue from the box beside the bed and
dabbed at her tears. "My poor Bets. You've been
through so much these past few days."

Brandon leaned down to kiss her gently on the lips
and she couldn't help smiling through the blur of tears.
"Better," she said with a sigh, then lifted her hand and
touched the tip of her nose. "There, too, please. It's
about the only other place on my body that doesn't
hurt."

"That's my girl." He kissed her nose carefully, then
suddenly nervous, cleared his throat. "Listen, Bets."
He stopped, cocked his head, gun-shy and waiting for
the interruptions. When only silence met his fierce
expression, he smiled. "You have to let me explain why
I acted the way I did and said the things I said when I
saw those damn pictures."

Her smile grew. Suddenly it didn't matter anymore.
She had been through too much to let a thing like those
pictures ruin her marriage. They had problems, she ac-
knowledged that, but none she couldn't live with. If
Brandon didn't love her the way she thought a husband should love a wife, then she'd accept *his* kind of
love. Death had been too close to both of them and she
realized that life was too short to waste. "I guess you've
got me captive and can do whatever you wish." She
tried to lighten the mood by waggling her eyebrows
suggestively, but the motion stung and she gave him a
pitiful smile. "How long am I going to be like this?"

"At least until I finish explaining—that's for sure."
He kissed her again, but this time he purposefully
deepened it, making her gasp with wanting when he was
through.

"You don't play fair."

"No? Who ever said love was fair, or a game? I've learned the hard way that it's deadly serious."

She couldn't believe her ears. Surely she'd heard him wrong....

"I went crazy when I saw those pictures, Bets. Angry, jealous and mad all at once."

"But why? Why would you believe I'd do something so ugly? What have I ever done to make you think I was a tramp with no morals at all?"

Brandon raked a hand through his hair. "You forget, Bets. I've witnessed the same scene before and the memory has stuck in my head like a canker sore for more than a year."

"What in the world are you talking about?" But suddenly she knew, and closed her eyes in agony.

"More than a year ago I walked in on a scene similar to the one in those pictures, with one exception. That time I knew the man. My brother."

"That's totally absurd and you know it," she sputtered, and struggled upright with a groan. "Damn, damn! Nothing happened in those pictures and nothing happened with Lucas. He was dead drunk and I was in his bed only to try to break up Jennifer and him." She slapped his helping hand away and hissed as she stuffed another pillow behind her back. What a hell of a time to be incapacitated. "That madman, Jean-Paul, played me for a fool, knowing how I felt about your family. He filled my head with lies about what Jennifer was doing to Lucas and how I needed to save him. He convinced me I was the only one who could do it."

"Hush, Bets. I know all that and it's not important."

"Well, it damn sure is if you think anything happened between Lucas and me. For God's sake, Brandon. Lucas is like a brother. I love him, yes, but never, never as a lover."

"Bets, don't get all upset. It will only make your head hurt worse. Then the doctor and Lucas will kill me for sure."

"But—"

"No. I know how you feel about Lucas . . . now." He wasn't ready to tell her of the years jealousy had eaten at him because he thought she was in love with his brother. "You're going to have to see this from my side of it, Bets. For a year I lived with the image of you in his bed. Reason told me it was a lie. Lucas told me it was a lie. Everyone told me it was a lie. But there it was, forever imprinted on my brain as if someone had taken a branding iron and seared it there. Then, when I saw those pictures of you and another man, it was like a resurrection of a nightmare. I was so Goddamn angry and hurt and yes, jealous when I opened that envelope and saw you that I didn't even stop to think."

This time, over the wild hammering of her heart she heard the love behind the words. "Brandon," she whispered softly, lovingly, and reached for him.

But he backed away from her touch. "There's something else. When I thought you were dead I wanted to die, too. I realized what a selfish bastard I'd been by not telling you . . . I love you, Bets. More than I'll ever be able to tell you, more than I'll ever show you, but I do. No, for the love of pete, don't interrupt. I guess I've loved you since you were a little girl, but I've fought it. You've known me long enough to realize I've always backed away from any strong entanglements. I know it's irrational, but it has to do with the pain of losing Mother and Elizabeth." He laughed a little shakily, rubbing his hands over his face as a shield. Then, dropping his hands to his thighs, he turned to her once more. "When I lost them I'd never been a loser before, never lost anything that truly meant anything to me. After their deaths, love, deep love, was something I isolated myself from. Oh, hell, yes, I could love casually for a while, but nothing serious. Never forever. Till you. When you disappeared after your father died I was obsessed with finding you, and it had nothing to do with your oil shares, either." Brandon could no longer stand not being able to hold her, and grasped her shoulders, pulling her into his arms.

JoBeth bit her lip to keep from crying out. Fat tears spilled from her eyes and dropped onto his shirt. How long had she waited to hear those words from him? A million nights, it seemed. Despite the protest of her muscles and her throbbing head, she wrapped her arms around his neck. "Do you have any idea how I've longed to hear you say you love me, love me like a woman and not some kid you grew up with? Oh, Brandon, I love you so much."

"Hush, Bets. You don't have to say you love me just because I have. If you can love me a little, I'll be content."

She pulled back in the circle of his arms and looked deeply into his eyes. What she saw there stunned her. He truly didn't know how much she loved him. His family and friends knew, the world knew, but he didn't. "I've loved you for as long as I can remember. Why do you think I was always hanging around you? Why do you think I did all those mean things to you when I saw you with a girl? Damn you, Brandon DeSalva, I've cried buckets for you over the years. A young girl's unrequited love is a tearful experience."

"This isn't necessary, Bets. Honestly. I love you without the reassurance."

"You fool," she growled, then grinned when he kissed her fiercely. But the grin immediately returned. "You really don't believe me, do you?" She was struggling to get up, but Brandon pinned her flat to the bed.

"Talk about a fool. You're supposed to stay in bed. Now what has upset you so that you want to leave me?"

Though he kept her down, his body hovering achingly close, he never truly touched her. She could feel his body heat radiating and she grinned. "You're crazy and I'm mad, but you know what? As bad as I hurt, I want you."

Brandon swore under his breath and moved off her. "Damn it, Bets, you have a way of making a man forget everything."

He was back to sitting on the bed beside her. "Good. Now that you're not going to attack me, would you please go find the big straw bag I brought back from my old house the other night?"

Brandon frowned, not wanting to leave her side, but did as she asked, returning a few minutes later.

"Sit down." She patted the bed and once again he made himself comfortable next to her. One by one she handed him the three diaries. "This is the first one, when I was very young. The second, I was about twelve, and the last one, about seventeen. Turn to the first and last pages of all three. Go ahead." She watched him closely as he did as she requested.

Brandon closed the last diary and squeezed his eyes shut. He'd never dreamed she'd loved him so much. It made him feel small. He dropped his hands and the book he held fell open in the middle. His eyes devoured the words, words of love and wanting and hope.

He was her dream. "I'm humbled, Bets." He looked up, his eyes swimming in tears. "I'll never do anything again unworthy of your love."

She threw back her head and began to laugh. "Silly man. If I wanted someone perfect I certainly wouldn't have fallen in love with a hardheaded nag and tease like you."

"I mean it, Bets. I love you and would do anything for you."

She was quiet for a long while, then began to chuckle. "Does this mean that you're willing to give up your side of the bed for me?"

Brandon groaned, buried his face in the crook of her neck and began to laugh. "That's pushing things a little far, Bets."

"Come on, sweet cheeks. You said 'anything.'" She patted his jean-clad bottom, caressing the firm curve, until he was forced to straighten up.

"Now, Bets. The bed is not open for negotiation."

"No, but it's the best starting place I know of."

"It's the beginning, Bets, the beginning of the rest of our lives."

Harlequin Superromance

COMING NEXT MONTH

#234 THE FOREVER PROMISE • Meg Hudson
Fourteen years ago Claire Parmeter left King Faraday at
the altar when she discovered that another woman was
carrying his child. Now King and Claire meet again.
Mutual desire draws them together, but the ghosts of
their past threaten to separate them once more....

#235 SWEET TOMORROWS • Francine Christopher
Valerie Wentworth thinks she's put Wall Street behind
her forever. But that is before an irate financial planner
waltzes into her antique-doll shop. Not only is Cutter
the most gorgeous man she's ever seen, but he has the
formidable wits to match her own, and their bodies,
well . . . they fit together perfectly.

#236 HALFWAY TO HEAVEN • Pamela Bauer
Designer Rachel Kincaid can't afford to fall in love with
sexy department store magnate Cole Braxton III. She is
still holding out hope that her missing fiancé will return
home. But Cole isn't about to wait around forever.
Faced with a barrage of difficult choices, Rachel finally
realizes the answers lie within her heart....

#237 CHILD'S PLAY • Peggy Nicholson
Snatching a small boy from under his bodyguard's nose
is no mean trick, even for Tey Kenyon. She can't let
Mac McAllister interfere with her plans, but interfering
with her heart is another matter!

ATTRACTIVE, SPACE SAVING BOOK RACK

Display your most prized novels on this handsome and sturdy book rack. The hand-rubbed walnut finish will blend into your library decor with quiet elegance, providing a practical organizer for your favorite hard-or soft-covered books.

Only $9.95

Approximately 16" x 8" when assembled

Assembles in seconds!

To order, rush your name, address and zip code, along with a check or money order for $10.70 ($9.95 plus 75¢ postage and handling) (New York residents add appropriate sales tax), payable to *Harlequin Reader Service* to:

In the U.S.

Harlequin Reader Service
Book Rack Offer
901 Fuhrmann Blvd.
P.O. Box 1325
Buffalo, NY 14269-1325

Offer not available in Canada.

BKR–

Can you keep a secret?

You can keep this one plus 4 free novels

FREE BOOKS/GIFT COUPON

Mail to   **Harlequin Reader Service®**

In the U.S.
901 Fuhrmann Blvd.
P.O. Box 1394
Buffalo, N.Y. 14240-1394

In Canada
P.O. Box 609
Fort Erie, Ontario
L2A 9Z9

YES! Please send me 4 free Harlequin Superromance® novels and my free surprise gift. Then send me 4 brand-new novels every month as they come off the presses. Bill me at the low price of $2.50 each—a 10% saving off the retail price. There are no shipping, handling or other hidden costs. There is no minimum number of books I must purchase. I can always return a shipment and cancel at any time. Even if I never buy another book from Harlequin, the 4 free novels and the surprise gift are mine to keep forever.

134-BPS-BP6F

Name _____ (PLEASE PRINT)

Address _____ Apt. No.

City _____ State/Prov. _____ Zip/Postal Code

This offer is limited to one order per household and not valid to present subscribers. Price is subject to change.   MSSR-SUB-1RR

Janet Dailey
Americana

Don't miss a single title from this great collection. The first eight titles have already been published. Complete and mail this coupon today to order books you may have missed.

Harlequin Reader Service

In U.S.A.
901 Fuhrmann Blvd.
P.O. Box 1397
Buffalo, N.Y. 14140

In Canada
P.O. Box 2800
Postal Station A
5170 Yonge Street
Willowdale, Ont. M2N 6J3

Please send me the following titles from the Janet Dailey Americana Collection. I am enclosing a check or money order for $2.75 for each book ordered, plus 75¢ for postage and handling.

_____	ALABAMA	Dangerous Masquerade
_____	ALASKA	Northern Magic
_____	ARIZONA	Sonora Sundown
_____	ARKANSAS	Valley of the Vapours
_____	CALIFORNIA	Fire and Ice
_____	COLORADO	After the Storm
_____	CONNECTICUT	Difficult Decision
_____	DELAWARE	The Matchmakers

Number of titles checked @ $2.75 each = $_____

N.Y. RESIDENTS ADD
   APPROPRIATE SALES TAX $_____

Postage and Handling $__.75____

TOTAL $_____

I enclose _____

(Please send check or money order. We cannot be responsible for cash sent through the mail.)

PLEASE PRINT

NAME _____

ADDRESS _____

CITY _____

STATE/PROV. _____

BLJD-A-